Happy Birthday

The Wedding Jester

We wish you 60
more great years.
So sorry we cannot
be at the celebration

love,

Penina & Mickey

The Wedding Jester

Steve Stern

Graywolf Press
Saint Paul, Minnesota

Publication of this volume is made possible in part by a grant provided by the Minnesota State Arts Board through an appropriation by the Minnesota State Legislature, and by a grant from the National Endowment for the Arts. Significant support has also been provided by Dayton's, Mervyn's, and Target stores through the Dayton Hudson Foundation, the Bush Foundation, the McKnight Foundation, the General Mills Foundation, the St. Paul Companies, and other generous contributions from foundations, corporations, and individuals. To these organizations and individuals we offer our heartfelt thanks.

Published by Graywolf Press
2402 University Avenue, Suite 203
Saint Paul, Minnesota 55114
All rights reserved

www.graywolfpress.org

Published in the United States of America

ISBN 1-55597-279-9

2   4   6   8   9   7   5   3   1
First Graywolf Printing, 1999

Library of Congress Catalog Card Number: 98-88488

"The Tale of a Kite" first appeared in *Doubletake Magazine*, and was subsequently reprinted in *The Pushcart Prize XXI*, and again in *Jewish American Fiction, a Century of Stories* (from the U. of Nebraska Press); "Romance" was printed in *The Alaska Quarterly Review*; "Bruno's Metamorphosis" appeared in the collection, *Isaac and the Undertaker's Daughter* (Lost Roads Press), and was reprinted in *Here I Am, Contemporary Jewish Stories from Around the World*. "The Sin of Elijah" first appeared in *Prairie Schooner* and was reprinted in *The Prairie Schooner Anthology of Contemporary Jewish American Writing*, and again in *The Year's Best Fantasy and Horror* (11th annual collection), and also in the forthcoming *Neurotica, an Anthology of Jewish Erotic Writing*. "Swan Song" first appeared in *Raccoon Magazine*. "Sissman Loses His Way" appeared in *The Jewish Forward* and was reprinted in *Many Lights in Many Windows, Twenty Years of Fiction and Poetry from the Writer's Community*. "The Wedding Jester" appeared in *The New England Review*.

Cover photograph: Walter Garschagen

Cover design: Julie Metz

Contents

The Tale of a Kite   3

Romance   21

Bruno's Metamorphosis   57

The Sin of Elijah   81

Swan Song   111

Yiddish Twilight   119

Sissman Loses His Way   149

The Wedding Jester   161

A String around the Moon:
   A Children's Story   215

The Wedding Jester

The Tale of a Kite

It's safe to say that we Jews of North Main Street are a progressive people. I don't mean to suggest we have any patience with freethinkers, like that crowd down at Thompson's Café; tolerant within limits, we're quick to let subversive elements know where they stand. Observant (within reason), we keep the Sabbath after our fashion, though the Saturday competition won't allow us to close our stores. We keep the holidays faithfully, and are regular in attending our modest little synagogue on Market Square. But we're foremost an enterprising bunch, proud of our contribution to the local economy. Even our secondhand shops contain up-to-date inventories, such as stylish automobile capes for the ladies, astrakhan overcoats for gentlemen—and our jewelers, tailors, and watchmakers are famous all over town. Boss Crump and his heelers, who gave us a dispensation to stay open on Sundays, have declared more than once in our presence, "Our sheenies are good sheenies!" So you can imagine how it unsettles us to hear that Rabbi Shmelke, head of that gang of fanatics over on Auction Street, has begun to fly.

We see him strolling by the river, if you can call it strolling. Because the old man, brittle as a dead leaf, doesn't so much walk as permit himself to be dragged by disciples at either elbow. A mournful soul on a stick, that's Rabbi Shmelke; comes a big wind and his bones will be scattered to powder. His eyes above his foggy pince-nez are a rheumy residue in an otherwise parchment face, his beard (Ostrow calls it his "lunatic fringe") an ashen broom gnawed by mice. Living mostly on air and the strained generosity of in-laws, his followers are not much more presentable. Recently transplanted from Shpink, some Godforsaken Old-World backwater that no doubt sent them packing, Shmelke and his band of crackpots are a royal embarrassment to our community.

We citizens of Hebrew extraction set great store by our friendly relations with our gentile neighbors. One thing we don't need is religious zealots poisoning the peaceable atmosphere. They're an eyesore and a liability, Shmelke's crew, a threat to our good name, seizing every least excuse to make a spectacle. They pray conspicuously in questionable attire, dance with their holy books in the street, their doddering leader, if he speaks at all, talking in riddles. No wonder we judge him to be frankly insane.

It's my own son Ziggy, the *kaddish*, who first brings me word of Shmelke's alleged levitation. Then it's a measure of his excitement that, in reporting what he's seen, he also reveals he's skipped Hebrew school to see it. This fact is as troubling to me as his claims for the Shpinker's airborne faculty, which I naturally discount. He's always been a good boy, Ziggy, quiet and obedient, if a little withdrawn, and it's unheard of that he should play truant from his Talmud Torah class. Not yet bar mitzvah'd, the kid has already begun to make himself useful around the store, and I look forward to the day he comes into the business as my partner. (I've got a sign made up in anticipation of the event: J. Zipper & Son, Spirits and Fine Wines.) So his conduct is distressing on several counts, not the least of which is how it shows the fanatics' adverse influence on our youth.

"Papa!" exclaims Ziggy, bursting through the door from the street—since when does Ziggy burst? "Papa, Rabbi Shmelke can fly!"

"Shah!" I bark. "Can't you see I'm with a customer?" This is my friend and colleague Harry Nussbaum, proprietor of Memphis Bridge Cigars, whose factory supports better than fifteen employees and is located right here on North Main. Peeling bills from a bankroll as thick as a bible, Nussbaum's in the process of purchasing a case of Passover wine. (From this don't conclude that I'm some exclusively kosher concern; I carry also your vintage clarets and sparkling burgundies, blended whiskeys and sour mash for the yokels, brandies, cordials, brut champagnes—you name it.)

Nussbaum winces, clamping horsey teeth around an unlit cigar. "Shomething ought to be done about thosh people," he mutters, and I heartily concur. As respected men of commerce, we both belong to the executive board of the North Main Street Improvement Committee, which some say is like an Old Country *kahal.* We chafe at the association, regarding ourselves rather as boosters, watchdogs for the welfare of our district. It's a responsibility we don't take lightly.

When Nussbaum leaves, I turn to Ziggy, his jaw still agape, eyes bugging from his outsize head. Not from my side of the family does he get such a head, bobbling in his turtleneck like a pumpkin in an eggcup. You'd think it was stuffed full of wishes and big ideas, Ziggy's head, though to my knowledge it remains largely vacant.

"You ought to be ashamed of yourself."

"But, Papa, I seen it." Breathless, he twists his academy cap in his hands. "We was on the roof and we peeped through the skylight. First he starts to pray, then all of a sudden his feet don't touch the floor . . ."

"I said, enough!"

Then right away I'm sorry I raised my voice. I should be sorry? But like I say, Ziggy has always been a pliant kid, kind of an amiable mediocrity. Not what you'd call fanciful—where others dream, Ziggy merely sleeps—I'm puzzled he should wait till his twelfth year to carry such tales. I fear he's fallen in with a bad crowd.

Still, it bothers me that I've made him sulk. Between my son and me there have never been secrets—what's to keep secret?—and I don't like how my temper has stung him into furtiveness. But lest he should think I've relented, I'm quick to add, "And never let me hear you played hooky from *cheder* again."

And that, for the time being, is that.

But at our weekly meeting of the Improvement Committee—to whose board I'm automatically appointed on account of my merchant's credentials—the issue comes up again. It seems that others of our children have conceived a fascination for the Shpinker screwballs, and as a consequence are becoming wayward in their habits. Even our chairman Irving Ostrow of Ostrow's Men's Furnishings, in the tasteful showroom of which we are assembled—even his own son Hershel, known as an exemplary scholar, has lately been delinquent in his studies.

"He hangs around that Auction Street shtibl," says an incredulous Ostrow, referring to the Chasids' sanctuary above Klotwog's feed store. "I ask him why and he tells me, like the mountains should tremble"—Ostrow pauses to sip his laxative tea—"'Papa,' he says, 'the Shpinker rebbe can fly.' 'Rebbe' he calls him, like an *alter kocker!*"

"Godhelpus!" we groan in one voice—Nussbaum, myself, Benny Rosen of Rosen's Delicatessen—having heard this particular rumor once too often. We're all of a single mind in our distaste for such fictions—all save old Kaminsky, the synagogue beadle ("Come-insky" we call him for his greetings at the door to the shul), who keeps the minutes of our councils.

"Maybe the Shmelke, he puts on the children a spell," he suggests out of turn, which is the sort of hokum you'd expect from a beadle.

At length we resolve to nip the thing in the bud. We pass along our apprehensions to the courtly Rabbi Fein, who runs the religious school in the synagogue basement. At our urgency he lets it be known from the pulpit that fraternizing with Chasids, who are after all no better than heretics, can be hazardous to the soul. He hints at physical consequences as well, such as warts and blindness. After that nothing is heard for a while about the goings on in the little hall above the feed store that serves as the Shpinkers' sanctuary.

What does persist, however, is a certain (what you might call) bohemianism that's begun to manifest itself among even the best of our young. Take for instance the owlish Hershel Ostrow: in what he no doubt supposes a subtle affectation—though who does he think he's fooling?—he's taken to wearing his father's worn-out homburg; and Mindy Dreyfus, the jeweler's son, has assumed the Prince Albert coat his papa has kept in mothballs since his greenhorn days. A few of the older boys sport incipient beards like the characters who conspire to make bombs at Thompson's Café, where in my opinion they'd be better off. Even my Ziggy, whom we trust to get his own hair cut, he talks Plott the barber into leaving the locks at his temples. He tries to hide them under his cap, which he's begun to wear in the house, though they spiral out like untended runners.

But it's not so much their outward signs of eccentricity as their increasing remoteness that gets under our skin. Even when they're present at meals or their after-school jobs, their minds seem to be elsewhere. This goes as well for Ziggy, never much of a noise to begin with, whose silence these days smacks more of wistful longing than merely having nothing to say.

"Mama," I frown at my wife Ethel, who's shuffling about the kitchen of our apartment over the liquor store. I'm enjoying her superb golden broth, afloat with eyes of fat that gleam beneath the gas lamp like a peacock's tail; but I nevertheless force a frown. "Mama, give a look on your son."

A good-natured, capable woman, my Ethel, with a figure like a brick *mikveh*, as they say, she seldom sits down at meals. She prefers to eat on the run, sampling critical spoonfuls as she scoots back and forth between the table and the coal-burning range. At my suggestion, however, she pauses, pretending to have just noticed Ziggy, who's toying absently with his food.

"My son? You mean this one with the confetti over his ears?" She bends to tease his sidelocks, then straightens, shaking her head. "This one ain't mine. Mine the fairies must of carried him off and left this in his place." She ladles more soup into the bowl he's scarcely touched. "Hey, stranger, eat your knaidel."

Still his mother's child, Ziggy is cajoled from his meditations into a grudging grin, which I fight hard against finding infectious. Surrendering, I make a joke: "Mama, I think the ship you came over on is called the *Ess Ess Mein Kind*."

Comes the auspicious day of Mr. Crump's visit to North Main Street. This is the political boss's bimonthly progress, when he collects his thank-yous (usually in the form of merchandise) from a grateful Jewish constituency. We have good reason to be grateful, since in exchange for votes and assorted spoils, the Red Snapper, as he's called, has waived the blue laws for our district. He also looks the other way with respect to child labor and the dry law that would have put yours truly out of business. Ordinarily Boss Crump and his entourage, including his hand-picked mayor du jour, like to tour the individual shops, receiving the tributes his *shwartze* valet shleps out to a waiting limousine. But today, tradition notwithstanding, we're drawn out-of-doors by the mild April weather, where we've put together a more formal welcome.

When the chrome-plated Belgian-Minerva pulls to the curb, we're assembled in front of Ridblatt's Bakery on the corner of Jackson Avenue and North Main. Irving Ostrow is offering a brace of suits from his emporium, as solemnly as a fireman presenting a rescued child, while Benny Rosen appears to be wrestling a string of salamis. Harry Nussbaum renders up a bale of cigars, myself a case of schnapps, and Rabbi Fein a ready blessing along with his perennial bread and salt. Puffed and officious in his dual capacity as neighborhood ward heeler and commit-tee chair, Ostrow has also prepared an address: "We citizens of North Main Street pledge to be a feather in the fedora of Mayor Huey, I mean Blunt . . ." (Because who can keep straight Mr. Crump's succession of puppet mayors?)

Behind us, under the bakery awning, Mickey Panitz is ready to strike up his *klezmer* orchestra; igniting his flash powder, a photographer from the *Commercial Appeal* ducks beneath a black hood. Everyone (with the exception, of course, of the Shpinker zealots, who lack all civic pride) has turned out for the event, lending North Main Street a holiday feel. We bask in Boss Crump's approval, who salutes us with a touch to the rim of his rakish straw skimmer, his smile scattering a galaxy of freckles. This is why what happens next, behind the backs of our visitors seems doubly shameful, violating as it does such a banner afternoon.

At first we tell ourselves we don't see what we see; we think, maybe a plume of smoke. But looks askance at one another con-firm that, not only do we share the same hallucination, but that the hallucination gives every evidence of being real. Even from such a distance it's hard to deny it: Around the corner of the next block, something is emerging from the roof of the railroad tenement that houses the Shpinker shtibl. It's a wispy black and gray something that rises out of a propped open skylight like vapor from an uncorked bottle. Escaping, it climbs into the cloudless sky and hovers over North Main Street, beard and belted caftan aflutter. There's a fur hat resembling the rotary brush of a chimney sweep, a pair of dun-stockinged ankles (to one of which a rope is attached) as spindly as the handles on a scroll. Then it's clear that, risen above the telephone wires and trolley lines, above the water tanks, Rabbi Shmelke floats in a doleful ecstasy.

We begin talking anxiously and at cross-purposes about mutual understanding through public sanitation, and so forth.

We crank hands left and right, while Mickey Panitz leads his band in a dirgelike rendition of "Dixie." In this way we keep our notables distracted until we can pack them off (photojournalist and all) in their sable limousine. Then, without once looking up again, we repair to Ostrow's Men's Furnishings and convene an extraordinary meeting of the Improvement Committee.

Shooting his sleeves to show flashy cufflinks, Ostrow submits a resolution: "I hereby resolve we dispatch to the Shpinkers a *delegatz*, with the ultimatum they should stop making a nuisance, which it's degrading already to decent citizens, or face a forceable outkicking from the neighborhood. All in agreement say oy."

The only dissenting voice is the one with no vote.

"Your honors know best," this from Kaminsky, a greenhorn till his dying day, "but ain't it what you call a miracle, this flying rebbe?"

For such irrelevance we decide it also wouldn't hurt to find a new secretary.

En route across the road to the *shtibl*, in the company of my fellows, I give thanks for small blessings. At least my Ziggy was telling the truth about Shmelke. Though I'm thinking that, with truths like this, it's maybe better he should learn to lie.

We trudge up narrow stairs from the street, pound on a flimsy door, and are admitted by one of Shmelke's unwashed. The dim room lists slightly like the deck of a ship, tilted toward windows that glow from a half-light filtering through the lowered shades. There's a film of dust in the air that lends the graininess of a photogravure to the bearded men seated at the long table, swaying over God-only-knows-what back-numbered lore. By the wall there's an ark stuffed with scrolls, a shelf of moldering books, spice boxes, tarnished candelabra, amulets against the evil eye.

It's all here, I think, all the blind superstition of our ancestors preserved in amber. But how did it manage to follow us over an ocean to such a far-flung outpost as Tennessee? Let the goyim see a room like this, with a ram's horn in place of a clock on the wall, with the *shnorrers* wrapped in their paraphernalia mumbling hocus-pocus instead of being gainfully employed, and right away the rumors start. The yids are poisoning the water, pishing on communion wafers, murdering Christian children for their blood. Right away somebody's quoting the *Protocols of Zion*. A room like this, give or take one flying rebbe, can upset the delicate balance of the entire American enterprise.

Returned at least in body from the clouds, old Shmelke sits at the head of the table, dispensing his shopworn wisdom. An unlikely source of authority, he appears little more substantial than the lemon shaft pouring over him from the open skylight.

"It is permitted to consult with the guardian spirits of oil and eggs . . . ," he intones, pausing between syllables to suck on a piece of halvah; an "Ahhh" goes up from disciples who lean forward to catch any crumbs. ". . . But sometimes the spirits give false answers." Another sadder but wiser "Ahhh."

When our eyes adjust to the murk, we notice that the ranks of the Shpinkers (who until now have scarcely numbered enough for a *minyan*) have swelled. They've been joined this afternoon, during Hebrew school hours no less, by a contingent of the sons of North Main Street, my own included. He's standing in his cockeyed academy cap, scrunched between nodding Chasids on the rebbe's left side. To my horror Ziggy, who's shown little enough aptitude for the things of this world, never mind the other, is also nodding to beat the band.

"Home!" I shout, finding myself in four-part harmony with the other committee members. Our outrage since entering having been compounded with interest, we won't be ignored anymore. But while some of the boys do indeed leave their places and make reluctantly for the door, others stand their ground. Among them is Ostrow's brainy son Hershel and my nebbish, that never before disobeyed.

Having turned toward us as one, the disciples look back to their *tzaddik*, who God forbid should interrupt his discourse on our account. Then Hershel steps forth to confront us, pince-nez identical to Shmelke's perched on his nose. "You see," he explains in hushed tones, though nobody asked him, "figuratively speaking, the rebbe is climbing Jacob's Ladder. Each rung corresponds to a letter of tetragrammaton, which in turn corresponds to a level of the soul . . ." And bubkes-bobkes, spouting the gibberish they must've brainwashed him into repeating. I look at Ostrow who's reaching for his heart pills.

Then who should pipe up but the pipsqueak himself, come around to tug at my sleeve. "Papa," like he can't decide whether he should plead or insist, "if they don't hold him down by the rope, Rabbi Shmelke can fly away to paradise."

I can hardly believe this is my son. What did I do wrong that he should chase after moth-eaten *yiddishe* swamis? Did he ever want for anything? Didn't I take him on high holidays to a sensible synagogue, where I showed him how to mouth the prayers nobody remembers the meaning of? Haven't I guaranteed him the life the good Lord intends him for?

Not ordinarily combative, when the occasion calls for it I can speak my mind. To the papery old man whom I hold personally accountable, I ask point-blank, "What have you done to my child?"

Diverted at last from his table-talk, Rabbi Shmelke cocks his tallowy head; he seems aware for perhaps the first time of the presence among his faithful of uninvited hangers-on.

"*Gay avek!*" he croaks at the remaining boys. "Go away." When nobody budges, he lifts a shaggy brow, shrugs his helplessness. Then he resumes in a voice like a violin strung with cobweb, "Allow me to tell you a story . . ."

"A story, a story!" The disciples wag their heads, all of them clearly idiots.

The rebbe commences some foolishness about how the patriarch Isaac's soul went on vacation while his body remained under his father's knife. Along with the others I find myself unable to stop listening, until I feel another tug at my sleeve.

"Papa," Ziggy's whispering, Adam's apple bobbing like a golf ball in a fountain, "they have to let him out the roof or he bumps his head on the ceiling."

"Do I know you?" I say, shaking him off. Then I abruptly turn on my heel and exit, swearing vengeance. I'm down the stairs and already crossing Auction Street, when I realize that my colleagues have joined me in my mortification. I suggest that drastic measures are in order, and as my anger has lent me an unaccustomed cachet, all say aye.

They agree there's not a minute to lose, since every day we become more estranged from our sons. (Or should I say sons and daughters, because you can't exclude old Kaminsky's orphaned granddaughter Ida, a wild girl with an unhealthy passion for books.)

But days pass and Rabbi Fein complains that even with the threat of his ruler, not to mention his assistant Nachum (whom the boys call Knock 'em), he can't keep his pupils in Hebrew class. Beyond our command now, our children are turning their backs on opportunity in favor of emulating certifiable cranks. They grow bolder, more and more of them exhibiting a freakish behavior they no longer make any pretense to conceal. For them rebellion is a costume party. They revel in the anomalous touch, some adopting muskrat caps (out of season) to approximate the Chasid's fur *shtreimel*. Milton Rosen wears a mackintosh that doubles for a caftan, the dumb Herman Wolf uses alphabet blocks for phylacteries. My own Ziggy has taken to picking his shirttails into ritual tassels.

He still turns up periodically for meals, silent affairs at which even Ethel is powerless to humor us. For his own good I lock him in his bedroom after dinner, but he climbs out the window, the little pisher, and scrambles down the fire escape. "Not from my side of the family does he get such a streak of defiance," I tell Ethel, who seems curiously resigned. "I think maybe comes the fairies to take him back again," she says, but am I worried? All right, so I'm worried, but I'm confident that, once the Shpinkers have been summarily dealt with, my son will return to the fold, tail between legs.

Still the problem remains: What precisely should we do? Time passes and the Shpinkers give no indication of developing a civic conscience; neither do they show any discretion when it comes to aiding their blithering rebbe to fly. (If you want to dignify what he does as flying; because in midair he's as bent and deflated as he is on Earth, so wilted you have to wonder if he even knows he's left the ground.) In response to their antics, those of us with any self-respect have stopped looking up.

Of course we have our spies, like Old Man Kaminsky who has nothing better to do than ogle the skies. He tells us that three times a day, morning, noon, and evening, rain or shine, and sometimes nonstop on Shabbos, Shmelke hovers above the chimneys. He marks us from a distance like some wizened dirigible, a sign designating our community as the haven of screwballs and extremists. We're told that instead of studying (a harmless enough endeavor in itself), the shiftless Shpinkers now spend their time testing various grades of rope. From the clothesline purchased at Hekkie's Hardware on Commerce Street, they've graduated to hawser obtained from steamboat chandlers down at the levee. They've taken to braiding lengths of rope, to splicing and paying them out through the skylight, so that Shmelke can float ever higher. Occasionally they might maneuver their rebbe in fishtails and cunning loop-the-loops, causing him to soar and dive; they might send him into electrical storms from which he returns with fluorescent bones. Sometimes, diminished to a mote, the old man disappears in the clouds, only to be reeled back carrying gifts—snuffboxes and kiddush cups made of alloys never seen on this planet before.

Or so says Old Man Kaminsky, whom we dismiss as having also fallen under Shmelke's mind control. We're thankful, in any case, that the Shpinkers now fly their *tzaddik* high enough that he's ceased to be a serious distraction. (At first the yokels, come to town for the Saturday market, had mistaken him for an advertising ploy, their sons taking potshots with peashooters.) But out-of-sight isn't necessarily to say that the rebbe is out-of-mind, though we've gotten used to keeping our noses to the ground. We've begun to forget about him, to forget the problems with our young. What problems? Given the fundamental impossibility of the whole situation, we start to embrace the conviction that his flights are pure fantasy.

Then Ziggy breaks his trancelike silence to drop a bombshell. "I'm studying for *bar mitzvah* with Rabbi Shmelke," he announces, as Ethel spoons more calf's-foot jelly onto my plate. But while his voice issues the challenge, Ziggy's face, in the shadow of his academy cap, shows he's still testing the water.

Ethel's brisket, tender and savory as it is, sticks in my gorge. I want to tell him the *tzaddik*'s a figment of his imagination and let that be an end to it, but Ziggy's earnestness suggests the tactic won't work.

"What's wrong," I ask, clearing my throat with what emerges as a seismic roar, "ahemmm . . . what's wrong with Rabbi Fein?"

"He ain't as holy."

Directly the heartburn sets in. "And what's holy got to do with it?"

Ziggy looks at me as if my question is hardly deserving of an answer. Condescending to explain, however, he finds it necessary to dismount his high horse, doffing his cap to scratch his bulbous head. "Holy means, you know, like scare . . . I mean sacred."

"Unh-hnh," I say, folding my arms and biting my tongue. Now I'm the soul of patience, which makes him nervous.

"You know, *sacred*," he reasserts, the emphasis for his own sake rather than mine.

"Ahhh," I nod in benign understanding, enjoying how his resolve begins to crack.

"That's right," pursues Ziggy, and tries again to fly in the face of my infernal tolerance, lacking wings, "like magic."

I'm still nodding, so he repeats himself in case I didn't hear.

"Oh sure, ma-a-agic," I reply, with the good humor of a parent introduced to his child's imaginary friend.

Flustered to the point of fighting back tears, Ziggy nevertheless refuses to surrender, retreating instead behind a wall of hostility.

"You wouldn't know magic if it dumped a load on your head!"

You have to hand it to the kid, the way he persists in his folly; I never would have thought him capable of such high *mishegoss*. But when the admiration passes, I'm fit to be tied; I'm on my feet, jerking him by the scrawny shoulders, his head whipping back and forth until I think I'm maybe shaking it clear of humbug.

"I'll magic you!" I shout. "Who's your father anyway, that feeble-minded old scarecrow or me? Remember me, Jacob Zipper, that works like a dog so his son can be a person?" Then I see how he's staring daggers; you could puncture your conscience on such daggers, and so I pipe down.

I turn to Ethel cooling her backside against the hardwood icebox, an oven mitten pressed to her cheek. "So whose side are you on?" I appeal.

She gives me a look. "This is a contest already?"

But tempted as I am to make peace, I feel they've forced my hand; I cuff the boy's ear for good measure and tell my wife, "I don't know him anymore, he's not my son."

Understand, it's a tense time; the news from the Old Country is bad. In Kiev they've got a Jew on trial for blood libel, and over here folks are grumbling about swarms of Hebrews washing onto our shores. Some even blame the wreck of the Titanic on the fact that there were Guggenheims onboard. It's a climate created by ignorance, which will surely pass with the coming enlightened age—when our sons will have proved how indispensable we are. But in the meantime we must keep order in our own house.

At the next meeting of the North Main Street Improvement Committee I propose that the time is ripe to act.

Ostrow and the others stir peevishly, their hibernation disturbed. "Act? What act?" It seems they never heard of fanatics in our bosom or the corruption of our youth.

"Wake up!" I exhort them. "We got a problem!"

Slowly, scratching protuberant bellies and unshaven jaws, they begin to snap out of it; they swill sarsaparilla, light cigars, overcoming a collective amnesia to ask me what we should do.

"Am I the chairman?" I protest. "Ostrow's the chairman." But it's clear that my robust agitation has prompted them to look to me for leadership, and I'm damned if I don't feel equal to the test.

"Cut off the head from the body," I'm suddenly inspired to say, "and your monster is kaput."

At sundown the following evening the executive board of the Improvement Committee rounds the corner into Auction Street. There's a softness in the air, the stench of the river temporarily overwhelmed by potted chicken wafting from the windows over the shops. It's a pleasant evening for a stroll, but not for us, who must stay fixed on the critical business at hand. We're all of one mind, I tell myself, though yours truly has been elected to carry the hedge shears—donated for the deed by Hekkie Schatz of Hekkie's Hardware. Ostrow our titular chair, Nussbaum the treasurer, Benny Rosen the whatsit, all have deferred the honor to me, by virtue of what's perceived as my greater indignation.

This time we don't knock but burst into the dusty shtibl. As it turns out our timing is perfect: A knot of disciples—it appears that several are needed to function as anchors—are unravelling the rope beneath the open skylight. Rising into the lemon shaft (now turning primrose), his feet in their felt slippers arched like fins, Rabbi Shmelke chants the *Amidah* prayer: "*Baruch atoh Adonoy*, blessed art Thou, our God and God of our Fathers . . ."

The Shpinkers start at our headlong entrance. Then gauging our intentions by the sharp implement I make no attempt to hide, they begin to reel their rebbe back in. My colleagues urge me to do something quick, but I'm frozen to the spot; though Shmelke's descending, I'm still struck with the wonder of watching him rise. "Decease!" cries Ostrow, to no effect whatsoever; then he and the others shove me forward.

Still I dig in my heels. Disoriented, I have the sensation that the room is topsy-turvy; above is below and vice versa. Standing on the ceiling as the rebbe is hauled up from the depths, we're in danger of coming unglued, of tumbling headfirst through the skylight. I worry for our delinquent sons, who now outnumber the Shpinkers, and in their fantastic getups are almost indistinguishable from the original bunch. Among them, of course, is Ziggy, elflocks curling like bedsprings from under his cap, perched on a chair for the better view.

Then the room rights itself. Holding the handles of the hedge shears, I could say that I'm gripping the wings of a predatory bird, its mind independent of my own. I could say I only hang on for dear life, while it's the shears themselves that swoop forth to bite the rope in two. But the truth is, I do it of my own free will. And when the rope goes slack—think of a serpent when the swami stops playing his pipe—I thrill at the gasps that are exhaled ("Ahhh") all around. After which: quiet, as old Shmelke, still chanting, floats leisurely upward again, into the primrose light that is deepening to plum.

When he's out of sight, my Ziggy is the first to take the initiative—because that's the type of person we Zippers are. The rascal, he bolts for the open window followed by a frantic mob. I too am swept into the general exodus, finding myself somehow impelled over the sill out onto the fire escape. With the others I rush up the clattering stairs behind (incidentally) Ida Kaminsky, who's been hiding there to watch the proceedings. I reach the roof just in time to see my son, never an athletic boy—nor an impulsive or a headstrong or a rebellious one, never to my knowledge any of these—I see him swarm up the slippery pane of the inclined skylight (which slams shut after) and leap for the rope. Whether he means to drag the old man down or hitch a ride, I can't say, but latched onto the dangling cord, he begins, with legs still cycling, to rise along with the crackpot saint.

Then uttering some complicated mystical war cry, Hershel Ostrow, holding onto his homburg, follows Ziggy's lead. With his free hand Hershel grabs my boy's kicking right foot, and I thank God when I see them losing altitude, but this is only a temporary reversal. Because it seems that Rabbi Shmelke, handicaps notwithstanding, has only to warble louder, adjusting the pitch of his prayer to gain height. I console myself that if he continues ascending, the fragile old man will come apart in the sky; the boys will plummet beneath his disembodied leg. Or Ziggy, whose leap I don't believe in the first place, unable to endure the burden of his companion, will let go. I assure myself that none of this is happening.

From beside me the wild Ida Kaminsky has flung herself onto Hershel's ankle, her skirt flairing to show off bloomers—which make a nice ribbon for the tail of a human kite. But even with her the concatenation doesn't end: The shambling Sanford Nussbaum and Mindy Dreyfus, the halfwit Herman Wolf, Rabbi

Fein's own pious Abie in his prayer shawl, Milton Rosen in his mackintosh, all take their turn. Eventually every bad seed of North Main Street is fastened to the chain of renegade children trailing in the wake of old Shmelke's ecstasy.

One of the rebbe's zealots, having mounted a chimney pot, makes a leap at the flying parade, but for him they're already out of reach. Then another tries and also fails. Is it because, in wanting to pull their *tzaddik* back to the earth, his followers are heavy with a ballast of desire? This seems perfectly logical to me, sharing as I do the Chasids' despair.

Which is why I shout "Ziggy, come back! All is forgiven!" and make to jump into the air. In that instant I imagine I grab hold and am carried aloft with the kids. The tin roofs, the trolley lines, the brand new electric streetlights in their five-globed lamps, swiftly recede, their incandescence humbled by the torched western sky. Across the river the sunset is more radiant than a red flare over a herring barrel, dripping sparks—all the brighter as it's soon to be extinguished by dark clouds swollen with history rolling in from the east. Then just as we're about to sail beyond those clouds, I come back to myself, a stout man and no match for gravity.

Romance

＿＿•＿＿

I.

The tale is told in my family of my mother's father Eli Goldfogle, who was engaged at birth to his future wife Esther in the Old Country, what the immigrants called "the other side." Nobody believes the story; the married couple themselves could not have known the whole of it, which is to say they were in no position to pass it along to their children, who passed it on to me. But ours is a family of disappointed dreamers, many of whom, like myself, live alone, and it's our penance to carry such tales. This one begins at the end of the last century in the Byelorussian village of Utsk, when arranged marriages were à la mode. It was a *mitzvah*, a good deed, and an act of faith that families should pledge to each other, over honey cakes and brandy, infants born at approximately the same time.

Since the Goldfogles and Esther's parents—call them the Bluesteins, though nobody used surnames in those days; since the Goldfogles and the Bluesteins inhabited separate villages several rolling versts apart, Eli and his pledged one, his *mash-kin*, managed to grow up without ever meeting. There had of course been occasions when they might have, market days and celebrations when the communities converged. But while they were aware of a mutual fate, which they accepted the way the young accept their mortality, never really believing they will die, neither child was especially curious about the other. Each had his own more pressing interests, and as the marriage contract was an accomplished fact, what after all did it have to do with either of them?

Young Eli was in any case engaged in his studies. While he wasn't counted among the prodigies—he couldn't perform, like some, those dazzling feats of memory whose fame in the Pale of Settlement were equal to virtuosity on the violin—he was nonetheless a fervent scholar. From his tenderest years it had been the boy's ambition to become a Talmud *khochem*, "an uprooter of mountains," like the wise men who sat in their bearded serenity by the synagogue's eastern wall. Like them he would devote himself to the Five Books and their commentaries, and to a total adherence to the precepts ordained therein. *"Torah min hashamayim*, the Torah is from heaven; *hashamayim min Torah*, heaven is from the Torah." This was Eli's watchword, which he intoned with an earnestness that caused his unlettered father, Moishe the Pit (so called for his work in a quarry or his bottomless appetite, take your pick), to scratch his head.

What he lacked in breadth of intellect, Eli made up for with his zeal and fidelity to the letter of the Law. And if it didn't appear that, by such application, he would ascend to the ranks of the saints, so be it; Eli had small patience with saints, who seemed to him in their mystical transports a largely irresponsible lot. Under the benevolent eye of the sage Rabbi Ben Bag Bag in the dilapidated study house, he had himself been tempted, through chanting the words of certain texts, to fly clear of the rotting rooftops of his village. But since such flights were not compatible with the social contract implicit in his prayers, Eli, however reluctantly, stuck close to home.

His industry notwithstanding, Eli grew up ramrod straight, his cheekbones high and pronounced, with the fine hawkish nose and sable hair that distinguished him from his rough-hewn tribe. His eyes, despite their severity, were large and doe-soft, dark as twin inkwells, which could weep—this was his unspoken fancy—words of Holy Writ.

"Your son," the village marriage broker would sigh to Eli's mother, lamenting a match already made, "a Daniel, a regular prince."

In her neighboring hamlet of Putsk, Esther Bluestein, Eli's betrothed, had a bookish bent of her own. But since girls could not attend *cheder*, her childhood reading had been necessarily confined to collections of Yiddish proverbs for women, and to the fairy tales contained in the *Maaseh*, *Shmuel*, and *Bovo* books. The last of these, Esther's favorite, recounted the implausible adventures of the daring Prince Bovo, who courted the ladies even as he confused his enemies with magic. As she grew older, Esther purchased from itinerant book peddlers romances of historical thunder by the popular author N. M. Shaikevitch, whose pen name was "Shomer." In them, Jewish sons and daughters defied hypocrisy and overcame fanatical constraints to seek their destinies in the world at large. Reading the books in fevered secrecy, Esther would later discard them, lest she be caught and accused of a frivolous self-indulgence.

She was a pretty girl, Esther, small-bosomed and stately, with a waist that might have been cinched by a velvet choker. She had olive skin, onyx eyes, sparrow hands, cocoa brown hair that, when freed of its kerchief, floated in billows like the grain of finished mahogany. As a consequence Esther was not without her portion of vanity, which declared itself whenever she polished the solitary heirloom of her mama's samovar. Rubbing hard as if to release the burnished image of herself trapped in brass, she would step back admiringly.

"It's a maideleh fit for a hero," she'd say.

It was a time of great stirrings among the Jews of the Russian Pale; there was much talk of enlightenment, of impending revolution that would throw off for good and all the yoke of the Czar.

A new kind of Jewish hero was abroad in the land, not so much warrior as poet and idealist, young firebrands sacrificing themselves on the altar of their beliefs and getting exiled to Siberia by the trainload. That they never seemed to pass through Putsk, these heroes, didn't mean the village wasn't alert to their legends; and no one was more alert than Esther, who imagined that her star was crossed with one of these. No matter that her future was already fixed to that of her plighted husband, whose reputation for a drudge had preceded him to her parents' door. Still Esther could dream, couldn't she? She could picture his handsome countenance next to hers in the cloudy samovar, his scholar's disguise laid bare to reveal the bold revolutionist. Then she would wish their wedding delayed a little longer, that his image might not yet have to come clear.

As it happened, the proposed date of the Goldfogle/Bluestein alliance was moved forward, due to its coinciding with Eli's call to appear at the induction center in Berditchev. There his eligibility for immediate conscription into the army of the Czar would be reviewed. That he'd be taken was a foregone conclusion, since nothing short of a bribe far beyond the humble resources of Moishe the Pit could secure his deferment. Moreover, it was generally understood that the Russian draft, quite nearly a life sentence, spelled a virtual death sentence for a Jewish lad. If he didn't perish from abuse or exposure, he would suffer at the very least a spiritual death by separation from the community of Israel. This was especially true in the case of a boy such as Eli, who drew his very sustenance from the holy books.

Thus it was decided that the family Goldfogle would employ a strategy taken by so many in those days: They would scrape together the funds to pack their scholar off to America. The Utskers might be relied on for contributions, since, his zealotry having made Eli something of a local spoilsport, most would be eager to see him go. It was further decided that the prearranged nuptials would take place as planned, prior to Eli's departure.

That way, no longer a bachelor, he would be proof against the temptations for which America was famous, temptations he already considered himself a bulwark against. Once established in the Golden Land, he could purchase the *shiffs-carte* for his wife's passage over; and later on, when he became a millionaire, a relatively predictable stage in an immigrant's progress, he would send for the rest.

The wedding canopy had been erected in the courtyard behind the Bluesteins' ancestral hovel in their ditch-side village, to which half of Eli's own village had traveled for the event. Consisting of a prayer shawl that had once belonged to an illustrious ancestor, the canopy would be passed on to Eli after his nuptials. He'd often coveted it, convinced it had properties that rendered one impervious to sin. But as he stood beneath it on that soft night in the month of Nisan, surrounded by a mob of wedding guests holding candles, Eli took small comfort in the bequest.

Although the marriage had always loomed on his horizon, he'd given little thought to it until now. What, frankly, had he given thought to other than the books in Rabbi Ben Bag Bag's study house, which contained worlds? Granted, Eli had no special taste for the more fanciful portions of Torah, but if he'd ever yearned for exotic places, he had only to read descriptions of the flora and fauna of paradise. Should he feel the urge to travel, he read about the patriarchs, who'd done enough wandering to last the Jews for all time. Hadn't Joseph, torn from his father's house and thrust into alien lands, made such dramas redundant for future generations? But here he was on the eve of departing the Pale forever, a prospect that had thus far filled him only with dread—until tonight, when the dread was nudged aside by a secret thrill. Undignified though it was to be roused by circumstances outside of Scripture, Eli found himself looking forward to the journey; the wedding was an awkward formality he had to suffer through before taking flight.

As his old teacher and rabbi shpritzed the seven benedictions in his face, Eli could scarcely contain his impatience. He chafed in the top hat and stiff white *kittl*, which he had reason to think made him look like an ornamental saltcellar. It didn't help that he was center stage in an unfamiliar setting, at a spectacle catered by a wealthy merchant for his own greater glory, where one and all, be they relations or beggars, had been invited to witness the banns of a scholar and a reputed beauty—seeing whom Eli would believe. But there was something else that troubled him beyond the vulgarity, though he'd known all his life this night must come. After all, it was written: "It is the duty of every man to take to himself a wife, in order to fulfill the precept of propagation." Indeed, a Jew without a wife, without children, was not a Jew in the eyes of the community. Although wasn't it also written: "When one is deeply engrossed in the study of Torah, and is afraid that marriage may interfere with his studies, he may delay marrying, provided of course he is not lustful." Too late did it occur to Eli that the wedding should have been postponed.

To try and filter out the proceedings, he mustered his powers of concentration to rehearse the *midrash* he intended to deliver at the wedding feast. In that way he managed to ignore the entrance of the bride and the ritual raising and lowering of her veil—which hadn't in fact revealed very much, since Esther, according to tradition, was blindfolded. She was furthermore positively giddy, enjoying herself hugely as her attendants led her in circles around her betrothed. For as long as she couldn't see anything anyway, she was free to erect a palace in the goat-reeking courtyard, to make a prince of the groom; or, forgetting the groom, imagine the wild Yeshiva student from Shomer's *Hershele Hotspur* leaping over the trestle tables on horseback to steal the bride away. Then the scarf was removed from her eyes and Esther peered through layers of lace at the bridegroom, who might as well have been a figure behind a waterfall.

When he placed the ring on her finger, Eli had occasion to note its tapered slenderness, thinking, "He who gazes at even the small finger of a woman in order to enjoy its sight commits a sin." He might have quibbled as to whether he'd actually enjoyed the sight, from which he was in any case distracted by the rabbi's pronouncement: "Behold, thou art consecrated according to the Law of Moses and Israel." Eli squashed the goblet like an offensive bug.

At the banquet, though bride and groom sat side-by-side, neither found cause to turn toward the other. Flanked by their respective families, who talked animatedly over them to their counterparts-in-law, Eli and Esther kept their eyes fixed on the entertainment. The wealthy merchant, rather than embarrass the poor with overmuch prodigality, had provided well within his means. Beet soup and groats, which the merchant intimated were a concession to the toothless rabbi, comprised the main courses, chased by a paint-thinning kvass. The hired jester, too arthritic to climb on the table, advertised his sidelines—love philtres and abortifacients—even as he performed his shtik. He told a medley of tasteless jokes ("It's the wedding night and the newlyweds are packing their bags for the honeymoon, while the *machetonim*, the in-laws, they're listening through the wall. 'Let me sit on it,' says the bride . . ." and so forth), after which he broke into sentimental song. The songs were accompanied by a skeleton orchestra of gypsy *klezmorim:* shrill horn, hammered dulcimer, a fiddle that set one's teeth on edge, a double bass that the musician seemed to be trying to saw in half.

It was a circus, thought Eli, arranged for his personal humiliation, whereas Esther was thankful for any diversion that put off a little longer the reckoning between husband and wife. Having summoned a composure befitting her newly elevated station, she received the blessings of her maiden friends; she nodded with regal approval at the festivities, clapping in time to the dancers— the men with men, women with women, mother-in-law in mock quarrel with mother-in-law, the old bubbeh swaying with a loaf of challah bread. Nor was she disappointed that the groom had foregone the custom of offering her an end of his handkerchief, following which they'd have been expected to dance a *mitzvah tantz* face-to-face.

During a lull between songs Eli rose to make his speech. Not wanting to invite more attention to himself than was necessary, he nevertheless felt obliged to lend some sanctity to an otherwise pagan affair. "If a man sets out to take a wife . . . ," he muttered, then cleared his throat and repeated the phrase like a call to arms. This was the passage from Deuteronomy to which Rabbi Simeon had applied a famous analogue, concerning a man who seeks something he's lost. But no sooner had Eli launched into Simeon's sermon than the wedding party applauded, the band struck up a quadrille, and everyone demanded he kiss the bride. Next to him Esther closed her eyes, but other than a zephyrlike stirring at the fringes of her still unlifted veil, she felt nothing at all. Then "Mazel tov!" and the pair of them were hustled from the courtyard, Eli prompting laughter with his protests that this wasn't Jewish; it was some *goyishe* sacrifice he'd been lured into unawares.

Left alone in the dark "bridal chamber," which was merely the close little room Esther shared with her younger sisters (chased out for the night), Eli was ashamed for his outburst. Determined to steel himself for what lay ahead, he tried to calm his stampeding heart, to curb his fingers from fanning the pages of imaginary books. In the dirty window the tilted ewer of a yellow moon spilled light onto the quilted bed, which Eli gazed at like a country spied from the gondola of a balloon. Waiting for Esther, who'd retired behind a gunny-cloth curtain, he reviewed what Rabbi Ben Bag Bag—Eli could feel the old man's whistling exhalations in his ear—had instructed him to think of as his duty. It was a distasteful business, but he believed himself more or less equal to the task. He was aware that some misguided souls were said to take delight in it, as was written: "Since the destruction of the Temple, sexual pleasure was taken from those who obey Torah and given to those who transgress it." But Eli didn't think himself in any danger of succumbing to pleasure.

Naked behind the curtain for the instant after she'd shed the brittle silk dress (which both her mother and mine were also married in), Esther felt a warm flickering begin in her belly and travel to her extremities. Hurriedly she pulled on her muslin gown as if pouring water to douse a flame. She presented herself in shadows to the groom, whose silhouette in its unremoved top hat resembled a trembling beaker on the boil. If unstopped, would he evaporate or explode? As she waited for him to speak—they'd yet to exchange a word all evening—Esther admitted to herself that he was perhaps no Prince Bovo, no valiant Yossel from Shomer's *The Convicted*, who fights a duel with the gentile count that made advances toward his sweetheart. But surely this Eli Goldfogle was *someone*, and Esther bit her lip in anticipation of who he might be.

However, as generosity had its limits, she presently judged his time to be up, satisfied that his silence had confirmed his nonentity. Taking the initiative, Esther was astonished that her first words to her husband should be a lie.

"I'm unclean."

"Ah," replied Eli, as if she'd imparted an interesting conversational tidbit rather than confessed herself ineligible for ritual immersion. The *Shulchan Arukh* was unequivocal on this point: One must never sleep with his wife during her menstrual flow. As it was written: "The husband in that period should not touch her even with his little finger . . ." With heartfelt gratitude for his eleventh-hour reprieve from intimacy, Eli announced, "Then I'll sleep on the floor."

From what he knew of the mysteries of the female body, he pictured a bloody tide, a red sea upon which the Ark itself might have foundered. Happy to have escaped inundation, Eli pulled down the gunny curtain and made a pallet at the foot of the bed. He curled up like a weary castaway and praised God for making his marriage the minor interruption it had so far proved to be.

At dawn, when the sexton rattled his clapper to call the men to prayer, Eli rose, having slept not a wink. He gathered the stiff *kittl* about him so that its rustlings wouldn't awaken his bride, who lay with the covers pulled over her head. Shrugging, he stepped out into the grease-fetid hovel, where the men in their boots and patched caftans were already abroad. A rowdy bunch of mostly blacksmiths and beekeepers, Eli's in-laws greeted him with rough embraces and swept him off to shul. Along the way their ranks, and high spirits, were swelled by Eli's own father and uncles, mostly smugglers, who'd stayed the night at a local inn. They joked and made rude references to the marriage bed, the rudest emanating from Moishe the Pit himself, who made amends with his hardihood for his son's bloodless reticence. Services over, all returned to the Bluestein abode for a breakfast of pot cheese and blintzes, a standard fare for weddings and funeral wakes alike. It was served by bustling wives, one of whom, supposed Eli, his swimming head bent toward the table, belonged to him.

Afterwards, while the *machetonim* made their noisy farewells, Eli climbed onboard the wagon to wait for his father, holding his breath lest someone should call him back. Although it was understood that he would return home immediately to start preparing for his journey overseas, he couldn't believe they'd allow him to make such a clean getaway. You might almost think Esther's family were as glad to be rid of him as he was to go. The caravan pulled into the ruts of the unpaved street, and Eli gave a look over his shoulder at a row of waving women like kerchiefed pears, again idly wondering which was his.

When they were gone, Esther finally came out of her room. All morning long, resisting her mother's pleading, she'd lain in bed imagining what might have been, but now she emerged as if nothing had happened. Her mama scolded her roundly and thanked God that the groom had not made a scandal by demanding she appear.

The next few days were filled with the flurry of arrangements surrounding Eli's departure. For the scholar himself, who'd made a curious peace with leaving his village, if not the entire continent of Europe, the preparations were simple: He had only to select what books to take along. Under his old rabbi's tutelage he learned the traveler's benedictions, which to say after having passed thirty cubits, which before traveling the first parasang, and so forth. It wasn't until the end of the week, when he was placed in the bed of his father's wagon and buried under a bale of beaver pelts, that Eli had doubts, and once more sensing the magnitude of the journey he was about to undertake, grew afraid.

He was spirited across the border by his father and his uncle Pishke, neither of whom (along with the rest of his family) would Eli ever see again. Outside Bialystok he was disinterred and consigned to a good-natured peasant, in whose rattletrap droshky he traveled by easy stages to Poznan, thence on to Hamburg by train. There, thanks to the forged passport and papers that were the speciality of the Utsker scribe, the red tape was kept to a minimum. The swindling ticket agents, the doctors' prods, a rat-infested wharfside quarantine, all took their turns at him, but insulated against torment and loneliness by his devotions, Eli endured. And one breezy afternoon in his eighteenth year, he found himself standing at the rusty taffrail of the S.S. *Gravenhage*, bound for the port of New York.

Watching the shoreline sink in the distance under an emerald swell, he asked aloud, "Ribbono Shel-Oylem, if it pleases You, what have I done?" and straightaway ducked into *The Ethics of the Fathers*. He recited his Psalms with the intensity that some claimed would mend the rift between heaven and earth, though Eli had always disdained such notions. Hadn't Maimonides in his *Guide* inveighed against the illogic of viewing prayers as "holy aphrodisiacs," the chanting of which would hasten the birth of Messiah? They should be uttered, such prayers, with measured breathing, of the type Eli associated with that of the girl back home in the so-called bridal chamber.

But this was the stuff of forbidden texts, which made otherwise serious scholars into crackpots and would-be saints—the kind who might see, in place of say the rolling green ocean, Satan's own rippling cloak, its folds concealing biblical monsters and frogs sixty houses high. To allay such phantasms, Eli increased the fervor of his spiritual exercises; he fasted as well, which wasn't difficult given the weevil-ridden kasha served in steerage from a common pot. In his hunger he remembered the tale of Rabbi Fertig, called the Armrest of Ha-Shem—how he was nourished by words of Torah, which, as he pronounced them, had both texture and taste. Although it smacked of arrogance, Eli decided that his case was much the same, or how else, on an empty stomach, should he have been so often sick over the rail?

II.

As she passed through the gates of the processing shed at Ellis Island, Esther muffled her face with her shawl against a blustering March wind. The shawl covered a wig, like a sat-upon ball of yarn, that in turn concealed her once-shorn hair, grown back in abundance since her marriage. What she hadn't been able to stuff into a canvas seabag, Esther wore, so that dresses ballooned about her slender frame. In a coat graffiti'd with chalk marks, bristling with tags, reeking of carbolic acid, she supposed herself indistinguishable from the other arrivals. How would he identify her, her husband, and vice versa? she wondered, although it was somehow the least of her concerns.

Outside at the head of the water stairs, in a roped-off receiving area, Esther saw what she mistook at first for a crowd of striking workers. Already begins the freedom, she thought. But their upheld placards, instead of radical slogans, bore the scrawled names of friends and relations they'd come to meet. Spying her own name in the stark Hebrew characters grown familiar to her over the years, Esther made her way toward the sign with modestly lowered eyes. She teased herself by prolonging the moment of mutual recognition with her husband, then wondered, when she didn't raise her eyes, if she'd missed forever the moment favorable for looking.

But if she didn't look at the man with the sign, who shouldered her bag in lieu of an embrace then led her up a gangplank into the steam launch, Esther took in everything else. Weary as she was from the voyage, eyes still smarting from an examination that turned their lids inside out, nothing was lost on her—not one tower among the fog-wreathed cluster, like a clutch of swords in a hand, rising before them as the ferry ploughed the harbor toward the Golden Land. Later, when they'd boarded the Second Avenue Elevated at dusk, she noted the horse cars startled by electric broughams; she recorded a thousand rime-bordered windows framing a thousand beige repetitions of mother, child, and sewing machine. There was the man on a platform who might have been a fugitive masquerading as a consumptive tailor, the woman bundled on a fire escape banked with airing mattresses like alfresco madhouse walls. She saw bazaars lit by bonfires, a billboard advertising the Uwanta Pill, King of Cathartics, a theater marquee for *Lula, the Beautiful Hebrew Girl.*

If the man beside her spoke, Esther never heard him over the din of the screeching train, too absorbed was she in any case with getting an eyeful of America. How long had she fed her imagination on books alone? The *shundromans* printed by New York's Yiddish presses and exported abroad, hawked in the market platz of Putsk, all of them depicting the Lower East Side of that city, rather than Warsaw or Kiev or Siberian exile, as the international seat of heartbreak and romance. "You want heroes?" the peddlers would tease her. In America they came by the job lot—artists and actors, poets and playwrights, revolutionists who lived on air in the attics of skyscrapers, close to the stars and high above the Law.

"Shomer" Shaikevitch, Esther's old favorite, had himself relocated abroad, and now set his penny dreadfuls, replete with disguises and mistaken identities, in the teeming streets of New York. Then there were the traveling players. Although Yiddish theater had been outlawed in Russia, by cleverly germanizing the dialogue, wandering troupes had staged the dramas of Messrs Hurwitz and Lateiner, Shomer's spiritual sons. On boards thrown over barrels in the market, they'd portrayed the ruptures and passions of the East Side ghetto—the wayward sons in conflict with unyielding fathers, pious daughters with cruel stepmothers, the wayward sons and pious daughters conceiving for one another impossible loves. The players also performed the lively songs of Tin Pan Alley, such as "Yiddle on Your Fiddle Play Ragtime" by Izzy Balin, now Irving Berlin. Eventually it had begun to seem to Esther as if life itself had emigrated to America.

True, she had at first been in no hurry to leave. Why travel so far to join a perfect stranger about whom she'd lost all curiosity? Nor was it easy to abandon one's family at a time when the shtetl was so threatened with government ukases, dispossessions, and peasant pogroms. Turn away, and before you turned back, the entire Pale of Settlement might be swallowed up by history like the sea swallows a mythical continent. So in the end her departure had less in common with leave-taking than escape. But as she made ready to exchange her old world for a new one, Esther had felt that, in a sense, she already enjoyed the best of two: She was, on the one hand, the honored spouse of a husband who'd made a place for her in *di goldeneh medina,* while on the other hand, she hardly felt married at all.

During the five years it had taken him to save the money for his wife's *shiffs-carte,* Eli had worked in a cloakmaker's loft on Rivington Street. It still rankled him that a scholar should have been reduced to a common wage-slave, whereas on the other side they would have competed for his upkeep. Here the scholar was indiscernible from the ordinary shnorrer peddling door-to-door notions and secondhand clothes, bags of ersatz Jerusalem dirt. Here a "mister" must become a "shister," and even the most devout began to question whether or not the Almighty ever condescended to visit the Lower East Side.

"Golden Land," they scoffed, "some joke! No wonder they call it America—*ama reka,* which it means hollow people, the disciples of Moloch."

But in time Eli had made a virtue of necessity, for as it was written: "Where there's no bread, there's no Torah." He became a Columbus tailor, one of the multitude who learned their needle skills in the New World. He even began to take some satisfaction in his handiwork, the neat stitchery that brought to mind the sainted Enoch, who, by sewing shoe leather, stitched together the upper and lower realms. When the shop foreman commended his labor, comparing it favorably to the inferior work of the young wags Eli's own age, Eli made no attempt to conceal his pride.

The wags in the cloakmaking factory had nicknames for everyone. Old Man Markish was the Goat for the way his pinking shears munched blindly at a bolt of chintz; Fischel the foreman was Polka Dotz, because the cough from his galloping-shop disease speckled his garments in blood. Mrs. Grinspan, owing to a prodigious endowment of bosom, was Froy Two-Bags-Full, and Eli was naturally the Rabbi. Although no one escaped their raillery, Eli, who'd refused to trim his beard and persisted in winding his phylacteries at his sewing machine, posed a special challenge to his "oysgreened" coworkers. They teased him mercilessly, making certain he was in earshot whenever they vaunted their amorous escapades.

They congratulated one another on their conquests at the Nonpareil Dancehall, on heated encounters with soubrettes in red tights backstage at the Bowery burlesques. They spoke openly of affairs with the ethical-culture ladies in the progressive East Broadway cafés, of their dalliance among handkerchief girls under the Allen Street El. Aware that much of this talk was for his benefit, Eli sometimes doubted its veracity; after all, their jobs were no less toilsome than his. So where did they find the pep, let alone the spare time, for such degradation? Then he remembered that the *yetser hora*, the evil intention, was said to be an inexhaustible source of fortitude.

Generally Eli kept his own counsel as Scripture prescribed, suffering a martyrdom that was its own reward. But as his silence only served to spur them on to more fiendish taunts, someone occasionally crossed a line beyond which even Eli couldn't hold his tongue. Such as the time Ari Baumgart lifted Sophie Gluck's skirt in front of him, asking his professional opinion of the picot stitch on her finespun drawers.

Scarlet to the gills, Eli rose to his feet. "Baumgart, shame!" he protested. "Are you not, like me, a married man?"

In fact, several of the young men had wives and families for whom they were theoretically saving money to import from the other side. But out-of-sight, their families were also out-of-mind, a condition that Baumgart illustrated, enlisting the help of his fellows in looking under pressing tables and bundles of cloth.

"Wife? I don't see no wife."

Then Eli had had to struggle against admitting they had a point. Over the years he'd been making regular, albeit token, weekly deposits at the draft and passage office, but the gesture had always seemed empty. Who was it exactly he was supposed to be sending for? Dutifully he had written to advise her of his progress, stiff and impersonal letters beginning: "I greet you, my esteemed and exemplary bride [he omitted using her name, which seemed too intimate] in accordance with Proverbs 5:18– 'Have a joy in the wife of thy youth, etc . . .'" Her replies were of an equal formality, in a hand like a water spider's tracings. But so neutral were the events she recounted that they might have belonged to anyone, and therefore invoked an image of no one in particular. Further, her letters suggested that she was no more eager than he was for their reunion, which vindicated the dawdling pace at which Eli saved for her fare.

Meanwhile he'd pursued his studies and ritual observances unimpeded, and with an increased sense of urgency. In the Old Country the Ark of the Covenant was synonymous with the Ark of the Flood, a vessel that kept the Jews perpetually afloat. But here in America the vessel had run aground, and Torah was a broken rudder you clung to for dear life. It was Babylon, this new world, where the Jews were no sooner off the boat than they shaved their beards and traded their *shtreimels* for narrow-brimmed fun hats. They haunted the blasphemous Yiddish music halls, the dancing academies, stuss parlors, and disorderly houses, operated by Jewish gangsters celebrated in the ballads of the day. They made journeys on Shabbos to a city erected for the sake of pleasure at Coney Island, and took trains into the mountains to worship flowers and trees.

One had always to be on his guard against such enticements—a worthy enterprise, reasoned Eli, since resistance to temptation had no value where temptation was not tempting. As Rabbi Yohanan of blessed memory once said: "A bachelor who lives in a great city and does not sin—the Holy One Himself daily proclaims his virtue." No matter that, technically, Eli was not a bachelor.

Twice a day he attended the storefront cloakmaker's shul on

East Broadway, where he davened with a handful of bareboned relics who still adhered to old ways. On Friday nights he treated himself to a seat in the opulent Eldridge Street synagogue. After hours, fatigued though he was from his daily labors, he pored over his tractates and commentaries by guttering lamplight. The cramped quarters of the Widow Winkelman's Ludlow Street apartment, where he boarded, was not conducive to the task, nor were his fellow boarders sympathetic to Eli's diligence. Waxman, the dipsomaniacal fruit peddler, would comment on it by means of a musical sphincter that corrupted the air as he fit-fully dozed; and Fiedler, a freight-handler and voluptuary, com-plaining that Eli's murmuring kept him from sleep, would abandon his own bed for the Widow's, whence was heard a rau-cous frolicking through the wall. But Eli persevered.

He lived with the utmost frugality, as how could he not on such meager wages? His only expenses beyond his room and board, and the pennies he socked away toward the steamship passage, were the books he bought from the Essex Street stalls. He deemed them essential, since not only did he require them for study, but they afforded him a measure of privacy—this by virtue of the parapet he stacked them in to separate his cot from the bed shared by the other boarders. And if the purchase of books meant that it took a bit longer to save for his wife's ticket over, where was the harm? Better she should find him steadfast and faithful, still girded against wickedness by word and deed.

At length Eli had begun to expand the base of his scholar-ship, which is not to say that he ventured into the secular—far from it. But along with the intensified rigor of his prayers had come a new development: a concentration so heightened that Eli often experienced what could only be called ecstasy. It was a sensation that had at first embarrassed him, then prompted an inquisitive itch that made him look beyond the purely *halakhik*, or legal, dimension of his studies. He became interested in the kinds of texts that one was discourgaged from reading outside the covenant of marriage—the otherwise forbidden books found in obscure and cavernlike shops presided over by shriveled ancients in dusty gabardines; books that some called "sacred pornography," though Eli thought the term far-fetched. Still, the books did sometimes embrace unorthodox concepts, such as casting the union of heaven and earth in the respective roles of husband and wife. Thus it was said that God engaged with His creation, personified as the Holy Shekhinah, the feminine aspect of the divine, through the medium of physical love. In his own rapturous meditations Eli, clutching a book to his breast, might believe he held the shimmering Shekhinah Herself, wearing only Sophie Gluck's ash gray drawers.

It was hard to know which had exacted the greatest toll, work, study, or prayer (never mind loneliness—who was lonely?), but Eli was aware that he'd aged. He'd aged considerably more than five years could account for. Barely twenty-three, he walked with a stoop from the arduous hours of bending over his machine. His hair was thinning, his beard grizzled, brow creased, eyes red-rimmed and clouded by the cheap spectacles he bought off the Hester Street carts. His spare frame was wracked with nameless aches, not all of which could be ascribed to his job. Some might have said he'd acquired character, though one thing was clear: he was no longer the fresh-faced *bocher* of Utsk. Which made Eli wonder if his wife, whose advent he'd put off for as long as his conscience allowed, would even recognize him when she arrived?

She was to work for the Widow Winkelman, whose parlor was transformed by day into a pillow-making sweatshop. Alongside the other girls in the Widow's employ, Esther would stuff the pillow slips with feathers for a nominal salary; in addition she would help with domestic tasks to defray her board. Later on, when their combined incomes permitted, the wedded couple would take a flat of their own, or so Eli assumed. But for the time being—Waxman having been banished to the parlor sofa; Fiedler having moved in with the Widow, neither of whom bothered to make a pretense of chastity anymore—husband and wife would have the second bedroom to themselves. It was a situation in keeping with the general depravity of American life, but that wasn't what aggravated Eli most. As the Widow, a generous woman for all her salaciousness, welcomed Esther and showed her to her room, Eli realized with a sinking heart that he'd looked forward to her coming. Having deferred the event for half a decade, he'd found himself counting the days until her arrival, and now, God help him, he thought he knew why.

That evening, to commemorate Esther's disembarkation, the Widow had the supper table dragged into a space designated as the parlor. Separated from the kitchen by a curtain, the parlor was no less crowded, its bins of eiderdown spilling over in drifts about the pier glass and the potbellied stove. It was as if a stuffy New York tenement had been invaded by its occupants' homesick dreams of the snowy steppes. That was anyway Waxman's sodden observation made for the benefit of the new arrival, whose attentions the freight-handler also competed for. His bluff spirits enlivened by the Widow's savory brisket and a growler of beer sent up from Max Schure's saloon, Fiedler outdid himself. He stroked his mustache like a music-hall villain, suggesting that Mrs. Goldfogle was the toothsomest dish at the table; while at the same time he played footsie under her chair with their hostess, who cackled throatily. Eli, who'd yet to lift his head since saying his benedictions, might have felt more ashamed for the others had he not been so ashamed of himself.

Having identified the source of his anticipation, he was mortified to discover that its name was not Esther but "sexual intercourse." Eli tried to dismiss his feelings as merely the natural impulse, so long restrained, to perform the mitzvah of making children, but who was he kidding? Call it what you will, he knew he was guilty of wanton desire, and that intercourse—as the rev-

erend Joseph Caro strenuously asserted in the *Shulchan Arukh*—
must never be entered into to satisfy desire. It must only be performed in the fulfillment of the obligation of one's conjugal
duty, like paying a debt. As the sages said: "A man has a small
organ; if he starves it, it is contented, but if he pampers it, it is
hungry." The sages also said flatly that a man should avoid
women, and it was immaterial to Eli, who still didn't feel like a
husband, that such precepts did not apply to man and wife.

Albeit the lumpish woman he'd met at the Immigration Bu-
reau, her face hidden in her shawl, hadn't exactly been the type
to inflame the loins; Eli's ache was of a less localized nature.
That she'd changed into a contoured pearl shirtwaist, her face
scrubbed to incandescence, the tendrils of cocoa hair peeping
out from under her *sheitel* wig, made no difference. For lest she
read his thoughts in his eyes, Eli never raised his head. Nor did
he look up when the Widow, mistaking Esther's abstraction for
an eagerness to be alone with her man, said complicitly, "*Fay-
geleh*, you're tired. *Gay shlufn* already, go to bed." Esther's voice,
as she excused herself, sounded to Eli a touch melodic, recalling
the maxim: "It is forbidden to hear the voice of a woman singer,
or even to gaze at her hair."

He put off the inevitable for as long as he could stand, but
having endured a surfeit of unsolicited advice from the boarders,
Eli finally removed himself from their company. In the bedroom
the turned-down gas flame shivered like a distant blue star. The
window giving onto the airshaft was also blue, ice like silver foil
at its edges, a woman's garments hanging limply from the elbow
of a stovepipe that impaled a corner of the room. In the sagging
brass bed vacated by its former tenants, a slight form relieved
the covers, and Eli felt the scalding urge to crawl in and possess
it. Embracing it, he would inhale its attar of earth, warming his
blood, which had suffered from poor circulation of late. After all,
as it said in *Pirke Avot*, "A man may do with his wife what he
pleases." Though it said elsewhere that it was forbidden to share

a bed except for the purposes of procreation, out of the question before the woman had attended to her ablutions, and so on. She in any case appeared to be sleeping, and Eli's thoughts were not fixed on the purpose, and it was moreover forbidden to do this and forbidden to do that . . . So he lay down on his cot, surrounded by the books like the sandbags around a soldier's redoubt.

Neither husband nor wife slept that night. Eli chanted to himself the Psalms intended to exorcise impure thoughts, wondering at the character of the king who'd conceived them, a man driven by lust even into his dotage. Esther, in a counterfeit repose that left her alone with her impressions, lay cherishing every sound. The airshaft contained a babel of voices the way a shell contains an ocean; but it was possible, if you paid attention, to discern now a curse, now a pleading endearment, a child bawling beyond the thin tenement walls. Somewhere a gramophone played "*Nyu York kokht vi a keslgrib*, New York bubbles like a pot . . ." A cough rattled, a siren wailed, a ferry moaned, the frozen clothes creaked on the lines, and Esther listened, committing noises to memory like the words of a lullabye.

In the morning, despite her vigil, she rose refreshed, though not until she was certain her husband had already set off for the cloak factory. The Widow Winkelman, in her billowing house wrapper, greeted Esther with a suggestive wink and introduced her to the other girls as they arrived. They were standoffish at first, suspicious of the pretty greenhorn, but Esther's artlessness soon won their assurances that they would take her under their wing. The work was tedious but not difficult, and once she'd gotten the hang of pillow-stuffing, the inverse of the chicken-flicking she was used to since childhood, Esther enjoyed the lively conversation. When they weren't advising her about the stylish shops on Grand Street, or describing a dance (which they called a "racket") at the Teutonia Hall, the girls talked of love.

One spoke candidly of her Litvak fiddler, another of a young professor at the Alliance night school, with an open affection that would have scandalized Putsk. But here they seemed to feel, as Esther had known they must, that love was their due. Conducted mainly in Yiddish, their talk was peppered with American phrases, such as "bloff" and "fifti-fifti" and "vane-makerz depodmn stor," conjurations Esther made note of for future reference.

In all things, especially affairs of the heart, the girls deferred to the Widow. She was a gentle taskmistress, who pretended not to notice when her employees made a game of their labor, some-times flinging more feathers at each other than they stuffed in the cases. Instead, as she fed the pillow-ticking to her droning machine, she would recall for their instruction the landmark events of her past. These usually began with the example of her dead husband Jakie, peace on his soul, and advanced through a number of subsequent amours. Frequently, however, she waived personal experience in favor of keeping her girls abreast of the complicated liaisons of local celebrities: of stars like Tomashef-sky and Rudolph Shildkraut, Adler the Eagle, Madames Liptzin and Kalish, the poet Leivick, the playwright Peretz Hirshbein.

On that first morning, stirred to intoxication by the mention of such legendary names, Esther had interrupted the Widow's narrative to exclaim, "It's a dreamland, I think, this America!" Smiling from their worldly vantage, her companions patiently corrected her: Dreamland was a place you went to by the Coney Island Ferry on Saturdays. But the great moment came when, in late afternoon, the Widow Winkelman asked Esther to accom-pany her to the market. Later, when she'd accustomed herself to the neighborhood, she could go alone.

That same day at the cloakmaking loft on Rivington Street, Eli's coworkers gave him no quarter. Aware of his bride's arrival and remarking the deeper circles under his eyes, they made coarse allusions to marital monkeyshines. "So when do we get to see her, your Queen Esther?" they needled, posing the question Eli might as easily have asked himself. In the evening he lingered overlong at his prayers and, on his return to Ludlow Street, walked past the Widow's building without stopping. He wandered the neighborhood, buffeted by a spectacle impervious to the chill and inclement weather. Boys fed broken kegs and mattresses to the flames of a cremated truck horse, around which couples in storm coats practiced their two-step. Peddlers hugged themselves behind naphtha-lit carts. A crowd on a corner abandoned a speaker indicting the capitalist cockroaches to chase after a runabout rumored to contain Anna Held. Saloons and pawnshops blazed; pianos rolled. On Allen Street painted girls in loose kimonos beckoned from open windows, their breath rivaling the plumed exhalations from manhole covers.

When Eli entered the dark bedroom, his wife was already asleep. He lit a lamp and took up a book, *The Palm Tree of Deborah*, a mystical text that ordinarily would have provided him the means to transcend his dismal predicament. But tonight such an ascent seemed inaccessible, not to say inappropriate under the circumstances, an ethereal seduction Eli would do well to resist. Instead he opted for the *Yesod Yosef*, grounded in its sober legalities. He forced himself to focus on an especially thorny passage, which debated whether laughter on a fast day constituted an excess of joy, to the point of exhaustion. His eyes grown heavy, Eli lay back on his cot, thinking that things might be worse: So long as he and the woman kept to their tacit agreement that neither existed for the other, life was tolerable. But no sooner had he started to doze, lulled by the rhythm of her breathing, than Eli succumbed to a sweetness beyond reason. Immediately he woke to the realization that he had spilled his sticky seed.

"Master of the Universe," he appealed, "I have done this unwittingly, but it was caused due to evil musings. Erase this iniquity and save me from sinful thoughts, so may it be Thy will!"

After that, Eli's path was clear, outlined as it was in detail in the *Shulchan Arukh*: he must endeavor whenever convenient to have circumcized infants on his lap, increase his donations to charity, be the first to arrive at the *minyan* and the last to leave, and rise every midnight to lament the destruction of the Temple. As for his wife, accessory though she was to his pollution, he must not look her in the face until his heart was pure.

As the Widow's particular pet, Esther received the lion's share of her sympathy. "Your husband that he's in heaven a saint already," the landlady would repine. "Which it makes you *almuneh* like me, a widow." Though she sometimes said *aguneh*, abandoned wife. In either case Esther would heave a wistful sigh, acknowledging the hollow charade of her marriage, but the truth was that she couldn't have been happier. Dreaming was after all her element, her true native country the land of heart's desire. Having spent her days in a diaspora of longing, what more could she ask than to have found herself in what she took to be the capital of dreams?

It was a conviction she reaffirmed each afternoon, when, dispatched into the East Side streets to do the marketing, Esther was set free. Veteran of countless traffickings among village peddlers, she was unintimidated by the Hester Street throngs. With a practiced eye she distinguished the fresh from the festering among the noisome chicken coops and herring tubs, confident that her bargaining skills had traveled well. In this way Esther made short work of the shopping, which left her time to linger awhile in the neighborhood before she was missed.

She took a daily excursion through what the Widow called the Yiddish Rialto, up to Second Avenue and down along the Bowery, where there were palaces built for the adoration of dreams. There were nickelodeons and automatic one-cent vaudevilles, a life-size mock-up of David Kessler under the Thalia marquee, brooding over a skull in "Hamlet, the Yeshiva Boy."

There was the great Jacob Adler tearing a passion to tatters on a poster for "God of Vengeance" outside his playhouse at the corner of Chrystie and Grand. No matter that Esther had yet to set foot inside one of these theaters; she was content to bide her time in anticipation of the day, just as she'd savored her coming to America. Then there was the fear that what went on in the theaters might fall short of what she'd imagined; it might pale by comparison to the continuous drama of the streets.

She made a loop through Seward Park past black-sleeve photographers and balladmongers performing topical songs—here an ode to the victims of the Triangle Fire, there a hymn to the heroism of Ida Strauss, who went down with her financier husband onboard the Titanic. She walked past the offices of the Yiddish dailies on East Broadway, then farther along past the cafés, which Esther saved for last. This was her destination, the end of the avenue where romance was run to ground, the very cradle of dreamers. And there they were, congregated in the Café Royal and Glickman's Odessa Tearoom, the writers indistinguishable from the creatures of their own invention—poets, revolutionists, renegade scholars in threadbare cutaways, their frayed collars upstanding, hair fallen in crescent forelocks over their face. They crowded around the tables as if ideas were dice in a crapshoot; as if they were surgeons and the muse was a patient under the knife. Wild-eyed, they gesticulated with monocles and Russian cigarettes, their animation a thing that could only have been borne of valor, or so Esther believed. They were a species not to be witnessed this side of the pages of books; though these, she had to remind herself, backing away from the plate-glass windows with a mortal shudder, these were flesh and blood.

Sometimes, before returning to Ludlow Street, Esther might pause to watch the ordinary men, toiling to and from the sweat factories in their molting alpacas, and wonder if one of them might have been her husband. She was grateful beyond measure not to know.

But ultimately there came an afternoon in early spring when the looking was no longer enough. Or rather, it seemed to Esther, leaning forward to peer through the sun's reflection on the window of Glickman's Odessa Tearoom, that she'd lost her balance and fallen in. How else would she have found the nerve to hide her market basket (into which she'd stuffed her wig) under a neighboring stoop and enter the café? At a corner table she ordered a glass of tea, stirring in the amber honey and discreetly eavesdropping.

"What you call art, I call it *shmaltzgrub*. Put Chekhov's pince-nez on Jacob Gordin and he's still another son of Esau."

"Libin and Kobrin—feh! Better Weber and Fields. By Act Two of 'Prince Lulu' I had already calluses on the brain."

"Cross your Social Darwinist with a Tolstoy vegetarian and what you get is . . ."

"*Di gas?*"

"From your mouth to Trotsky's ear."

Among the assembled there were girls Esther's age, clever girls unafraid to vie in irreverence with the men. They made daring remarks ("For her Yom Kippur penance she's shtupping Harry Fein at the Labor Bund picnic") and performed variations on the personals column of the *Arbeiter Zeitung:* "I'm a young man with a good job that's got only on the back a slight hump, which it will bring, so they tell me, much *mazel* to my bride . . ." A pair of them sang in chorus: "We get our knowledge from the College of the Circumcized Citizens of New York . . ."

Vacillating between shock and envy, Esther determined to stay seated until she felt at home. Then she observed that some of the younger men were trying to catch her eye, and brought to herself, she abruptly rose and fled the café. So flushed was she on her return to Ludlow Street that her landlady hinted she must have had an assignation. Coquettishly, Esther neither affirmed nor denied, feeling that, in a sense, it was true, and afterwards the glass of tea at Glickman's Odessa became a part of her daily routine.

Insomnia having compounded Eli's anguish, no amount of prayer and mortification could calm him down, or help to reduce his desire. He was further galled by the incessant jibes in the cloakmakers' loft, convinced that his coworkers were encouraged by the benighted thoughts writ on his brow. They could read in his features how the sound of his sleeping wife's breathing blew through his head all day like a desert wind. So why not just get it over with and consummate the marriage? Eli reasoned. It was after all his sacred obligation—though he saw through his own sophistry. What he contemplated was nothing other than the means to an evil end, to the satisfaction of his lust, and it was written that children born of such unions were tainted; they were the offspring of the left-hand side.

As part of his atonement, Eli forbade himself the mystical texts that might have released him awhile from despair, and concentrated exclusively on legal tractates. Instead of saying his benedictions at his sewing machine, he now attended afternoon services at the cloakmakers' shul. Since time in the factory was measured not by hours but the number of garments one made in a day, he was forced to stay later at work, which also suited his program. On his afternoon walks to and from the East Broadway shtibl, Eli had to pass the cafés, the *kibbitzarnia*, where he was irked at the sight of so many idlers talking through their noses. He marveled at their license, these *apikorsin*, these heretics, who had no use for guilt, let alone God Himself. Art, they claimed, was their God, or idolatry, to call it by its rightful name. So why was it they who had all the robustness of spirit, while Eli had only his shame?

What was it about these lumpen do-nothings that made them

so fascinating to Jewish daughters, though such daughters as one would wish on no pious father! For these had discarded modest apparel for loose blouses and uncorseted waists, skirts with peekaboo pleats; they'd exchanged cowls and wigs for jaunty bonnets, for hair streaked with henna and braided like the devil's own challah, when not allowed to flow free. They smoked cigarettes, these sisters of Lilith, and insinuated themselves into arguments, striking adventurous poses. As he observed them through the window of Glickman's Odessa, one of their more infamous haunts, Eli's heart would irately rattle the cage of his chest. His custom was to walk away in disgust, though today, an especially sultry late May afternoon, he stood his ground; he told himself he needed a closer look, if only to prove he could face provocation with self-command. Then doing the unthinkable, Eli entered the café and ordered a glass of tea.

He glanced about with contempt at his surroundings, the framed chromo of Theodore Herzl, the broadside above the buffet advertising last year's Yom Kippur Ball. The air was caustic with pickle brine, thick with the names they conjured with: Kropotkin, Zhitlowsky, Zola, Beiliss, Cahan . . . , all of whom meant nothing to Eli. What interested him was the aggressive behavior of the young women, whose every gesture, while pantomiming devotion to this or that cause célèbre, was an enticement. Neither was Eli deceived by their faces, whose engaged expressions thinly veiled a wantonness bred in the bone. Though there was one, seated alone over her tea in an adjacent corner, whom he excused from his general assessment. This one had a dignified beauty that needed no extravagant airs, a smooth olive complexion and searching onyx eyes. Her cocoa hair, strands of which had come loose from a tidy bun, was as undulant as the grain in dark mahogany. Obviously out of place here, she might have been a young rebitsin; she had the look of a fit companion for a Torah scholar, were that scholar—a hammer fell in Eli's head—not already married.

Still he was unable to take his eyes off the girl. Sipping this tea, he drank the elixir of her presence, which warmed his vitals and tickled his brain, and presently he felt he wanted her more than anything on earth. Here was a desire that knew no remorse, a passion that purged the mind of all impurities. He sat studying her face as intently as he might have a page in *The Book of Mirrors*, and experienced rapture. Lit from within, he was convinced that beams shot from his every orifice; a radiance escaped his eyes, ears, and nostrils as if the moon were captured in a helmet full of holes. This was a higher order of lasciviousness; call it love, which emanated from the supernal realm, its beguiling physical complement notwithstanding. A holy delirium was upon him, in the throes of which Eli understood that this was the woman he'd been saving himself for. Then he noticed that she was observing him with an equally unflinching stare, and dropping his eyes, he paid his bill and left the café.

On her way back to Ludlow Street Esther may as well have been sleepwalking, so thoroughly had the image of the young man in the tearoom displaced everything else in her consciousness. She was drawn to his solitude, the melancholy that set him apart from the rest, the haunting quality of his inkwell eyes. Those eyes, so sunken and limned in red, possessed a molten sadness that belied their best efforts at severity. They belonged to a poet who lived alone in a drafty attic near the river and stayed awake nights composing verses to one such as her. It was a hero's face, the gaunt face of a martyr to dreams, whose details came clearer in his absence: the furrowed cheeks and untrimmed beard, the sidelocks twined about the temples of his lopsided spectacles. Then he'd removed the spectacles, as if to show how the badges of his bookishness failed to repudiate the sensuality of his eyes.

Had she known about the tripartite soul—the *nefesh, ruah,* and *neshomah*—Esther might have concluded (as had the learned Eli with respect to her) that the young man completed her *neshomah*, her highest soul, which meant that they were destined for each other.

That night, as she undressed for bed, Esther felt she was waiting for him; she'd been waiting for him all her life. And so, when the door opened and he entered, her expectancy was at such a pitch that she was hardly surprised, only thankful that she'd thus far kept herself pure and inviolate. There was a moment when she thought the visitor might be her husband; she had a husband. But the gas lamp, dim as it was, suggested the striking visage of the young man from the café. Besides, it was a certainty that her husband could never have embraced her so impulsively, never "taken" her—a thrilling notion!—without a thousand preliminary rites. He could never have cried out, "*Ikh vil ayk ufesn!* I want to eat you up!" so that the whole household must have been alerted, but who cared? Let them listen at the door if they must to the groaning bedsprings, the straw mattress crackling like flames, Esther's heated assurances that she was his.

For a time Eli held her tightly, the way a rabbi hugs his scrolls on Simchas Torah: *dveikuss*, this was called, a cleaving in ecstasy to the sublime. Then he drew back and lifted her muslin gown. A fragrance as of moist clay tinged with cloves went to his head, and in his dizziness Eli had to close his eyes. With his fingers he explored the sloping expanse of her hip, the trough of her abdomen, the close-pored dunes beyond—the geography of a new world whose shores he'd reached after years of voyaging. He pulled the ruck of her gown from beneath her chin as if unfolding petals, opening his eyes to find her face. The kiss that she so hungrily returned was the kiss of the Holy Shekhinah, which rendered powerless the Angel of Death and allowed one to enter paradise alive. It was the kiss that sealed the union of a soul cleft in two in heaven, prior to birth, and reunited in the lower world with its other half.

Afterwards, remembering the words of the masters, Eli invited regrets. "Do not suppose," said the masters, "that only he who commits the act with his body is called an adulterer. He who commits it with his eyes is also considered unfaithful." And they said: "If a wife is alone with her husband and is engaged in intercourse, while her heart is with another man she met on the road, no act of adultery is greater." Surely this applied to the husband as well, Eli conceded, rolling desolately out of bed to resume his former place on the cot.

Relieved to be alone with her musings, Esther sighed in the afterglow of passion and imagined that her lover had left her bed before her husband's return. Unable to contain his inspiration, the poet had gone back to work at his poems.

III.

At first Eli had to force himself to avert his eyes whenever he walked past the café, but after a couple of months the habit had become second nature. He'd continued to go doggedly through the motions of his three-part regimen, but of work, study, and prayer, only work could still hold his attention. Otherwise he remained in a walking stupor, wondering at the exquisite felicity attached to sin. Then there was a day toward the end of summer, as he plodded along the sidewalk toward his afternoon minyan, when thoughts of the girl had momentarily slipped his mind, and Eli chanced to look through the window of Glickman's Odessa. She was seated at her table, looking out, sullenly watching him watch her.

Riveted to the pavement, Eli was seized by a sudden recklessness. Here I stand a fallen creature, he brooded, who, having already lost heaven, has nothing else left to lose. So why shouldn't he take some pleasure on this side of the grave? He might as well step into the tearoom, state his case, and let the chips fall where they may. "Shalom, my name is Eli Goldfogle and I adore you." Hesitating, Eli allowed his gaze to caress her perfect cheek, the not-so-slight curve of her breast, her waist, where he noted a subtle difference: Despite its tightness, her corset had failed to confine a telltale swelling. She belonged, it seemed, to another, and carried his child. She was heavy with the get of some un-washed scribbler, he would wager, a ragged pipe-dreamer, blind to her condition, who tilted with windmills all night in a garret room. But was this really any of Eli's business? Her life was something alien, probably wicked, which he could never in any case enter into, and so there it was—she could never be his.

Of course, it shouldn't be forgotten that Eli had a companion of his own, a woman named Esther with whom he'd had relations that tarnished them both for all eternity. It was a situation that, beyond dissolute, was more than the Law allowed. How could he have strayed so far from the path of righteousness?— such a distance that, should his holy books ever speak to him again, he wouldn't hear them.

He returned to the loft on Rivington Street where he pumped the treadle so furiously that his machine traveled several feet across the floor. Quipped the wags: "The rabbi is racing his chariot." That very evening he was advised that the ailing old Polka Dotz Fischel had finally succumbed to a bout of the white plague. Since none of the other young men in the shop were half so conscientious as Eli, the boss, Leyzer Cohen, designated him the foreman's successor, with a substantial raise in salary. The position was his provided he discontinue the practice of nipping out for afternoon prayers, a stipulation to which Eli readily agreed.

He moved himself and his expectant wife into an apartment of their own in a railroad-style tenement on Cherry Street. It was a grim building of baleful odors and thunderous toilets, even shabbier than the Ludlow Street flat, but it had a parlor that might also function as a nursery. It had a cookstove, black and solid as an anvil, on which Esther could prepare the Widow Winkelman's tempting recipes. Liberated from the pillow-stuffing sweatshop, Esther's time was now her own, which meant there was more of it to spend in the East Side streets. Never again, however, was she disposed to go back to the tearoom. Since the day she'd watched her young man walk away, she'd mourned him, but Esther nonetheless accepted as inevitable the end of their affair. It was enough to have participated in a tragedy that elevated her above the commonplace. Although regretful, she was serene in the knowledge that, in a place deep inside her only he had touched, a child was growing.

She'd begun to cultivate a long dormant fondness for domestic pursuits. Employing talents she came by naturally, Esther took pride in her ability to, for instance, judge a capon's kosherness by pinching its intimate parts. In time, having driven hard bargains with the contract peddler, she'd cozily feathered her nest. She acquired a pier glass and a china cabinet, and determined that, when the baby (a boy Nathan) was old enough, they would have a piano. From the sweet compotes and noodle puddings she plied her husband with to fatten him up, Esther also put on weight, its ballast serving her well in her "pig market" campaigns. Become formidable, she was fiercely protective of her little Nathan, a difficult child whom she spoiled like a prince.

After my uncle Nathan, whose excessive pampering left him a petulant parasite all his days, came others: my malcontent maiden aunt Millie, whose favorite wish (gleaned from Talmud) was never to have been born; and my mama, the bedeviled Sara Rochel, whose bedroom games drove my milquetoast father, a grocer, to an early grave. (She was forever goading him—or so says Aunt Millie the Tongue—to make believe he was, alternately, Adolph Menjou, Dutch Schultz, and Clifford Odets.) There was my scapegrace uncle Shmuel, the bluebeard, who told me this story in exchange for the loan of a couple of bucks. But for all the energy she devoted to her homemaking, my grandmother Esther still found time for the back-numbered romances of "Shomer" Shaikevitch and his ilk. She read them openly now, without embarrassment, titles such as *The Secrets of the Czarist*

Court, which nudged from the shelves the sacred texts her husband had relegated to a closet.

Sometimes, of an evening, Eli would look up from his *Daily Forward*, which he preferred to the less progressive *Tageblatt*, and shake his head over his wife's lifelong addiction to fluff. All the same, he dutifully saved her the section containing Mrs. Bronstein's popular serial, "Woman in Chains." Handing it over, he might wonder when it was he'd first begun to look at her, this dowdy *balebosteh* who kept his house in such apple-pie order, who raised the offspring that would pray for him after he was gone. When had she not been an indispensable part of his world? Then he would resolve to take her out one of these nights to the theater, and afterwards for tea and pastries on Second Avenue. When his eyes were again lowered, Esther might steal a glance at her slump-shouldered man with his stubbled chins, his paunch like a pet in his lap, and smile inwardly, resolving that her children would marry for love.

Bruno's Metamorphosis

—— —

Someone was playing a prank on Bruno Katz. A teacher who made no great claims to imagination, he had been trying to write a story. Only just emerged from an abortive love affair, he thought that the writing might distract him from unhappiness.

The affair in question, his first of any endurance, had ended in a literal abortion, when Bruno at thirty-five confessed to his girlfriend Goldie Shapiro his unreadiness to have a child. In terminating her pregnancy, Goldie had terminated her relationship with Bruno as well. Walking, despite some pain, all the way from the clinic where Bruno had preferred not to accompany her, she burst unannounced into his small but tidy West Side apartment.

"You nebbish!" she called him, and blowing her nose, "You spineless worm! You slob!" Then she turned on her heel and slammed out the door, causing a medley of Broadway show tunes on Bruno's phonograph to skip.

This was unfair, Bruno thought, objecting to her latter accusation. Call him what you will, he was not a slob. Although somewhat overweight, he dressed well enough and was neat in his personal habits.

Later on that evening—lonely, downhearted, bored with the routine of his days—he put on his pajamas and bathrobe and sat down to write a story. Though writing had long been a secret ambition of Bruno's, he always found excuses not to begin. Too little experience, he told himself; or was it that he merely lacked inspiration? In any case, there was a drama about the end of Goldie that prompted him to try to write again. And moreover, by depicting himself as a character in a tale, he might find the perspective to help him through this trying time.

Thus, pushing his bifocals over the hump of his nose, he commenced typing. But rather than draw from his present still-sensitive circumstances, he chose for his subject a distant episode. Not untypical of his childhood, the episode nonetheless haunted and frustrated him even now. As what in his life, come to think of it, did not?

The episode recalled an outing to Coney Island with his mother. Game for showing her son a good time, she had taken him on some of the gentler rides, then bought tickets for the funhouse. Little Bruno, frail and scrawny then (the baby fat would come later), had reluctantly taken his mama's hand. He had followed her down a dark corridor at the end of which a neon clown flashed off and on. Past the clown, however, the corridor turned a corner into utter darkness; where Bruno, looking over his shoulder for a light that was no longer there, started to cry. Although his mama assured him there was nothing to fear, he insisted that they turn back. Nor would he stop crying until she had led him safely out into the sunshine, where his terror subsided into shame.

It had been the mature Bruno's intention to finally resolve the incident, to redeem himself by allowing the boy and his mother, if only on paper, to continue on through the funhouse. What they would encounter—for their intrepid exploits would comprise the story—he wasn't quite sure. He knew only that they would pass from darkness into light, this time without turning around.

Although aware that the word was unpopular, Bruno would have admitted, if pressed, that his method was a kind of therapy. But for the sake of his wounded pride, he was calling it fiction.

The problem, however, had come when, in the course of developing his story, he arrived at the point where the mother and son turn the corner past the clown. Beyond which he could not write. So there he was decades after the fact, educated and grown-up, but still paralyzed in the face of the unknown. A failure of imagination, he'd called it, what was by any other name a failure of nerve. How true to form that on this, his first attempt, he should be stricken with writer's block.

"Give it up," he told himself, shrugging, resting in the assurance that there were other means of diverting oneself. There was, for instance, a whole world beyond his room.

He thought he might try to get back in trim, though who was he kidding? When, in a life led almost exclusively indoors, had he ever been in trim? All right, so he was soft, his flesh pale and tallowy, his frown yielding two or three chins. Still, in rare daydreams he disowned the endomorph, fancied himself angular and spry, leaping from place to place instead of walking. And toward this vision of himself, he tried jogging one evening through Riverside Park.

Winded after a few hundred yards, chafed by ill-fitting sweat clothes, leery of shady characters along the benches, he resorted to a nearby bar. Exercise having failed him, he surrendered to its inverse: debauchery. He would drink himself into a state of indifference. But as drink was never his medium, his overindulgence left him instead only crapulous and irritable.

Then there was food which—giving himself over to an orgy of eggrolls and blintzes—he flattered himself that he understood. He would eat to forget. But overeating and its attendant dyspepsia were, after all, nothing new to Bruno. What he needed was a more radical change of focus, something to get him over his broken heart. If broken heart he had.

So what was next? And of the extremes of behavior left open to him, sex was most certainly the ticket. Albeit a ticket he'd always found hard to get punched. Undeceived by his natty attire and complacent potbelly, women, sensing the driven nature of his needs, had kept their distance. Except of course Goldie, who, with her strabismus and thinning hair, had been as desperate as he.

And thinking of her, Bruno had a sudden realization: that there were no regrets. From what then, if not from Goldie, had he been so strenuously trying to divert his thoughts? Why departed from his customary routine? The answer came like the handwriting on the wall, or maybe the absence of same. He was still feeling baited by the unfinished page in the typewriter, still hounded and absorbed. All other activities apart from working at his story—so randomly begun—seemed extracurricular, merely the tactics of evasion.

Insomnia, a nuisance of longstanding, kept him constantly fatigued. He brooded through the night over his page, wondering how he'd stumbled into such a first-class obsession. He, Bruno Katz, who'd successfully eluded commitments for thirty-five years. How was it that his future seemed suddenly to depend on the advancement of a mother and son through a carnival funhouse?

He'd been lying in bed worrying about what the headmaster had said. This was the headmaster at the prep school where Bruno taught English to rich kids too smart for their own good. He'd told Bruno that afternoon how his preoccupation had been noticed, not to mention his uncharacteristic slovenliness. Though the headmaster, his face grown around his pipe like an old tree around a post, had used a milder word. "Discomposure," that was it.

"If there's anything wrong, feel free to confide in us," he said. But Bruno, tempted, usually such a glutton for sympathy, held his tongue. Who would understand?

Then clearing his throat the headmaster had told him he must understand, there were standards to be maintained. This after seven years.

"I'm expendable," Bruno chanted all the way home, trying to get used to the idea.

Complementing his worries was the evidence that he was going to hell. His appearance, in which he'd always taken pride, bore it out: the crest come unstitched from his blazer, the coarse hair grown over an unwashed collar. His pants sagged from the weight he'd lost in the absence of his appetite. What's more his apartment, kept usually spotless, had fallen into disarray. Nor would Bruno, for all his fretting, lift a finger to halt the deterioration—not if it meant taking time from the primary fretting over his unfinished page.

Then it happened, what had to be someone's idea of a joke. Somewhere during the small hours he'd managed to doze off. He'd dreamed a crazy dream about a skeleton tap-dancing on a tin roof, then was awakened by the cold. Sitting up he saw that his window, always shut, was now open to the midwinter winds. He remembered the broken lock that he'd meant for some time to repair. Fearful of burglars he switched on a lamp and made an inventory of his effects: his books, his dirty clothes, old phonograph, portable typewriter. What in fact did he have worth stealing? And wrapping himself in a blanket, trembling from more than the cold, he got out of bed to investigate further.

At first he noticed nothing out of the ordinary, neither in bedroom nor kitchenette. Though it dawned on him, after he'd inspected the contents of his impoverished refrigerator, that a pint of milk which he'd swear to having purchased yesterday was missing.

"What's going on!" Bruno demanded aloud, hurrying to slam shut the window. Taking up a broom that he broke over his knee, he wedged the handle above the window frame. And stooping to recover his blanket, he happened to glance again at his desk, at the typewriter about which his world had revolved for some weeks. Then he observed what minutes before had escaped his attention, what astonished him so much he forgot to be afraid.

For the page, which had lain so long in his typewriter three-quarters blank, was now replete with words. Tentatively Bruno edged closer to the desk and examined the page. He saw that, without so much as a paragraph break, his story—stalled forever, he'd thought—had been continued.

"Okay, very funny," he affirmed, not to be caught off guard, unconsciously smoothing back hair that stood on end. "Ha ha," he added without much heart. Then rubbing his eyes against their possibly deceiving him, he read the sentence that took up where his own manuscript left off: at the point where the mother and son turned their corner.

"Then the boichik," it began, "he is cryink in the dark and the mama she is sayink shaineh kin she is strikink a match . . ." In this pidgin manner the typescript rambled on, careless of syntax and punctuation. But despite the homeliness of the language, its lapses into Yiddish, Bruno found himself warming to its tone. He felt that, their primitiveness aside, the words seemed to fairly dance down the page.

The story itself told how the mother led her son through a maze of pitch-black passages, through rooms of tableaux vivant (which may or may not have been wax) that depicted frightening scenes from the little boy's life. In this way, without losing sight of the burning match, the boy followed his mother in wonder past a bully at school, past his own angry father in the act of removing his belt. Then he was led into scenes outside of his own life and times: a Cossack with a whip, a Spanish inquisitor beside an iron maiden. And following the artless narrative to the bottom of the page, Bruno shared in the little boy's wonder, how it mitigated the horrors and rendered them benign.

When the narrative inconclusively ended, Bruno, wanting more, tore the page from the typewriter and turned it over. He looked furiously about the desk as if for clues. But the spell was broken and Bruno was left feeling duped and scared. Trying to catch his runaway breath, he was struck by two propositions:

First, that there were maybe more things in heaven and earth, etc. And second, that he must be losing his mind.

He lay awake until dawn feeling vulnerable, trying to make sense, unable to clear his head for the ringing in his ears. At school during the next few days, stuporously inattentive, he lost what little control he had over his classes. Once the headmaster, alerted by the noise, entered his classroom to find the students amok, some of them smoking marijuana, while Bruno stood gazing perplexedly out the window. After which it was suggested he seek counseling.

Meanwhile Bruno was spending his nights poring over the mysterious manuscript. Unable to explain it, having only ascertained that it was real, he fell back on his original notion that someone was playing a prank. But who? He tried to picture Goldie creeping over the windowsill, but stealth was never her strong point. Only after her there was no one he could think of who would have taken such pains for his sake. Nor, by the same token, was there anyone to whom he could unburden himself of such a thing. He had few acquaintances outside of his colleagues at school, whose growing suspicions he didn't want to aggravate further.

Beyond this there was his instinct, new to Bruno, to preserve the secrecy of what had happened. For overriding even his bewilderment was his continuing fascination with the story thus far. Living with it, with its humor and simplicity, he was coming to feel protective of the story and to regard it as a kind of gift. Had it not in fact carried his own narrative further than he'd been able to carry it himself? And for this he felt, leaving aside the question of its origin, that the story was pointing the way for him. Somehow, he felt, he was meant to complete it.

Only now he was back where he'd started. He was beating his brains out for the solution to the tale, the telling of which had a drollery that Bruno, at the best of times, could not have mustered. His frustration compounded, he came that close to ripping the text to shreds, to throwing it out the window from where it came.

With his situation so was his presence—given the neglect of his former good grooming—degenerating. Passing a mirror, he was interested and appalled at the sight of his alteration: his previously brilliantined hair now matted and elflocked, his face showing cheekbones for the first time in several decades. He would pause for a moment's consideration of how, having pampered himself for so long, he could now forget himself so completely. Then it was back to worrying about the matter at hand.

After a series of warnings he was notified of his dismissal from the preparatory school, an event he'd dreaded as the very worst that could happen. Though when it came it seemed scarcely worthy of his attention, so consumed was he by the story.

"It never rains but it pours," was all he could spare by way of appropriate response. But security was no longer his theme. Money, of which there remained only a couple of weeks' worth in the bank, was the least of his problems. The story was the thing. And impotent to coax the mother and son a syllable further in their progress, unable to leave them alone, Bruno was at his wit's end.

Then one night at the brink of delirium, no longer responsible for his actions, he yanked the broomstick out of the window. Giddy with anticipation, he lay down with one eye open and waited. Doubts assailed him, apprehension toward his extreme state of mind. Was this what came of keeping too much to one's own company? Then he would have risen to replace the broomstick had not weariness kept him prone, the intensity of the preceding days having worn him out. Amazed that his native insomnia should have failed him on this particular night, he felt himself drifting off to sleep.

He awoke to the cold, leapt from his bed, and rushed to his desk without bothering to close the window. The typewriter was empty, but beside it was a small stack of manuscript pages. These Bruno abruptly pounced upon.

By his goosenecked lamp he read the continued story, marveling again how its ingenuous style lured one with impunity through a gallery of horrors.

Having passed through a few more preliminary tableaux, the mother and son came to a scene depicting a medieval atticlike room littered with scrolls. The figures in the room included a rabbi of evil countenance stuffing a parchment into the mouth of a diminutive clay golem. And while the rabbi remained frozen in this posture, the golem, who was the spit and image of the little boy, clamped his teeth over the parchment and began to shuffle slowly forward. Looking on in mortal terror, screaming, "Lemme out of here!" the boy clung to his mama's skirts. But his mama only told him, "Happy bar mitzvah!" and shoved him in the direction of the golem. She said, "Zuninkeh, give him a patsch! Show him what my son is made of."

Then the boy, his heart bursting with fear and pride, begins wrestling with the golem.

"Ridiculous!" exclaimed Bruno, laughing out loud. But if so ridiculous, why the tears streaming down his cheeks, the thrill beyond reason?

Still, he wanted more, wanted to see the fight resolved, the mother and son leaving the funhouse triumphant. But calming down he listened to his better judgment, which told him that the story had ended as it should. Critical faculties engaged, he realized that, for all its ungainliness, it was a modern story. Its unresolved climax was ambiguous enough to satisfy the contemporary reader. There was little left for him to do.

Closing the window, lodging the broomstick in place, he sat down then and there to give the manuscript his finishing touches. Respectful of the tone, interfering as little as possible with the rhythm of the sentences, he discreetly inserted punctuation, dropping the more obscure Yiddish phrases. He was unconcerned now with who might be responsible for the story, feeling that in a sense he was himself responsible, the manuscript being the gift of his muse. Drinking black coffee as the milk in his refrigerator had vanished, he worked through the early morning. By noon the story was completed but for a title. Too impatient to think of anything more fitting, Bruno labeled it simply "A Modern Fable," then stuffed it into an envelope with an ingratiating cover letter and sent it off to an eminent magazine.

In a couple of weeks he got word from the magazine, saying sorry they were unable to use the story at this time, saying that but for the title, which could stand improvement, the piece had been much admired; by all means he should try them again. This was all the encouragement that Bruno needed.

"So I'm not crazy," he sighed, rereading the editor's response, as if his sanity had been the issue all along. And having suspended his efforts while awaiting a verdict, having done nothing in fact since submitting his story, Bruno launched immediately into another.

In keeping with the tradition of the funhouse episode, this one also concerned an occasion during which a young boy exhibits faintheartedness. It was drawn of course from Bruno's endless repertoire of such occasions. This particular episode had occurred when, for the purpose of his initiation into a neighborhood gang, Bruno had agreed to crawl through the tunnel of a sewer. This without the benefit of his mama's accompaniment.

He'd been doing all right, had managed maybe fifty yards on his hands and knees through nauseating swill, when the tunnel suddenly turned a corner. At that point the light from the entrance, which he'd kept for reference over his shoulder, disappeared. It was then he reasoned that he didn't like the other boys much anyway. He made a token effort to force himself forward in the dark. But panic overtaking him, he turned around and scrambled wildly toward daylight, toward certain and undying humiliation. Which the older and wiser Bruno prepared himself to erase.

But again he could get no farther on his own steam than the story's, that is the sewer's, turning point. There his invention jammed and his newfound confidence slipped away. Nothing left to do but sleep on it, though Bruno was as usual too agitated to sleep.

"I've been here before," he complained to his pillow. In nocturnal vigils he wondered how something undertaken so blithely could change so quickly to headaches and futility.

Meanwhile, his money spent and no more where it came from, he contemplated last resorts. Such as pawning his typewriter or looking for a job. How had he let things come to such a pass? His weight loss was now tantamount to atrophy. Seriously gaunt, dark hollows beneath the eyes, hooked nose and Adam's apple prominent, he was swallowed by his once sartorial wardrobe. Furthermore it appeared that his thick and unruly hair had begun to recede. Who was so recently enchanted seemed now to be cursed.

Never far from it, he succumbed to self-pity. Here he was destitute on the threshold of middle age, living in a pigsty of a room and a half that he was incapable of dreaming himself out of.

"What I've got," he sulked, "is nothing to lose. What I need," a little heartened by the obvious rhyme, "is a visit from my muse."

And again removing the broomstick from the window, he asked himself why he hadn't done it sooner.

As an afterthought he put a pint of milk on the desk and went to bed. Closing his eyes, he fell into a semiconscious doze, as deep as his slumber ever got these nights. He was listening to what he thought was a rattling radiator, what he came gradually to realize was the sound of typing. Opening his eyes by degrees, he was presented with the sight of a wizened old man at his desk, his feet not quite reaching the floor. Bearded, earlocked, with an embroidered skullcap perched atop his wispy gray hair, he was slouched in a threadbare and shiny black gabardine. His face, creased and glaucous, squinted over his pair of crooked forefingers, which hopped about the keys like a jig on hot coals.

In a film, thought Bruno, this is where I shut my eyes and say it's only a dream. But how should Bruno, who never sleeps, be dreaming? Then shaken by the grotesque and impossible truth of the situation, he sat bolt upright and shouted.

"Go away!"

The little man turned with rust-rimmed eyes and studied Bruno's face, as if looking there for something lost. Instantly Bruno was sorry.

"Come back!" he cried, as his visitor, nimble despite his years, leapt from the chair and vaulted through the open window.

With the covers still pulled to his chin, Bruno dared to picture himself giving chase, pursuing the little rabbi through the streets in his pajamas, carrying a butterfly net. In the end, worn out with imagining, he ventured as far as the window. He looked out past the fire escape to the tops of the neighboring roofs, to the moon disentangling itself from a skirmish of aerials. It was, he concluded, an unusually balmy night for early March.

He snapped out of his reverie at the sight of the empty milk bottle. Remarking its drabness in his drab apartment he felt vaguely disappointed. So that was his muse, that shrunken chasidic gargoyle looking more like a scholar than a scribe. Well, what had he expected, an archangel with wings of flame? Beggars, as the saying went, could not be choosers.

In this way he checked his astonishment with ingratitude. He tore the page out of the typewriter, a little thrilled as he examined its contents that he could handle it with such disdain. Which turned to astonishment as soon as he began to read.

Picking up where Bruno'd left off, the story recounted the further adventures of the boichik: how, turning a corner, he gets lost in a maze of black tunnels. He gropes along in terror until he stumbles into a cell beneath a manhole cover. In the cell illumined by oil lamps he encounters a hermit, living there in the sewer to escape, so he says, history and a yenteh wife. He has brought with him some holy books, a few zlotys, and a tiny iron stove for cooking his tsimmes on—all mementoes of the Old Country, whose denizens and houses he has crayoned over the concrete walls.

"Don't tell nobody," he entreats the boichik, "and some day all this is yours."

Undiscouraged when the manuscript ended abruptly, Bruno whistled as he worked, playing show tunes on the phonograph as he refurbished the sentences in hand. Later on he went out and borrowed some money from a former colleague who failed to recognize him at first. Then he treated himself to a decent meal.

"I deserve this," he said, but left his cheesecake uneaten. It saddened him that his old relish for food had vanished along with his belly. That night however, though briefly disturbed by the sound of typing, Bruno slept extremely well.

In the morning he applauded the details of the completed story: the touching friendship between the boy and the old man, lasting through the years until the old man passes away. Then the boichik, without a candle, lugs the body wreathed in a kapok life preserver a mile through subterranean drek. He then drops it in the East River, giving it a shove in the direction of paradise. Afterwards, having come into the old man's estate, he says to himself, "I am blessed!" Which fact becomes small comfort during the course of an otherwise lonely and uneventful life.

As he affectionately edited the manuscript, Bruno, so capti-
vated by the manuscript itself, gave scarcely a thought to its
strange originator. Such familiar, if unnameable, chords did it
strike in his breast that the story might as well have been his own.

Aware that the title of the previous piece had not been satisfactory, he tried to think of something catchy for the current.
Drawing a blank, he told himself it was no sin to be literal, and
hastily scrawled "Boichik Inherits" at the top of page one. Then
he paused as a maverick thought crossed his mind: "Maybe I
ought to concede the collaboration."

The thought past, Bruno signed his name to the story and
sent it off.

In a week he received a five-hundred-dollar check from the
magazine. Taking his second story they asked to reconsider the
first; they praised what they called his knockabout surrealism.
By the time the news arrived Bruno was already anticipating a
collection of Boichik tales, and had started another.

Great days ensued for Bruno Katz. His praises were sung in
many quarters, his stories the talk of the town. A mensch, as his
muse might have said, was what he'd become. His telephone,
silent since his breakup with Goldie Shapiro, was now ringing
off the hook. Agents and publishers wooed him; friends he'd
not heard from in years called to congratulate. Colleagues from
the prep school voiced their approval, hinted at his possible
reinstatement—but who needed it? Goldie herself had phoned to
say that she too had succumbed to the charms of his stories, and
would he maybe care to come to dinner? But no thank you
again. Why, with his brilliant future unfolding, should he be
content to pick up where he'd left off?

And while he tried to keep his notoriety in some kind of perspective, his head was already turned. On the one hand he told
himself don't be greedy, while on the other he was dizzily aware
of spoils for the taking. Already he was matching the money he

had against what he would make, his loneliness against the women that would inevitably surround him. Of course, he never failed to observe, such fringe benefits were nothing compared to the fulfillment of a finished story.

But for all its promise of glory his new life, as Bruno called it, had come to him a little too fast. Thirty-five years is fast? Yes, when the change came like this: when least expected, when you found yourself a late bloomer who never expected to bloom at all. And so he fell prey to second thoughts. Where he'd initially welcomed so many opening doors, he now feared the threat to this privacy. Solitude was after all the condition in which his stories had been nurtured. Perhaps a more public Bruno might lose touch with his materials. Perhaps he would find his "muse"—the word employed here in its figurative sense—perhaps he would find his muse reluctant to call.

Meanwhile, having signed a contract with the magazine, he was spending money on the strength of a story he'd yet to write. The deadline was drawing near and he'd started nothing. He was strapped for a premise, his new self-importance having eclipsed the old disgraces that had been his themes. The page in his type-writer remained blank, his muse—granted, in a literal sense—apparently not interested in initiating a tale.

So he indulged in expensive distractions, bought extrava-gant meals, although rich foods no longer agreed with him. To replace the clothes that were now too big, he bought a wardrobe of stylish others, ostensibly to show off his svelte new physique. But in the mirror the clothes mocked him, appeared too young for him, the loss of his baby fat having left him a cadaverous stranger.

His beard had grown unkempt along with his thinning hair, the sight of which prompted a hairdresser to cluck his tongue. Seeking comfort Bruno nearly engaged the services of a call girl, but was discouraged at the last minute by her swivel eye. He was beginning to wonder if good fortune was his cup of tea.

Thinking he might feel better in less shabby surroundings, he shopped around for a new apartment, maybe something over-looking Central Park. But still he lingered in his old cramped quarters, due in part to his exhausted advance, in part to cold feet. As the weather was warm he slept with the window wide open, his broken broom in the trash, a pint of milk souring on his desk.

But nothing happened. The magazine, after hounding him for a while left him alone. The phone ceased to ring. His star, which had so swiftly ascended, seemed just as swiftly to be in decline. The desolation that had been his lot was again his lot, only now he was spoiled. Having tasted success, however abortive and brief, how could he return to his squalid obscurity?

"Cinderella," he teased himself, but without humor.

He languished for days, sustaining himself on melba toast and sardines. Now and again an idea might present itself, though Bruno couldn't be bothered to get up and write it down. He preferred to lie across smelly sheets mourning the loss of his prospects, wasting away. But after a week or two even Bruno's misery began to tire of its own company. His resistance down, he concluded this about his ambitions: Easy come, easy go. He was damned in any case, incapable of enjoying the fruits of his labor. And asking himself, so why labor, he answered why not.

Thus prompted more by habit than afflatus, Bruno went to his desk and started another story.

It was about (what else?) a writer whose muse had abandoned him; who after a few windfall successes can think of nothing else to write. Who worries that he may have already used up in his stories what notable experiences his limited life has to offer. Then arriving in his composition at the point where the imaginary writer must do or die, must invent or resign himself to having been a flash in the pan, Bruno found himself stuck again.

In its familiarity Bruno's frustration was almost a homecoming. He relaxed amid the fragrances of tar and exhaust wafting through his open window. Gladly conceding defeat, what was there left to do but pack it in, but to put on his filthy pajamas and go to bed, to take off his pajamas against the unseasonable heat.

Lying in the dark, he picked at the scab of his conscience. Was his inadequacy, he wondered, some kind of vengeance of the muse, wrought for his failing to give credit where credit was due? If so, it was a vengeance he'd been subject to since birth. Perhaps he ought to reconsider the prep school if they'd have him back, reconsider Goldie. But when he compared what he had been with what he'd become—compared the chubby school-teacher with the spectre savaged by obsession—he found to his surprise that he still had no regrets. And besides, wasn't it already too late for turning back? On that note, curious to see what if anything the morning might bring, Bruno fell asleep.

He woke up to the heat, unnaturally intense, to the smoke that sent him coughing and choking to the window. Sticking his head out, gulping for air, he saw flames like ragged curtains flapping from the other windows of his building. He heard sirens and tenants hysterically shouting, saw them practically climbing over one another as they raced down the fire escapes. Then prompted by his own sleepless instinct for panic, Bruno wasted no time in following their lead.

He flung a leg over the windowsill and bolted down the metal stairs dodging flames. Gingerly he stepped onto the last flight that tipped vertically, spilling him and the others behind him onto the sidewalk. Disengaging himself from his neighbors, he scurried to get clear of the building as the fire trucks arrived.

In the street amid pandemonium—firemen and hoses, disconsolate families, squad cars with flashing lights—Bruno stood alone looking up at the burning building. He was scarcely aware of being jostled in all the activity, so transfixed had he become by the vision of his window burst into flame.

"My life!" he called to the window, dubiously, as if to confirm that no one was there. Fascinated by the disaster, he remained—despite bullhorns and squalling children and the infernal rumbling of the fire itself—surprisingly calm. Despair, he knew, would overtake him in a moment; it would crush him beyond comfort, as who was there to comfort Bruno? But despair didn't come, and in its place he felt (it was almost heretical) a sense of relief. Easy come, easy go.

And since no one stepped up to console him it was just as well, since he'd realized that he was standing mother-naked in the street. Turning, he shouldered his way through the throng of onlookers, who ignored him, beating it into the Laundromat adjacent to his building. Although brightly lit, it was empty of customers, everyone having run out to see the fire. In a sweat Bruno lunged for the first machine whose porthole showed tumbling clothes. But opening the dryer he hesitated, diverted by his own gaunt reflection in the windowpane. Beyond his reflection he could see the crowd watching the chaos, the men on ladders directing long arcs of water, the flames reaching an awesome height. His heart unexpectedly lifted to the height of the flames, Bruno waved and danced a few steps in his nakedness. Then he pulled out the clothes.

The pants, made out of an itchy black material, were too tight in the crotch, the cuffs reaching to just below his knees. The collarless white shirt, also too small, was stiff and smelled musty, though it had presumably just been washed. There was a vest which, while it constricted his armpits, he slipped on anyway—as his outfit had seemed incomplete. Then heading barefoot for the door he was again impressed with his reflection in the glass, and stood there a moment grinning at his antic transformation.

Once outside, shoving through the crowd that strained at the police barrier, Bruno hadn't a clue as to where to go next. Standing on tiptoe to get his bearings, he saw only confusion, saw the flames dissolving into a red morning sky. And down the street past the burning building, scuttling around the corner at the end of the block, he saw the little rabbi, his fleeing muse.

"Wait for me!" cried Bruno, ducking under a barrier, oblivious to the shouted warnings from the cops. And pumping his legs over aching feet, he gave chase.

Turning the corner, he was just in time to see the rabbi disappearing down the steps at a subway entrance. Calling to him in vain Bruno poured it on, taking the steps in a couple of strides, vaulting a turnstile with inspired agility. He reached the platform and leapt on to the waiting train, then about-faced to confirm what he thought he had seen. As there waiting on the platform sans anyone to fill them was a pair of battered black shoes.

"Any port in a storm," thought Bruno, stooping to snatch them up, as the doors closed and the subway jolted forward.

Forcing on the shoes that crimped his toes, he was launched again, sliding the doors between couplings, searching toward the front of the train. He charged down the aisle between the early morning passengers too drowsy to lift more than a brow at his zany attire. Rushing headlong into the foremost car, Bruno spotted his muse. He was seated beside some nurses in his long gabardine, its hem stopping short of his hairy ankles and unshod white feet.

Lunging forward Bruno was abruptly thrown backward, grabbing an overhead strap as the subway squealed to a halt. Risen, the little rabbi looked at him askance, wrinkling his whiskered features quizzically. Then he stepped out into a concourse of Grand Central Station with the former prep-school teacher at his heels.

How the figure in front of him, with his scuttling pace, stayed just beyond his reach was a mystery to Bruno. Though it might have had something to do with the fact that, on the point of overtaking him, Bruno was losing heart.

"Wait a minute," he panted, uncertain as to whether he were addressing his muse or himself. And besides, his feet were killing him.

He held onto a pretzel concession to catch his breath, suffering the stares of the passersby, watching the little rabbi hurry away up a ramp. So what—it seemed the moment to ask himself—what did he hope to gain from such meshugass?

He was bewildered at having come so far afield, at behaving with such mad impetuosity. And here he was looking forward to god-only-knew—to making more of a spectacle of himself than he already was, to springing upon a kosher leprechaun in the middle of Grand Central Station. Demanding what? Fairy gelt? Another story? Which he would transcribe on whose typewriter in what room?

He thought of the fire. He thought that in a film this is where the newsboy shouts: "EXTRA! PROMISING WRITER LOST IN FLAMES!" How buying a paper, he would sigh for the late Bruno Katz—what a waste. Though the prospect, rather than distress him, filled him with a sense of mischief, as if his very existence were a kind of prank. Then it occurred to Bruno, rootless in the world, that he didn't want so much to capture his muse as to follow him home. And as he loped up the ramp from the subway, it seemed that his shoes were giving a bit.

The ramp led to a corridor that opened onto a row of numbered gates. At the farthest of these was a queue of passengers that included the little rabbi, handing their tickets to a uniformed collector to be punched. Beyond the gate a train, breathing steam, stretched along the platform.

Bruno stepped to the rear of the line moving forward until he was asked for his ticket.

"Ticket!" he repeated. "Of course." Then he made a great show of searching his person, while the collector (Had he batted an eye at the rabbi?) frowned suspiciously. Fishing in the pockets of his trousers, which seemed to have grown baggier, he pulled out a slip upon which was printed: NEW YORK ONTARIO & WESTERN RR. Bruno's jaw hung open as the collector, snatching the ticket, punched it and handed it back. Its stamped destination read: LIBERTY.

Onboard the train, peering over upraised newspapers, Bruno prowled from car to car, but no little rabbi. Instead he found draped over a vacant seat next to the window, a tasseled prayer shawl. In need of accessories he took up the shawl and wrapped it with a flourish about his throat. Then, undiscouraged, feeling that everything—so to speak—was already written, Bruno occupied the seat himself. He sunk so far into its cushions that his feet barely touched the floor.

In a newspaper that a passenger was holding across the aisle, he could see if he squinted an article about an apartment-house fire. Leaning forward he could make out, toward the bottom of the column, something about a writer of promise presumed to have perished. Then the newspaper was fluttering, the train pulling out of the station. And Bruno, exhausted from the chase, lulled by the cadence of clacking wheels, was beginning to nod. He was asleep as the train snaked its way beneath the city, surfacing finally into daylight.

He woke to blue mountains, the train crossing a river flanked by granite cliffs. As the window—unusually high—began at the level of his chin, Bruno craned his neck to take it all in. He rubbed his eyes and tugged at his scraggly beard while the train hugged the tree-lined slopes. Pitching through tunnels, it burst upon vistas wherein towns appeared. Mountaindale, Woodridge, Fallsburgh, Liberty: its name painted across a broad shingle hanging from the eaves of a gingerbread station house.

As the voice of a conductor confirmed their arrival, Bruno, trying to shake himself into motion, sighted his barefoot rabbi through the window. He was crossing the wooden platform as if in a hurry to keep an appointment.

"I'm properly out of my skull," Bruno reflected, and shrugged.

Getting up he was conscious that, despite having slept in them, he was comfortable in his borrowed clothes; he was conscious that the other passengers seemed larger than himself. This left him hopeful that from now on everything would have extra dimensions. Then in a couple of bounds, sprightly for his years, he was off the train and again on the trail of his muse.

Not bothering to hail him, Bruno followed his man down a pleasant avenue lined with ornate shops. The shop windows bore posters announcing the bill of fare at Grossinger's, at the Concord. Then the rabbi, obviously accustomed to this route, turned into a shady residential street. In a block or two the houses ended, petering into a narrow unpaved lane. The lane in turn dead-ended in a garden path, with a gate that the rabbi left open as he quickly passed through.

Following, Bruno had to stifle his laughter, so intoxicating was the fragrant air. Holding his own with the rabbi's brisk pace, he was strolling through bluebells and clover. With his sidelocks borne on the breezes, occasionally tickling his nose, he was trotting down an incline that grew ever more treacherous and steep.

At the bottom of the defile was a brook with a few stones across it. Over these the little rabbi stepped smartly—a feat that Bruno, shoes no longer pinching, duplicated without effort. Not so effortless was the climb up the slope on the other side. Practically a precipice, up which the rabbi scrambled in defiance of gravity, it was obstacled with jutting rocks. There were grapevines and gnarled spruce trees, whose trunks Bruno clung to in his struggle to keep up. But even in his toiling, he found himself distracted by the flora, sniffing the sassafras and witchhazel whose scents he wondered how he knew. Where in his claustrophobic urban past had he gleaned such woodlore?

Eventually he reached an overhang where he clutched at roots, his feet dangling a dizzy moment in space. Managing at last to haul himself up over the brow of the cliff, he lay panting awhile in a bed of moss, then picked himself up and inhaled the view.

The mountains, their tops veiled in mist, were much nearer than they'd appeared from the train. They were distanced now by only a valley in whose hollow was a blue-green meadow, and in the meadow what appeared to be a village. Although he'd never set eyes on it before, Bruno felt that the scene possessed a certain familiarity. It was the kind you enjoyed when reading the little rabbi's stories, the credit for which he now regretted having taken. Then he realized, looking down through the clustering trees, that his muse was nowhere in sight.

Alarmed, half running, half sliding, Bruno flung himself down the long hill. Stumbling he rolled headfirst over pine needles and leaf mold, then got to his feet only to trip and sprawl again amid towering trees. So dense was their foliage that only the few odd coins of sunlight, falling on toadstools, could filter through. Bruno raised himself, dusting off thistles. Left to his own devices in this sinister place, abandoned one might say, he began to have serious misgivings. Although he proceeded, his bravado had left him, and in its place was his old and erstwhile companion fear. To which, having had enough, Bruno shouted, "Fuck off!"

Koff-foff-off: his voice came back to him in diminishing echoes. And when the echoes had faded away, so had the fear, departing into memory. Then memory itself had grown dim, absorbed by the fear that had fled, taking with it his recollection of why he was here, how he had come, where he had been in all the years (evaporating now) previous to this moment. Then he knew that he'd lost himself, that Bruno—portly, fastidious, fainthearted and friendless, childless—had turned around and gone back where he came from.

"Nu?" he wondered wiping away tears. "So who does that make me now?"

But in any case, as he toddled through shadows, he felt at peace with his emptiness; felt in fact that the grimacing stones, the waist-high ferns, that deserted quarry, that broken chimney, that oak, had at least as much significance as himself.

Picking his way down the remainder of the slope, whistling show tunes, he paused beneath a ruined tree, its barkless limbs as crooked as his fingers. From its bottom-most branch a long gabardine kapote was limply hanging. Taking it down from the tree he put it on and declared it a perfect fit. Then as if prompted by habit, he reached into one of its pockets, looking for maybe a compass? a map? And finding an embroidered skullcap, he placed it over the bald spot in the midst of his wispy gray hair.

He emerged from the trees into a meadow, across which he could clearly see the shingled roofs and smoking chimneys of the village, the cupola of its wooden synagogue. As he scuttled through the tall grass, he made up a story, secure in the knowledge that he had a million more. In this one the village, call it Bobolinka, appears for only a day every hundred years . . .

. . . Bruno Katz, the wandering *mayse*-teller, returns home for a night. Family and friends pour into the muddy streets bearing gifts—chicken livers, baked knishes, schnapps. These he gratefully declines, protesting that they mustn't spoil him. Later on they gather in the study house where he tells them of his travels. The young are spellbound while the older ones tease him that Broadway has turned his head. In the morning, shalom and he's off again. He goes on foot to the city, the world having broken down in his absence. But as some things never change, he climbs through an open window and, thirsty, looks in an icebox for milk. Then he sits at a desk, his back to the bed where someone is fitfully snoring. In the typewriter he reads an unfinished page about a man whose house catches fire, and making a face, he begins to type.

The Sin of Elijah

Somewhere during the couple of millennia that I'd been com-
muting between heaven and earth, I, Elijah the Tishbite—former
prophet of the Northern Kingdom of Israel, translated to Paradise in a chariot of flame while yet alive—became a voyeur. Call
me weak, but after you've attended no end of circumcisions,
performed untold numbers of virtuous deeds and righteous
meddlings in a multitude of disguises, your piety can begin to
wear a little thin. Besides, good works had ceased to generate
the kind of respect they'd once commanded in the world, a
situation that took its toll on one's self-esteem; so that even I,
old as I was, had become susceptible from time to time to the
yetser hora, the evil impulse.

That's how I came to spy on the Fefers, Feyvush and Gitl, in
their love nest on the Lower East Side of New York. You might
say that observing the passions of mortals, often with stern dis-
approval, had always been a hobby of mine; but of late it was
their more intimate pursuits that took my fancy. Still, I had standards. As a whiff of sanctity always clung to my person from my
sojourns in the Upper Eden, I lost interest where the dalliance of
mortals was undiluted by some measure of earnest affection.
And the young Fefer couple, they adored each other with a love
that surpassed their own understanding. Indeed, so fervent was
the heat of their voluptuous intercourse that they sometimes
feared it might consume them and they would perish of sheer
ecstasy.

I happened upon them one miserable midsummer evening when I was making my rounds of the East Side ghetto, which in those years was much in need of my benevolent visitations. I did a lot of good, believe me, spreading banquets on the tables of desolate families in their coal cellars, exposing the villains posing as suitors to young girls fresh off the boat. I even engaged in spirited disputes with the *apikorsin*, the unbelievers, in an effort to vindicate God's justice to man—a thankless task, to say the least, in that swarming, heretical, typhus-infested neighborhood. So was it any wonder that with the volume of dirty work that fell to my hands, I should occasionally seek some momentary diversion?

You might call it a waste that one with my gift for camouflage, who could have gained clandestine admittance backstage at the Ziegfeld Follies when Anna Held climbed out of her milk bath, or slipped unnoticed into the green room at the People's Theater where Tomashefsky romped au naturel with his zaftig harem, that I should return time and again to the tenement flat of Feyvush and Gitl Fefer. But then you never saw the Fefers at their amorous business.

To be sure, they weren't what you'd call prepossessing. Feyvush, a cobbler by profession, was stoop-shouldered and hollow-breasted, nose like a parrot's beak, hair a wreath of swiftly evaporating black foam. His bride was a green-eyed, pear-shaped little hausfrau, freckles stippling her cheeks as if dripped from the brush that daubed her rust red pompadour. Had you seen them in the streets—Feyvush with nostrils flaring from the stench, his arm hooked through Gitl's from whose free hand dangled the carcass of an unflicked chicken—you would have deemed them in no way remarkable. But at night when they turned down the gas lamp in their stuffy bedroom, its window giving on to the fire escape (where I stooped to watch), they were the Irene and Vernon Castle of the clammy sheets.

At first they might betray a charming awkwardness. Feyvush

would fumble with the buttons of Gitl's shirtwaist, tugging a little frantically at corset laces, hooks, and eyes. He might haul without ceremony the shapeless muslin shift over her head, shove the itchy cotton drawers below her knees. Just as impatiently Gitl would yank down the straps of her spouse's suspenders, pluck the studs from his shirt, the rivets from his fly; she would thrust chubby fingers between the seams of his union suit with the same impulsivness that she plunged her hand in a barrel to snatch a herring. Then they would tumble onto the sagging iron bed, its rusty springs complaining like a startled henhouse. At the initial shock of flesh pressing flesh, they would clip, squeeze, and fondle whatever was most convenient, as if each sought a desperate assurance that the other was real. But once they'd determined as much, they slowed the pace; they lulled their frenzy to a rhythmic investigation of secret contours, like a getting acquainted of the blind.

They postponed the moment of their union for as long as they could stand to. While Feyvush sucked her nipples till they stood up like gumdrops, Gitl gaily pulled out clumps of her husband's hair; while he traced with his nose the line of ginger fur below her navel the way a flame follows a fuse, she held his hips like a rampant divining rod over her womb. When their loins were finally locked together, it jarred them so that they froze for an instant, each seeming to ask the other in tender astonishment: "What did we do?" Then the bed would gallop from wardrobe to washstand and the neighbors pound on their ceilings with brooms, until Feyvush and Gitl spent themselves, I swear it, in a shower of sparks. It was an eruption that in others might have catapulted their spirits clear out of their bodies—but not the Fefers, who clung tenaciously to each other rather than suffer even a momentary separation from their better half.

Afterwards, as they lay in a tangle, hiding their faces in mutual embarrassment over such a bounty of delight, I would slope off. My prurient interests satisfied, I was released from impure thoughts; I was free, a stickiness in the pants notwithstanding, to carry on with cleansing lepers and catering the weddings of the honest poor. So as you see, my spying on the Fefers was a tonic, a clear case of the ends justifying the means.

How was it I contrived to stumble upon such a talented pair in the first place? Suffice it that, when you've been around for nearly three thousand years, you develop antennae. It's a sensitivity that, in my case, was partial compensation for the loss of my oracular faculty, an exchange of roles from clairvoyant to voyeur. While I might not be able to predict the future with certainty anymore, I could intuit where and when someone was getting a heartfelt shtupping.

But like I say, I didn't let my fascination with the Fefers interfere with the performance of good works; the tally of my *mitzvot* was as great as ever. Greater perhaps, since my broader interests kept me closer than usual to earth, sometimes neglecting the tasks that involved a return to Kingdom Come. (Sometimes I put off escorting souls back to the afterlife, a job I'd never relished, involving as it did what amounted to cleaning up after the Angel of Death.) Whenever the opportunity arose, my preoccupation with Feyvush and Gitl might move me to play the detective. While traveling in their native Galicia, for instance, I would stop by the study house, the only light on an otherwise deserted street in the abandoned village of Krok. This was the Fefers' home village, a place existing just this side of memory, reduced by pogrom and expulsions to broken chimneys, a haunted bathhouse, scattered pages of the synagogue register among the dead leaves. The only survivors being a dropsical rabbi and his skeleton crew of disciples, it was to them I appealed for specifics.

"Who could forget?" replied the old rabbi stroking a snuff yellow beard, the wen on his brow like a sightless third eye. "After their wedding he comes to me, this Feyvush: 'Rabbi,' he says guiltily, 'is not such unspeakable pleasure a sin?' I tell him:

'In the view of Yohanan ben Dabai, a man may do what he will with his wife; within the zone of the marriage bed all is permitted.' He thanks me and runs off before I can give him the opinion of Rabbi Eliezer, who suggests that, while having intercourse, one should think on arcane points of law . . . "

I liked to imagine their wedding night. Hadn't I witnessed enough of them in my time?—burlesque affairs wherein the child bride and groom, martyrs to arranged marriages, had never set eyes on each other before. They were usually frightened to near paralysis, their only preparation a lecture from some doting melammed, or a long-suffering mother's manual of medieval advice. "What's God been doing since He created the world?" goes the old query. Answer: "He's been busy making matches." But the demoralized condition of the children to whose nuptials I was assigned smacked more of the intervention of pushy families than the hand of God.

No wonder I was so often called on to give a timid bridegroom a nudge. Employing my protean powers—now regrettably obsolete, though I still regard myself a master of stealth—I might take the form of a bat or the shimmying flame of a hurricane lamp to scare the couple into each other's arms. (Why I never lost patience and stood in for the fainthearted husband myself, I can't say.) Certainly there's no reason to suppose that Dvora Malkeh's Feyvush, the cobbler's apprentice, was any braver when it came to bedding his own stranger bride—his Gitl, who at fifteen was two years his junior, the only daughter of Chaim Rupture the porter, her dowry a hobbled goat and a dented tin kiddush cup. It was not what you'd have called a brilliant match.

Still, I liked to picture the moment when they're alone for the first time in their bridal chamber, which was probably some shelf above a stove encircled by horse blankets. In the dark Feyvush has summoned the courage to strip to his *talis koton*, its ritual fringes dangling a flimsy curtain over his knocking knees.

Gitl has peeled in one anxious motion to her starchless shift and slid gingerly beneath the thistledown, where she's joined after a small eternity by the tremulous groom. They lie there without speaking, without touching, having forgotten (respectively) the rabbi's sage instruction and the diagrams in *The Saffron Sacrament*. They only know that the warm (albeit shuddering) flesh beside them has a magnetism as strong as gravity, so that each feels they've been falling their whole lives into the other's embrace. And afterwards there's nothing on earth—neither goat's teat nor cobbler's last, pickle jar, poppy seed, Cossack's knout, or holy scroll—that doesn't echo their common devotion.

Or so I imagined. I also guessed that their tiny hamlet must have begun to seem too cramped to contain such an abundance of mutual affection. It needed a shtetl, say, the size of Tarnopol, or a teeming city as large as Lodz to accommodate them; or better: For a love that defied possibility, a land where the impossible (as was popularly bruited) was the order of the day. America was hardly an original idea—I never said the Fefers were original, only unique—but emboldened by the way that wedded bliss had transformed their ramshackle birthplace, they must have been curious to see how love traveled.

You might have thought the long ocean passage, at the end of which waited only a dingy dumbbell tenement on Orchard Street, would have cooled their ardor. Were their New World circumstances any friendlier to romance than the Old? Feyvush worked twelve-hour days in a bootmaking loft above the butcher's shambles in Gouverneur Slip; while Gitl haggled with fishmongers and supplemented her husband's mean wages stitching artificial flowers for ladies' hats. The streets swarmed with hucksters, ganefs, and handkerchief girls who solicited in the shadows of buildings draped in black bunting. Every day the funeral trains of cholera victims plied the market crush, displacing vendors crying spoiled meat above the locust-hum of the sewing machines. The summers brought a heat that made ovens of the tenements, sending the occupants to their roofs where they inhaled a cloud of blue flies; and in winter the ice hung in tusks from the common faucets, the truck horses froze upright in their tracks beside the curb. But if the ills of the ghetto were any impediment to their ongoing conjugal fervor, you couldn't have proved it by the Feyvush and Gitl I knew.

They were after all no strangers to squalor, and the corruptions of the East Side had a vitality not incompatible with the Fefers' own sweet delirium. Certainly there was a stench, but there was also an exhilaration: There were passions on display in the music halls and the Yiddish theaters, where Jacob Adler or Bertha Kalish could be counted on nightly to tear their emotions to shreds. You had the dancing academies where the greenhorns groped one another in a macabre approximation of the turkey trot, the Canal Street cafés where the poets and revolutionaries fought pitched battles with arsenals of words. You had the shrill and insomniac streets. Content as they were to keep to themselves, the Fefers were not above rubbernecking. They liked to browse the Tenth Ward's gallery of passions, comparing them— with some measure of pride—unfavorably to their own.

Sometimes I thought the Fefers nurtured their desire for each other as if it were an altogether separate entity, a member of the family if you will. Of course the mystery remained that such heroic lovemaking as theirs had yet to produce any offspring, which was certainly not for want of trying. Indeed, they'd never lost sight of the sacramental aspect of their intimacy, or the taboos against sharing a bed for purposes other than procreation. They had regularly consulted with local midwives, and purchased an assortment of *bendls*, simples, and fertility charms to no avail. (Gitl had even gone so far as to flush her system with mandrake enemas against a possible evil eye.) But once, as I knelt outside their window during a smallpox-ridden summer (when caskets the size of bread pans were carried from the tenements night and day), I heard Feyvush suggest: "Maybe no babies is for such a plenty of pleasure the price we got to pay?"

You didn't have to be a prophet to see it coming. What could you expect when a pair of mortals routinely achieved orgasms like Krakatoa, their loins shooting sparks like the uncorking of a bottle of pyrotechnical champagne? Something had to give, and with hindsight I can see that it had to happen on Shabbos, when married folk are enjoined to go at their copulation as if ridden by demons. Their fervent cleaving to one another (*dveikuss* the kabbalists call it) is supposed to hasten the advent of Messiah, or some such poppycock. Anyway, the Fefers had gathered momentum over the years, enduring climaxes of such convulsive magnitude that their frames could scarcely contain the exaltation. And since they clung to each other with a ferocity that refused to release spirit from flesh, it was only a matter of time until their transports carried them bodily aloft.

I was in Paradise when it happened, doing clerical work. Certain bookkeeping tasks were entrusted to me, such as totting up the debits and credits of incoming souls—tedious work that I alternated with the more restful occupation of weaving garlands of prayers; but even this had become somewhat monotonous, a mindless therapy befitting the sanatariumlike atmosphere of Kingdom Come. For such employment I chose a quiet stone bench (what bench wasn't quiet?) along a garden path near the bandstand. (Paradise back then resembled those sepia views of Baden-Baden or Saratoga Springs in their heyday; though of late the place, fallen into neglect, has more in common with the seedier precincts of Miami Beach.) At dusk I closed the ledger and tossed the garlands into the boughs of the Tree of Life, already so festooned with ribbons of prayer that the dead, in their wistfulness, compared it to a live oak hung with Spanish moss. Myself, I thought of a peddler of suspenders on the Lower East Side.

I was making my way along a petal-strewn walk toward the gates in my honorary angel getup—quilted smoking jacket, tasseled fez, a pair of rigid, lint white wings. Constructed of chicken wire and papiér mâche, they were just for show, the wings, about as useful as an ostrich's. I confess this was a source of some resentment, since why shouldn't I merit the genuine article? As for the outfit, having selected it myself I couldn't complain; certainly it was smart, though the truth was I preferred my terrestrial *shmattes*. But in my empyrean role as Sandolphon the Psychopomp, whose responsibilities included the orientation of lost souls, I was expected to keep up appearances.

So I'm headed toward the park gates when I notice this hubbub around a turreted gazebo. Maybe I should qualify "hubbub," since the dead, taking the air in their light golfing costumes and garden-party gowns, were seldom moved to curiosity. Nevertheless, a number had paused in their twilight stroll to inspect some new development under the pavilion on the lawn. Approaching, I charged the spectators to make way. Then I ascended the short flight of steps to see an uninvited iron bed supplanting the tasteful wicker furniture; and on that rumpled, bow-footed bed lay the Fefers, man and wife, in flagrante delicto. Feyvush, with his pants still down around his hairy ankles, and Gitl, her shift rucked to the neck, were holding onto each other for dear life.

As you may know, it wasn't without precedent for unlicensed mortals to enter the Garden alive. Through the ages you'd had a smattering of overzealous mystics who'd arrived by dint of pious contemplation, only to expire outright from the exertion. But to my knowledge Feyvush and Gitl were the first to have made the trip via the agency of ecstatic intercourse. They had, in effect, shtupped their way to heaven.

I moved forward to cover their nakedness with the quilt, though there was really no need for modesty in the Upper Eden, where unlike in the fallen one innocence still obtained.

"I bet you're wondering where it is that you are," was all I could think to say.

They nodded in saucer-eyed unison. When I told them Paradise, their eyes flicked left and right like synchronized wipers on a pair of stalled locomobiles. Then just as I'd begun to introduce myself ("the mock-angel Sandolphon here, although you might know me better as . . ."), an imperious voice cut me off.

"I'll take care of this—that is of course if *you* don't mind . . ."

It was the archangel Metatron, né Enoch ben Seth, celestial magistrate, commissary, archivist, and scribe. Sometimes called Prince of the Face (his was a chiseled death mask with one severely arched brow), he stood with his hands clasped before him, a thin gray eminence rocking on his heels. He was dressed like an undertaker in a sable homburg and frockcoat, its seams neatly split at the shoulders to make room for an impressive set of ivory wings. Unlike my own pantomime pair, Enoch's worked. While much too dignified to actually use them, he was not above preening them in my presence, flaunting the wings as an emblem of a higher status that he seldom let me forget. He had it in for me because I served as a reminder that he too had once been a human being. Like me he'd been translated in the prime of life in an apotheosis of flames to Kingdom Come. Never mind that his assumption had included the further awards of functional feathers and an investiture as full seraph: He still couldn't forgive me for recalling his humble origins, the humanity he'd never entirely outgrown.

"Welcome to the Upper Eden," the archangel greeted the bedridden couple, "the bottommost borough of Olam ha-Ba, the World to Come." And on a cautionary note, "You realize of course that your arrival here is somewhat, how shall we say, premature?"

With the quilt hoisted to their chins, the Fefers nodded in concert—as what else should they do?

"However," continued Enoch, whose flashier handle I'd never

gotten used to, which insubordination he duly noted, "accidents will happen, eh? and we must make the best of an irregular state of affairs. So," he gave a dispassionate sniff, brushing stardust or dandruff from an otherwise immaculate sleeve, "if you'll be so good as to follow me, I'll show you to your quarters." He turned abruptly and for a moment we were nose-to-nose (my potato to Enoch's flutey yam), until I was forced to step aside.

Feyvush and Gitl exchanged bewildered glances, then shrugged. Clutching the quilt about their shoulders, they climbed out of bed—Feyvush stumbling over his trousers as Gitl stifled a nervous laugh—and scrambled to catch up with the peremptory angel. They trailed him down the steps of the gazebo under the boughs of the Tree of Life, in which the firefly lanterns had just become visible in the gloaming. Behind them the little knot of immortals drifted off in their interminable promenade.

"What's the hurry?" I wanted to call out to the Fefers; I wanted a chance to give them the benefit of my experience to help them get their bearings. Wasn't that the least I could do for the pair who'd provided me with such a spicy pastime over the years? Outranked, however, I had no alternative but to tag along unobtrusively.

Enoch led them down the hedge-bordered broadwalk between wrought-iron gates, their arch bearing the designation GANEYDN in gilded Hebrew characters. They crossed a cobbled avenue, ascended some steps onto a veranda where thousands of cypress rockers ticked like a chorus of pendulums. (Understand that Paradise never went in for the showier effects: none of your sardonyx portals and myriads of ministering angels wrapped in clouds of glory, no rivers of balsam, honey, and wine. There, in deference to the sensibilities of the deceased, earthly standards abide; the splendor remains human-scale, though odd details from the loftier regions sometimes trickle down.)

Through mahogany doors thrown open to the balmy air, they

entered the lobby of the grand hotel that serves as dormitory for the dead. Arrested by their admiration for the acres of carpets and carved furniture, the formal portraits of archons in their cedar of Lebanon frames, the chandeliers, Feyvush and Gitl lagged behind. They craned their necks to watch phoenixes smoldering like smudge pots gliding beneath the arcaded ceiling, while Enoch herded them into the elevator's brass cage. Banking on the honeymoon suite, I took the stairs and, preternaturally spry for my years, slipped in after them as Enoch was showing the couple their rooms. Here again the Fefers were stunned by sumptuous appointments: the marble-topped whatnot, the divan stuffed with angel's hair, the Brussels lace draperies framing balustraded windows open to a view of the park. From its bandstand you could hear the silvery yodel of a famous dead cantor chanting the evening prayers.

Inconspicuous behind the open door, my head wreathed in a Tiffany lamp shade, I watched the liveried cherubs parade into the bedroom, dumping their burdens of fresh apparel on the canopied bed.

"I trust you'll find these accommodations satisfactory," Enoch was saying in all insincerity, "and that your stay here will be a pleasant one." Rubbing the hands he was doubtless eager to wash of this business, he began to mince backward toward the door.

Under the quilt that mantled the Fefers, Feyvush started as from a poke in the ribs. He looked askance at his wife who gave him a nod of encouragement, then ventured a timid, "Um, if it please your honor," another nudge, "for how long do we supposed to stay here?"

Replied Enoch: "Why, forever of course."

Another dig with her elbow failed to move her tongue-tied husband, and Gitl spoke up herself. "You mean we ain't got to die?"

"God forbid," exhaled Enoch a touch sarcastically, his patience with their naiveté at an end: It was a scandal how the living lacked even the minimal sophistication of the dead. "Now, if there are no further questions . . . ?" Already backed into the corridor, he reminded them that room service was only a bellpull away, and was gone.

Closing the door (behind which my camouflaged presence made no impression at all), Feyvush turned to Gitl and asked, "Should we have gave him a tip?"

Gitl practically choked in her attempt to suppress a titter whose contagion spread to Feyvush. With a toothy grin making fish-shaped crescents of his goggle eyes, he proceeded to pinch her all over, and together they dissolved in a fit of hysterics that buckled their knees. They rolled about on the emerald carpet, then picked themselves up in breathless dishevelment, abandoning their quilt to make a beeline for the bedroom.

Oh boy, I thought, God forgive me; now they'll have it off in heaven and their aphrodisiac whoops will drive the neutered seraphim to acts of depravity. But instead of flinging themselves headlong onto the satin counterpane, they paused to inspect their laid-out wardrobe—or "trousseau" as Gitl insisted on calling it.

Donning a wing-collar shirt with boiled bosom, creased flannel trousers, and a yachting blazer with a yellow Shield of David crest, Feyvush struck rakish poses for his bride. Gitl wriggled into a silk corset cover, over which she pulled an Empire tea gown, over which an ungirded floral kimono. At the smoky-mirrored dressing table she daubed her round face with scented powders; she made raccoon's eyes of her own with an excess of shadow, scattered a shpritz of sparkles over the bonfire of her hair. Between her blown breasts she hung a sapphire the size of a gasolier.

While she carried on playing dress-up, Feyvush tugged

experimentally on the bellpull, which was answered by an almost instantaneous knock at the door. Feyvush opened it to admit a tea trolley wheeled by a silent creature (pillbox hat and rudimentary wings) who'd no sooner appeared than bowed himself out. Relaxing the hand that held the waived gratuity, Feyvush fell to contemplating the pitcher and covered dish on the trolley. Pleased with her primping, Gitl rose to take the initiative. The truth was, the young Mrs. Fefer was no great shakes in the kitchen, the couple having always done their "cooking" (as Talmud puts it) in bed. Nevertheless, with a marked efficiency, she lifted the silver lid from the dish, faltering at the sight of the medicinal blue bottle underneath. Undiscouraged, however, she tipped a bit of liver brown powder from the bottle onto the plate, then mixed in a few drops of water from the crystal pitcher. There was a foaming after which the powder assumed the consistency of clotted tapioca. Gitl dipped in a finger, gave it a tentative lick, smacked her lips, and sighed. Then she dipped the finger again, placing it this time on her husband's extended tongue. Feyvush too closed his eyes and sighed, which was the signal for them both to tuck in with silver spoons. Cheeks bulging, they exulted over the succulent feast of *milchik* and *fleishik* flavors that only manna can evoke.

Having placated their bellies, you might have expected them to turn to the satisfaction of other appetites. But instead of going back to the bedroom, they went to the open windows and again looked out over the Garden. Listening to the still warbling cantor (to be followed in that evening's program by a concert of Victor Herbert standards—though not before at least half a century'd passed on earth), they were so enraptured they forgot to embrace. Up here where perfection was the sine qua non, their felicity was complete, and they required no language or gesture to improve on what was already ideal.

Heartsick, I replaced the lamp shade and slunk out. I know it was unbecoming my rank and position to be disappointed on account of mere mortals; after all, if the Fefers had finally arrived at the logical destination of their transports, then good on them! What affair was it of mine? But now that it was time I mounted another expedition to the fallen world—babies, paupers, and skeptics were proliferating like mad—I found I lacked the necessary incentive. This is not to say I was content to stay on in Paradise, where I was quite frankly bored, but neither did a world without the Fefers have much appeal.

It didn't help that I ran into them everywhere, tipping my fez somewhat coolly whenever we crossed paths—which was often, since Feyvush and Gitl, holding hands out of habit, never tired of exploring the afterlife. At first I tried to ignore them, but idle myself, I fell into an old habit of my own. I tailed them as they joined the ranks of the perpetual strollers meandering among the topiary hedges, loitering along the gravel walks and bridle paths. I supposed that for a tourist the Garden did have its attractions: You've got your quaint scale reproductions of the industries of the upper heavens, such as a mill for grinding manna, a quarry of souls. There's a zoo that houses some of the beasts that run wild in the more ethereal realms: a three-legged "man of the mountain," a sullen behemoth with barnacled hide, a petting zoo containing a salamander hatched from a myrtle flame. But having readjusted my metabolism to conform to the hours of earth, I wondered when the Fefers would wake up. When would they notice, say, that the fragrant purple dusk advanced at only a glacial pace toward dawn; that the dead, however well-dressed and courteous, were rather, well, stiff and cold?

In the end, though, my vigilance paid off. After what you would call about a week (though the Shabbos eve candles still burned in the celestial yeshivas), I was fortunate enough to be on hand when the couple sounded their first note of discontent.

Hidden in plain sight in their suite (in the pendulum cabinet of a grandfather clock), I overheard Feyvush broach a troubling subject with his wife. Having sampled some of the outdoor prayer minyans that clustered about the velvet lawns, he complained, "It ain't true, Gitteleh, the stories that they tell about the world." Because in their discourses on the supernatural aspects of history, the dead, due to a faulty collective memory, tended to overlook the essential part of being alive: that it was natural.

Seated at her dressing table, languidly unscrolling the bobbin of her pompadour, letting it fall like carrot shavings over her forehead, Gitl ventured a complaint of her own. He should know that in the palatial bathhouse she attended—it was no longer unusual for the couple to spend time apart—the ladies snubbed her.

"For them to be flesh and blood is a sin."

She was wearing a glove-silk chemise that might have formerly inspired her husband to feats of erotic derring-do. Stepping closer, Feyvush tried to reassure her, "I think they're jealous."

Gitl gave a careless shrug.

At her shoulder Feyvush continued cautiously, "Gitl, remember how," pausing to gather courage, "remember how on the Day of Atonement we played 'blowing the shofar'?"

Gitl stopped fussing with her hair, nodded reflexively.

"Do you remember how on Purim I would part like the pages of Megillah . . ." here an intake of air in the lungs of both parties ". . . your legs?"

Again an almost mechanical nod.

"Gitl," submitted Feyvush just above a whisper, "do you miss it that I don't touch you that way no more?"

She put down the tortoiseshell hairbrush, cocked her head thoughtfully, then released an arpeggio of racking sobs. "Like the breath of life I miss it!" she wailed, as Feyvush, his own frustrations confirmed, fell to his knees and echoed her lament.

"Gitteleh," he bawled, burying his face in her lap, "ain't nobody fency yentzing in Kingdom Come!" Then lifting his head to blow his nose on a brocaded shirtsleeve, drying his eyes with same, he hesitantly offered, "Maybe we could try to go home ..."

"Hallelujah!"

This was me bursting forth from the clock to congratulate them on a bold resolution. "Now you're talking!" I assured them. "Of course it won't be easy; into the Garden you got without a dispensation but without a dispensation they won't never let you leave ..." Then I observed how the Fefers, not yet sufficiently jaded from their stay in heaven, were taken aback. Having leapt to their feet, they'd begun to slide away from me along the paneled walls, which was understandable: For despite my natty attire, my features had become somewhat crepe-hung over the ages, my rheumy eyes tending toward the hyacinth red.

Recalling the introduction I never completed upon their arrival, I started over. "Allow me to present myself: the prophet Elijah, at your service. You would recognize me better in the rags I wear in the world." And as they still appeared dubious, Gitl smearing her already runny mascara as if in an effort to wipe me from her eye, I entreated them to relax: "You can trust me." I explained that I wanted to help them get back to where they belonged.

This at least had the effect of halting their retreat, which in turn called my bluff.

"You should understand," I began to equivocate, "there ain't much I can do personally. Sure, I'm licensed to usher souls from downstairs to up, but regarding vicey-versey I got no jurisdiction, my hands are tied. And from here to there you don't measure the distance in miles but years, so don't even think about starting the journey on your own ..."

At that point Gitl, making chins (their ambrosial diet had endowed her with several extra), planted an elbow in Feyvush's ribs. He coughed once before speaking. "If it please your honor," his listless tone not half so respectful as he'd been with Enoch, "what is it exactly you meaning to do?"

I felt a foolish grin spreading like eczema across my face. "What I have in mind . . . ," I announced on a note of confidence that instantly fell flat, because I didn't really have a clue. Rallying nonetheless, I voiced my determination to intercede with the archangel Metatron on the couple's behalf.

But who was I kidding? That stickler for the letter of the Law, he wouldn't have done me a favor if his immortality depended on it. Still, a promise was a promise, so I sought out his high-and-mightiness in his apartments in the dignitaries' wing of the hotel. (My own were among the cottages of the superannuated cherubim.)

Addressing him by his given name, I'm straight away off on the wrong foot.

"Sorry . . . I mean Metatron, Prince of the Face (such a face!), Lesser Lord of the Seventy Names, and so forth," I said, attempting to smooth his ruffled pride. It seemed that Enoch had never gotten over the treatment attending his translation to heaven, when the hosts mockingly claimed they could smell one of woman born from parasangs away. "Anyhow," putting my foot in it deeper, "they had a nice holiday, the Fefers, but they would like already to go back where they came."

Seated behind the captain's desk in his office sipping a demitasse with uplifted pinky, his back to a wall of framed citations and awards, the archangel assumed an expression of puzzled innocence. Did I have to spell it out?

"You know, like home."

"Home?" inquired Enoch as if butter wouldn't melt on his unctuous tongue. "Why this is their home for all eternity."

Apparently I wasn't going to be invited to sit down. "But they ain't happy here," I persisted.

"Not happy in Paradise?" Plunking down his cup and saucer as if the concept was unheard of.

"It's possible," I allowed a bit too emphatically. Enoch clucked his tongue, which provoked me to state the obvious. "Lookit, they ain't dead yet."

"A mere technicality," pooh-poohed the archangel. "Besides, for those who've dwelt in Abraham's Bosom, the earth should no longer hold any real attraction."

Although I was more or less living proof to the contrary, rather than risk antagonizing him again, I kept mum on that subject. Instead: "Have a heart," I appealed to him. "You were alive when you came here . . ." Which didn't sound the way I meant it to. "Didn't you ever want to go back?"

"Back?" Enoch was incredulous. "Back to what, making shoes?"

That he'd lowered his guard enough to mention his mortal profession made me think I saw an angle. "Feyvush is a cobbler," I humbly submitted.

"Then he's well out of it." The seraph stressed the point by raising his arched brow even higher, creating ripples that spoiled the symmetry of his widow's peak. "Besides, when I stitched leather, it was as if I fastened the world above to the world below."

"But don't you see," I pleaded, the tassel of my fez dancing like a spider before my eyes till I slapped it away, "that's what it was like when Feyvush would *yentz* with his bride . . ." This was definitely not the tack to have taken.

"Like I said, he's better off," snapped Enoch, rising abruptly from his swivel chair to spread his magnificent wings. "And since when is any of this *your* business?"

The conversation closed, I turned to go, muttering something about how I guessed I was just a sentimental fool.

"Elijah . . . ," the angel called my name after a fashion guaranteed to inspire maximum guilt.

"Sandolphon," I corrected him under my breath.

". . . I think it's time you tended to your terrestrial errands."

"Funny," I replied in an insipid singsong, "I was thinking the same thing."

You'll say I should have left well enough alone, and maybe you're right. After all, without my meddling the Fefers would still be in heaven and I pursuing my charitable rounds on earth—instead of sentenced for my delinquency to stand here at this crossroads directing traffic, pointing the pious toward the gates, the wicked in the other direction, not unlike (to my everlasting shame) that Nazi doctor on the railroad platform during the last apocalypse. But who'd have thought that, with my commendable record of good works, I wasn't entitled to a single trespass?

When I offered the Fefers my plan, Gitl elbowed Feyvush, then interrupted his diffident "If it please your honor—" to challenge me herself: "What for do you want to help us?"

"Because," since my audience with the archangel I'd developed a ready answer, "I can't stand to see nobody downhearted in Paradise. This is my curse, that such *rachmones*, such compassion I got, I can't stand it to see nobody downhearted anywhere." Which was true enough. It was an attitude that kept me constantly at odds with the angelic orders, with Enoch and Raziel and Death (between whom and myself there was a history of feuding) and the rest of that cold-blooded crew. It was my age-old humanitarian impulse that compelled me to come to the aid of the Fefers, right? and not just a selfish desire to see them at their shtupping again.

Departing the hotel, we moved through whatever pockets of darkness the unending dusk provided—hard to find in a park whose every corner was illumined by menorahs and fairy lights. Dressed for traveling (Feyvush in an ulster and fore-and-aft cap, Gitl in automobile cape and sensible shoes), they were irked with me, my charges, for making them leave behind a pair of overstuffed Gladstone bags. Their aggravation signified an ambivalence which, in my haste to get started, I chose to ignore, and looking back I confess I might have been a little pushy. Anyway, in order not to call attention to ourselves (small danger among the indifferent immortals), I pretended I was conducting yet another couple of greenhorns on a sightseeing tour of the Garden.

"Here you got your rose trellis made out of what's left of Jacob's Ladder, and over there, that scrawny thing propped on a crutch, that's the *etz ha-daat*, the Tree of Knowledge . . ."

When I was sure no one was looking, I hauled the Fefers behind me into the shadows beneath the bloated roots of the Tree of Life. From a hanger in their midst I removed my universal *luftmensch* outfit—watch cap, galoshes, and patched overcoat—which I quick-changed into after discarding my Sandolphon duds. Then I led the fugitives into a narrow cavern that snaked its way under the Tree trunk, fetching up at the rust-cankered door of a dumbwaiter.

I'd discovered it some time ago while looking for an easier passage to earth. My ordination as honorary angel, while retarding the aging process, had not, as you know, halted it entirely; so I was in need of a less strenuous means of descent than was afforded by the branches of the Tree of Life. An antique device left over from the days when the Lord still frequented the Garden to send the odd miracle below, the dumbwaiter was just the thing. It was a sturdy enough contraption that, notwithstanding the sponginess of its wooden cabinet and the agonizing groan of its cables, had endured the test of time.

The problem was that the dumbwaiter's compactness was not intended to accommodate three people. A meager, collapsible old man, I'd always found it sufficiently roomy; but while the Fefers were not large, Gitl had never been exactly svelte, and both of them had put on weight during their "honeymoon." Nevertheless, making a virtue of necessity, they folded themselves into a tandem pair of S's and allowed me to stuff them into the tight compartment. This must have been awkward for them at first, since they hadn't held each other in a while, but as I wedged myself into the box behind them and started to lower us down the long shaft, Feyvush and Gitl began to generate a sultry heat.

They ceased their griping about cramped quarters and began to make purring noises of a type that brought tears to my eyes. I felt an excitement beyond that which accrued from our gathering speed, as the tug of gravity accelerated the dumbwaiter's downward progress. The cable sang as it slipped through my blistering fingers. Then came the part where our stomachs were in our throats and we seemed to be in a bottomless free fall, the dizzy, protracted prelude to the earth-shaking clatter of our landing. The crash must have alerted the cooks in the basement kitchen of Ratner's Dairy Restaurant to our arrival; because, when I slid open the door, there they were: a surly lot in soiled aprons and mushroom hats, looking scornfully at the pretzel the Fefers had made of themselves. I appeased them as always with a jar of fresh manna, an ingredient (scarce in latter-day New York) they'd come to regard as indispensable for their heavenly blintzes.

If the plummeting claustrophobia of the dumbwaiter, to say nothing of its bumpy landing, hadn't sufficiently disoriented my charges, then the shrill Sunday brunch crowd I steered them through would have finished the job. I hustled them without fanfare out the revolving door into a bitter blast of winter barreling up Delancey Street from the river.

"Welcome home!" I piped, though the neighborhood bore small resemblance to the one they'd left better than three-quarters of a century ago. The truck horses and trolleys had been replaced by a metallic current of low-slung vehicles squealing and farting in sluggish procession; the pushcarts and garment emporia had given way to discount houses full of coruscating gadgetry, percussive music shuddering their plate-glass windows. Old buildings, if they weren't boarded up or reduced altogether to rubble, had new façades, as tacky as hoopskirts on dowagers. In the distance there were towers, their tops obscured by clouds like tentpoles under snow-heavy canvas.

Myself, I'd grown accustomed to dramatic changes during my travels back and forth. Besides, I made a point of keeping abreast of things, pumping the recently departed for news of the earth, lest returning be too great a jolt to my system. But the Fefers, though they'd demonstrated a tolerance for shock in the past, seemed beyond perplexity now, having entered a condition of outright fear.

Gitl was in back of her husband, trying to straighten his crimped spine with her knee, so that he seemed to speak with her voice when she asked, "What happened to the Jews?" Because it was true that, while the complexions of the passersby ran the spectrum from olive to saffron to lobster pink, there were few you could've identified as distinctly yid.

I shrugged. "Westchester, New Rochelle, Englewood, the Five Towns they went, but for delicatessen they come back to Delancey on Sundays." Then I grinned through my remaining teeth and made a show of protesting, "No need to thank me," though who had bothered? I shook their hands, which were as limp as fins. "Well, good-bye and good luck, I got things to do . . ."

I had urgent business to attend to, didn't I?—*brisses*, famines, false prophets in need of comeuppance. All right, so "urgent" was an exaggeration. Also, I was aware that the ills of the century had multiplied beyond anything my penny-ante philanthropies could hope to fix. But I couldn't stand being a party to Feyvush and Gitl's five-alarm disappointment. This wasn't the world they knew; *tahkeh*, it wasn't even the half of what they didn't know, and I preferred not to stick around for the heartache of their getting acquainted. I didn't want to be there when they learned, for instance, that Jews had vanished in prodigious numbers from more places on the face of the planet than the

Lower East Side. I didn't want to be there when they discovered what else had gone out of the world in their absence, and I didn't want to admit I made a mistake in bringing them back.

Still, I wouldn't send them away empty-handed. I gave them a pocket full of heaven gelt—that is, leaves from the *Etz ha-Chaim*, the Tree of Life that passed for currency in certain neighborhood pawnshops; I told them the shops where you got the best rate of exchange. The most they could muster by way of gratitude, however, was a perfunctory nod. When they slouched off toward the Bowery, drawing stares in their period gear, I thought of Adam and Eve leaving the Garden at the behest of the angel with the flaming sword.

I aimed my own steps in the direction of the good deeds whose abandonment could throw the whole cosmic scheme out of joint. Then conceding there was no need to kid myself, it was already out of joint, I turned around. Virtually invisible in my guise as one more homeless old crock among a multitude of others, I followed the Fefers. I entered the shop behind them, where a pawnbroker in a crumpled skullcap greeted them satirically: "Reb ben Vinkl, I presume!" (This in reference to Feyvush's outdated apparel and the beard that had grown rank on his reentering the earth's atmosphere.) But when he saw the color of the couple's scrip, he became more respectful, even kicking in some coats of recent vintage to reduce the Fefers' anachronistic mien.

There was no law that said Feyvush and Gitl had to remain in the old ghetto neighborhood. Owing to my foresight they now had a nest egg; they could move to, say, the Upper West Side, someplace where Jews were thicker on the ground. So why did they insist on beating a path through the shrieking winds back to Orchard Street? via a scenic route that took them past gutted synagogues, *shtiblekh* with their phantom congregants sandwiched between the bodegas and Chinese takeouts, the *talis* shops manned by ancients looking out as from an abyss of years. Answer: Having found the familiar strange enough, thank you, they might go farther and fare even worse.

As luck (if that's the right word) would have it, there was a flat available in the very same building they'd vacated a decades-long week ago. For all they knew it was the same paltry top-floor apartment with the same sticks of furniture: the sofa with its cushions like sinkholes, the crippled wing chair, the kitchen table, the iron bed; not that decor would have meant much to Feyvush and Gitl, who didn't look to be in a nostalgic mood. Hugging myself against the cold on the fire escape, I watched them wander from room to room until the windows fogged. Then someone rubbed a circle in a cloudy pane and I ducked out-of-sight below the ledge. But I could see them nonetheless, it was a talent I had: I could see them as clearly in my mind as with my eyes, peering out into a street beyond which there was no manicured pleasure garden, no Tree.

They went out only once. Despite having paid a deposit and the first month's rent, they still had ample funds; they might have celebrated. But instead they returned with only the barest essentials—some black bread and farfel, a shank of gristly soup meat, a greasy sack of knishes from the quarter's one surviving knisherie. Confounded by the gas range that had replaced her old coal-burning cookstove, Gitl threw up her hands. Feyvush hunched his shoulders: Who had any appetite? Then they stared out the window again, past icicles like a dropped portcullis of fangs, toward a billboard atop the adjacent building. The billboard, which featured a man and woman lounging nearly naked on a beach, advertised an airline that offered to fly you nonstop to paradise.

Hunkered below the window ledge, I heard what I couldn't hear just like I saw what I couldn't see—Feyvush saying as if to himself, "Was it a dream?" Gitl replying with rancor: "Dreams are for *goyim*."

At some point one of them—I don't remember which—went

into the bedroom and sat on the bed. He or she was followed soon after by the other, though neither appeared conscious of occupying the same space; neither thought to remove their heavy coats. The sag of the mattress, however, caused them to slide into contact with one another, and at first touch the Fefers combusted like dry kindling. They flared into a desperate embrace, shucking garments, Gitl pulling at her husband's suspenders as if drawing a bowstring. Feyvush ripped open Gitl's blouse the way Cossacks part a curtain to catch a Jew; he spread her thighs as if wrenching apart the jaws of a trap. Having torn away their clothes, it seemed they intended to peel back each other's flesh. They marked cheeks and throats with bared talons, twisting themselves into tortured positions as if each were attempting to put on the other's skin—as if the husband must climb through the body of his wife, and vice versa, in order to get back to what they'd lost.

That's how they did it, fastened to each other in what looked like a mutual punishment—hips battering hips, mouths spitting words refined of all affection. When they were done, they fell apart, sweating and bruised. They took in the stark furnishings of their cold-water flat: the table barren of the fabric flowers that once filled the place with perpetual spring, the window overlooking a street of strangers and dirty snow. Then they went at it again hammer and tongs.

I couldn't watch anymore; then God help me, I couldn't keep from watching. When the windows were steamed, I took the stairs to the roof, rime clinging to my lashes and beard, and squinted through a murky skylight like a sheet of green ice. When they were unobservable from any vantage, I saw them with an inner eye far clearer than my watery tom-peepers could focus. I let my good works slide, because who needed second sight to know that the world had gone already to hell in a phylactery bag? While my bones became brittle with winter and the bread and knishes went stale, and the soup meat grew mold and was nibbled at by mice, I kept on watching the Fefers.

Sometimes I saw them observing each other, with undisguised contempt. They both shed the souvenir pounds they'd brought back from eternity. Gone was Gitl's generous figure, her unkempt hair veiling her pallid face like a bloody rag. Her ribs showed beneath breasts as baggy as punctured meal sacks, and her freckles were indistinguishable from the pimples populating her brow. Feyvush, always slight, was nine-tenths a cadaver, his eyes in their hunger fairly drooling onto his hollow cheeks. His sunken chest, where it wasn't obscured by matted fur, revealed a frieze of scarlet hieroglyphs etched by his wife's fingernails. So wasted were they now that, when they coupled, their fevered bones chuckled like matches in a box. Between bouts they covered their nakedness with overcoats and went to the window, though not necessarily together. They rubbed circles, looked at the billboard with its vibrant twosome disporting under a tropical sun; then satisfied they were no nearer the place where they hoped to arrive, Feyvush or Gitl returned to bed.

Nu, so what would you have had me to do? Sure, I was the great kibbitzer in the affairs of others; but having already violated divine law by helping them escape from *der emeser velt*, the so-called true world, was I now to add insult to injury by delivering them from the false? Can truth and deception be swapped as easily as *shmattes* for fancy dress: give me a break, the damage was done; human beings were not anyway intended to rise above their stations. The Fefers would never get out of this life again, at least not alive.

So I remained a captive witness to their savage heat. I watched them doing with an unholy vengeance what I never found the time for in my own sanctimonious youth—when I was too busy serving as a mighty mouthpiece for the still small voice that had since become all but inaudible. I watched the mortals in their heedless ride toward an elusive glory, and aroused by the driven cruelty of their passion, achieved an erection: my first full engorgement since the days before the destruction of the Temple, when a maiden once lifted her tunic and I turned away. At the peak of my excitement I tore open the crotch of my trousers, releasing myself from a choked confinement, and spat my seed in a peashooter trajectory over Orchard Street. When I was finished, I allowed my wilted member to rest on the frigid railing of the fire escape, to which it stuck. Endeavoring to pull it free, I let loose a pitiable howl: I howled for the exquisite pain that mocked my terminal inability to die, and I howled for my loneliness. Then I stuffed my bloody putz back in my pants and looked toward the window, afraid I'd alerted the Fefers to my spying. But the Fefers, as it turned out, were well beyond earshot.

I raised the window and climbed over the sill muffling my nose with a fingerless mitten against the smell, and shuffled forward to inspect their remains. So hopelessly entangled were the pair of them, however, that it was hard at first to distinguish husband from wife. Of course, there was no mistaking Feyvush's crown of tufted wool for Gitl's tattered red standard, his beak for her button nose, but so twined were their gory limbs that they defied a precise designation of what belonged to whom. Nor did their fused loins admit to which particular set of bones belonged the organ that united them both.

My task was as always to separate spirit from flesh, to extricate their immortal souls, which after a quick purge in the fires of Gehenna (no more than a millennia or two) would be as good as new. The problem was that, given the intricate knot they'd made of themselves, what was true of their bodies was true as well of their souls: I couldn't tell where Gitl's left off and her husband's began. It took me a while to figure it out but ultimately I located the trouble; then the solution went some distance toward explaining their lifelong predicament. For the

Fefers had been one of those rare cases where a couple shares two halves of a solitary soul. Theirs had indeed been a marriage made in heaven such as you don't see much anymore, the kind of match that might lead you to believe God Himself had a hand in it—that is, if you didn't already know He'd gotten out of the matchmaking racket long ago.

Swan Song

As Morris Silverman, a retired salesclerk for Lipsky's Discount Shoes, plummeted toward the sun-dappled river, he thought that this was a stupid way to end such a cautious life.

It happened on a perfect Sunday afternoon in April, when his son Nat and daughter-in-law Miriam had come to air him out in their sporty new Dodge sedan. They'd driven across the shuddering bridge into the bottomlands beyond the river, cruising along the flat roads among rice paddies and cotton fields. Then, after the hour it took for his father's chronic complaining to wear his patience thin, Nat turned the car around and headed home. They were back on the old cantilevered bridge, which Morris had contended for years was falling down, when the blowout occurred.

"*Gott in himmel!*" cried Morris, as if the gunshot sound of the puncture had penetrated his own rickety person. Fortunately, given the snail's pace of the Sunday traffic, Nat had no real difficulty in maintaining control of the sedan. But as the other vehicles were backed up and honking behind him, the situation was somewhat tense. Nor was the tension reduced by Morris, who hung onto his fluttering heart in the backseat, cataloguing calamities they'd narrowly escaped—"No thanks to my *meshugener* son!"

Nat was removing the jack from the trunk, placing it under the bumper.

"Miriam," he called out in a singsong voice that implied his temper was being tested, "will you help Papa out of the car?"

Holding her straw hat with silk violets against the wayward breezes, Miriam got out and opened the back door. She took hold of Morris's arm and began gently, then not so gently, pulling him to his feet. You would have thought she was dragging him over a precipice.

"What are you doing?" he demanded, his sallow eyes sprung from their sockets. "*Vildeh moid*, leave an old man in peace!"

From behind the car Nat shouted, no longer disguising his aggravation, that Morris must get out. Sulking, his father stepped uncertainly onto the sidewalk, tethered to Miriam of whom he'd never approved. "You see how she manhandles me," he moaned, inviting heaven to witness his treatment. To Nat he barked, adding his voice to the chorus of curses and honks, "You should of been more careful how you buy a new car. Shmo, you let them take you for a ride."

Then it bothered Morris the way the accusation redounded upon himself. He looked about, suddenly aware of his tenuous situation on the trembling span, and began to complain of vertigo and imminent peril.

Nat was muttering between clenched teeth that flat tires sometimes happened. Looking up from his labors, he called over his shoulder to Miriam to come please and collect the lug nuts. Before complying, Miriam took Morris's bony fingers and folded them one by one around the rusty guardrail. Morris stared daggers as if he were being marooned.

"Comes a big wind and Silverman's a goner!" he wailed, stealing a peek at the swollen river that turned him green.

Then came a big wind. Blown off his already precarious balance, Eli clung for dear life to the railing, at—as it happened—its weakest point. The corroded cast iron came loose under the pressure of even the old man's slight weight; and before he could appreciate his sudden gift of prophecy, Morris was gone, falling headlong toward the moiling water.

He fell for a very long time.

Before he'd fully understood his predicament, he saw, receding above him, the bewildered faces of his son and daughter-in-law, summoned to the broken rail by his forlorn cry. He saw a zephyr take Miriam's hat like a tossed bouquet.

Then he was tumbling head over fallen arches, the wind like a flock of mice running wild in his clothes. The rush of his descent rearranged the creases of his face and forced a grin, unknitting the ashen tufts of his brows. His throat and bowels played pitch with his delicate stomach, which made him indignant; he was doubly irate at realizing that the fear by which he set such store had abandoned him when it should have been most intense. Feeling cheated here in his extremity, Morris could have demanded a refund of all the years—which were passing swiftly (all seventy-six of them) before his eyes, a long life though you couldn't have called it happy. You'd have had to stretch it to call it a life.

There was a childhood spent, come to think of it, watching other boys throwing themselves off of high places. They jumped from fire escapes and trees, from bridges, leaping blindly into the future; while Morris, whom they guessed was born old, cautioned them against breaking their fool necks. They should think of the consequences; they should, for the sake of their poor mothers and later their wives, keep themselves in one piece. They should follow the example of Morris, who, in the employ of his old friend Lipsky, kept his head down and watched a procession—four decades long—of other people's feet. Then came retirement and the passing of his joyless wife Annie, after which, out of habit, he'd kept himself in one piece for the sake of . . .

Death, maybe?—which, in the shape of a river that glistened

like a dragon's tail, was rising up to the slap the daylights out of Morris Silverman.

But with respect to such an anticlimax, Morris could feel only contempt. Wasn't he, even as he dropped into oblivion, a survivor? Hadn't he come through this world unscratched? Disdainful of his brittle bones, he wanted to fling what remained of his caution to the winds. He wanted to spread his arms like the boys he used to warn against diving headfirst off the high board.

Then the wind stopped its shrill battery; the water kept its distance, as if he'd faced it down. A funnel of blackbirds whirled about him and Morris hung suspended in the eye of their storm. Then they'd risen above him, leaving the old man to float miraculously in midair: an extraordinary fellow after all, not only fearless but able to fly!

With some minimal adjustment to the horizontal and an occasional flap of his sticklike arms, Morris began to glide on a raft of air. Through his gaping jaw the inpouring gulf stream seemed to cleanse his creaking innards of age. What impressed him most (in a way that would have formerly made him fearful of a stroke) was the naturalness of his buoyancy; as if he'd come home to the element in which he truly belonged. He was born to the air, *shikkered* with vitality, sailing against the current above the turgid river they called the Old Man.

Clearing his throat of catarrh, he hooted obscenely, tore open his shirt to stretch the tails into wings, kicked off his shoes. In no time at all he had the hang of it; defiant of gravity, he was a regular Peter Pansky, somersaulting as he clutched his ribs to savor the joke. An exotic and fantastical creature, he was SILVERMAN—the bold letters emblazoned across his spangled underwear, as he barreled down out of the heavens, scourging Nazis in every walk of life.

Cunningly maneuverable now, Morris took in the sights. He hovered above a sandbar that featured, like a decaying snail shell, a beached paddle wheel. He swooped down over a forested island with a hermit's shack in a tree, over garfish like a school of torpedoes, a barge upon which a little man leaped and pointed at the flying *landsman*—yet another joke. Then having seen what the earth hereabouts had to offer, Morris aimed his tussocky beak toward the clouds—which were turreted and onion-domed like holy places, like palaces where maybe God kept his harem.

He lost his bearings among fleecy corridors embroidered in golden sunlight, caught (he could have sworn) fleeting glimpses of soaring alabaster wings. Then feeling a nosebleed coming on, he changed direction, doing a kind of pigeon breaststroke down through the billows until he rediscovered his Southern city perched on its bluff. With his moist eyes sharpened from gazing at impossible distances, he was delighted to see that life still carried on. People were fishing from the cobbled levee, window-browsing along the sidewalks, scattering doves in the fountained square. And north along Main Street, the sinking ship to which some of his neighbors still clung, Morris thought he could make out a couple of acquaintances.

Wasn't that Seligstein the druggist in his drooping suspenders, shambling across the street between a tin façade and a jungly vacant lot? And that freckled pate seated on marble steps leading up to the rubble of a collapsed synagogue, didn't it belong to Abe Plesofsky the jeweler? And there, leaning out of a window above the boarded-up front of Lipsky's Discount Shoes, wasn't that Morris's longtime boss, old sourpuss Lipsky himself? These were the boys who had long ago thrown themselves from high places instead of keeping themselves in one piece until they were old enough to take flight.

In his own variation on barnstorming Morris made a megaphone of his hands, frog-kicking above old North Main.

"Hey Lipsky, you fossil," he bawled, "this is Silverman! I'm flying and I don't care who knows it!" But Morris's neighbors, even as his shadow passed over them, were not in the habit of looking up.

He wanted to tell them how the neighborhood looked like a bombsite from his vantage. Whereas, beyond it there was modest but respectable housing; there were shimmering bayous, far-flung blue pastures, three hundred and sixty degrees of promising land. There was snow somewhere to the north, and to the south New Orleans and the sea. Morris had a sudden yen to see New Orleans, a fun-loving and romantic city he'd been led to believe. And while he was at it, why not solo on across the ocean, dropping benedictions on the heads of the crowds who would wave from the Eiffel Tower and the Wall of China; then continue his travels, island-hopping the South Pacific, stopping long enough to cure his constipation with fresh fruit. Who knew but he might fly off to the evening star, which winked a come-on in the cobalt sky over Morris's right shoulder? While on his left the sun, extinguishing itself behind mauve Delta fields, leaked flames into the smoldering river.

But Morris was growing tired. His lungs, unused to such exertion, wheezed like tuneless bagpipes in his ears. He'd developed a stitch in his side that was causing him to veer downward with a limp. Windmilling his arms in an attempt to tread thin air, he panicked at the thought that he might never be able to land. The flying *landsman*, he was maybe condemned, for having been always so earthbound, to bobbing about like a fugitive kite till Kingdom Come.

Eventually, however, he managed to alight by labored degrees on a graveled rooftop. Immediately his knees buckled under him. The dizziness, unexplainably deferred during his flight, caught up with him now he was stationary, so that he felt he might lose his lunch. Over by a cracked skylight there was a torn canvas deck chair that someone must have once dragged up to enjoy the view. With the same effort it had cost him to land on the roof, Morris made his way to the chair and lowered himself groaningly into its sling. Dabbing at runnels of perspiration with a shirttail, waiting to catch his breath, Morris had to admit that this flying stuff was for the birds, or at least for younger men.

"So I'm a late bloomer," he considered, though the howling of his joints argued against it.

Already the memory of flying had begun to fade. No match for his aches and pains, it was dissolving, like that sunset across the river whose only surviving trace was a warm ochre stain. Good riddance, thought Morris, who in his exhaustion had no more use for nostalgia than for dangerous fun. The thing was to watch your blood pressure and keep your health, such as it was. Only, what if he'd fallen off the bridge, say, seventy years earlier? With a lifetime in which to practice, he would have been some aerodynamic person, a thing of beauty able to stay aloft for days, to run a shuttle service between here and paradise. What a waste that his talent had been neglected for so long, that his own *nebbish* flesh had kept the secret from him all these years. What a crying shame.

Then it must have been his fatigue that prompted Morris, who didn't put up much of a fight, to succumb to a fit of sobbing. The tears welled up from his gut with a furious force, not unlike—if he weren't mistaken—the surge he'd felt upon receiving the gift of flight. For a moment he had the hope that such an eruption might lift him once more into the air, but instead he was only shaken to the roots of his feeble frame. He was wracked with lamentation until his false teeth chattered and his heart, tossed in the flood, could no longer keep itself in one piece.

Yiddish Twilight

for Howard Schwartz

Before he became a dissolute wanderer and corrupter of children, Hershel Khevreman was a devout student of Talmud. Son of an impoverished poulterer known as Itche Chicken in the Galician village of Zshldz, he'd far outdistanced the local scholars and soon after his bar mitzvah had set off on foot in search of a higher learning, landing eventually in the court of the Saczer Rebbe in the remote Carpathian outpost of Stary Sacz. There, beyond the diseases and rampaging Cossacks that plagued his native Zshldz, beyond the reach of his dowdy parents, Hershel flourished; he earned a reputation for scholarship that in turn brought him to the attention of Reb Avrom Treklekh, a prosperous distiller of fruit kvass, who offered Hershel his daughter's hand in marriage. Despite his youth (he was barely sixteen) and his absorption in the study of the Law, Hershel was no fool, and he anxiously looked forward to assuming his portion as a rich man's son-in-law.

On the Monday night before the wedding (Tuesday weddings were considered propitious because God had said thrice, "It is well" on the Third Day) Hershel and his fellow scholars were gathered in the *besmedresh* for an informal celebration. With its timeworn benches and sagging shelves of books, their weathered pages as scalloped as cockleshells, with its burbling samovar atop a barrel-shaped stove, the study house was more than a classroom; it was parlor, dining hall, and dormitory to the majority of yeshiva boys. Outside, the early autumn wind was indistinguishable from the howling of wolves on the heights above the town; while across the steppes below swept the armies of an emperor, a kaiser, a czar, for whom the *zhids* were cannon fodder or target practice. Below their mountain fastness were blood libels and legal pogroms, a night distinctly unfriendly to the Jews; but despite (or because of) the dangers, the house of study remained for its occupants as snug as a humidor.

For the eve of Hershel's wedding, the scholars, penniless all, had nevertheless managed to stockpile some refreshment: a little herring, zweiback and sour pickles, a couple of bottles of shabbes wine. This they did more out of a sense of tradition than from any love of the groom, whom they largely considered an arrogant prig. If they had anything to celebrate, it was that the self-styled Talmud *chochem*, the wise guy, would soon be moving in under Rev Avrom's ample roof, and hopefully out of their hair. Still, unaccustomed to excess, the lads found themselves growing festive with drink, the friskier among them teasing the groom in a spirit that betrayed their jealousy.

Velvl Spfarb, for instance, a fat boy who fancied himself a serious challenger to Hershel's standing as resident genius, raised his glass to propose: "If the shekels are there, the groom will appear." Meant to suggest Hershel's mercenary intentions, it was a hypocritical dig, since who among them wouldn't have liked to be in the scholar's shoes? Then Shloyme Aba, ungainly in peaked cap and patched gabardine, a permanent leer across his foxy face, went Velvl one better. "The uglier the piece, the luck will increase," he declared; because the truth was that Hershel's betrothed, Shifra Puah—Hershel had hardly noticed her at the contract-signing, so beguiled was he by the uncracked books in Rev Avrom's study—was not a very prepossessing young woman. In fact, just thirteen, with a body like an empty pillow slip and a pinched face the hue of a biscuit dipped in borsht, she was not a woman at all.

Seated stiffly in the place of honor at the head of a scored oak table, Hershel chafed at their disrespect. A proven prodigy who'd bested them all in the toe-to-toe *pilpul* discourse, he didn't like being used with such familiarity. Moreover, observing an obligatory prenuptial fast, the bridegroom was forbidden food and drink, which made it doubly hard to appreciate their sportive mood. Still, Hershel reminded himself that, given the degree of good fortune that had lately befallen him, he could afford to be a little indulgent. After all, what did he want beyond the leisure to pursue a lifelong exploration of Mosaic Law? And if that pursuit were sustained by the generosity of in-laws in a house like a Venetian palazzo, then how manifold were his blessings; and how small a price to pay for them was the sniping of his less accomplished peers.

The drudge, Muni Misery, shoulders drooping from what he liked to claim was the weight of history, offered this observation: "A wedding is like a funeral but with musicians." He was seconded by Yukie Etka Zeidl's, ordinarily a taciturn oaf but moved to speak up tonight: "A man goes to the bridal canopy alive and returns a corpse." More proverbs equating marriage with death were tendered as toasts, after which the boys took another sip of wine.

Then Shloyme Aba, the closest to an authentic wag the yeshiva could boast of, bounded onto the table to pose a riddle like a wedding jester. "Why," he asked, extending a finger from the ragged wing of his sleeve, "does a stretcher have only two poles while a wedding canopy has four? Because—" He was interrupted before he could answer himself.

"Because, with a stretcher you bury only one person," it was Hershel, unable to suffer in silence any longer, "while with a wedding canopy you bury two." Risen to his feet, he displayed the assurance that made him both the bane and envy of the other students.

There was a hush while the gathering fumbled for some

common attitude toward Hershel's intrusion, though none were perhaps more surprised than the bridegroom himself. Had he, by participating, given his blessing to these unseemly goings on? An asthmatic wheeze from Shloyme Aba signaled the others that the guest of honor had at last entered into the spirit of the occasion; raising his glass, he proposed another toast, this one more or less sincere. "God send you the wife you deserve!" Hershel, at some expense of dignity, forced a smile.

As the company joined in the toast, Shloyme Aba hopped down from the table and launched into an impersonation of their teacher, Rabbi Asher ben Yedvab, the Saczer Rebbe. Rattle-boned, with a nose like a spigot, Shloyme was eminently suited for the role. He bent his back, fluttered an eyelid, fidgeting a mock-palsied hand at the level of his crotch; while Velvl Spfarb, who'd done yeoman service in assisting the actual rebbe, stepped forward to lend his support to the sham. The hammer-headed Salo Pinkas took Shloyme Aba's other arm.

"P-place a drop of blood on the t-tip of a sword," he intoned in the rebbe's reedy stammer. "The instant it t-t-takes the drop to d-duh-duhhh [Salo Pinkas slapped him hard on the back] to divide into two parts, that is t-twilight."

It was a fair approximation of the Saczer's fanciful pro-nouncements, and the students cackled their approval. Goaded by the laughter, Shloyme Aba further exaggerated the rebbe's galvanic tics and spasms, joggling so that his supporters could barely hold on. Then he turned toward the eastern wall of the study house, where a ponderous piece of mahogany furniture stood. This was the hall tree the rebbe had brought with him on his journey from Przemysl over half a century before. Since the study house had no vestibule and the thing itself looked nothing like a tree—was in fact a tall, throne-like structure with a seat and a large oval mirror circumscribed by coat hooks—it was a constant source of amusement to the yeshiva boys. Especially amusing to them was their otherwise ascetic rebbe's attachment to his hall tree. He addressed it with a reverence typically reserved for the ark in the synagogue, wherein the scrolls of the Law were kept. This made Shloyme Aba's prayerful convulsions, body flapping like a shutter in a gale, all the more risible to his audience.

Even the haughty bridegroom succumbed to the comedy, which, fueled by drink and the zeal of his fellows, wildly exceeded Shloyme Aba's ordinary mischief. Having stooped to make an adjustment, he now turned back around to show a limp sock dangling from his fly—unbuttoned flies being one of the rebbe's frequent oversights.

"Rabbi Ishmael ben Yose's member was the size of a wineskin of nine *k-k-k-kav*," he proclaimed. "But Rav Papa himself had a shwantz like the b-baskets of Hip-hip-areenum . . ."

While most still hooted their encouragement, some of the younger boys had fallen silent, perhaps sensing that Shloyme Aba had crossed a line. Hershel, who for his part had never shared the others' unconditional affection for their rebbe, applauded the imposture. He had always been irritated by Rabbi ben Yedvab's overheated romance with Torah, an attitude he deemed lacking decorum and courting indecency. ("Like the s-sex of the gazelle is the Torah," the rebbe was wont to say, "for whose husband every t-t-time is like the first.") He disapproved of how the old *tzaddik* used Scripture as a stimulus to ecstatic transports. If Scripture was meant to be a stimulus for anything, thought Hershel, it was to inspire practical interpretations, such as Maimonides' *Mishneh Torah* or Rashi's commentaries—texts the scholar tended to prefer to the Pentateuch itself.

So when Shloyme Aba, whose performance was approaching the feverish, began reciting the betrothal benedictions, Hershel—reasoning that the burlesque was after all in the nature of a rehearsal—stepped up beside him. Velvl Spfarb, as if seized by conscience, backed furtively away, but Yukie Etka Zeidl's took his place, and together he and Salo Pinkas, in lieu of a wedding canopy, raised a threadbare caftan over the bride-groom's head.

"*Mi adir al ha-kol* b-b-biddle-bum . . . ," chanted Shloyme Aba, having faced the hall tree again; as over his shoulder Hershel took the measure of himself in the cloudy mirror. With his interest generally fixed on the abstract, the prodigy had seldom concerned himself with appearances—why should he care what kind of figure he cut in the tortured alleys of Stary Sacz? But tonight, no doubt infected by the high spirits of his companions (he hadn't thought of them as "companions" until tonight), Hershel felt peculiarly at home in his body, and noted that he wasn't a bad-looking chap. Slender as a taper, he stood remarkably straight for a boy who spent his days bent over books. His cheeks, still beardless, were unblemished by the eruptions afflicting so many other students; his nose was imperially aquiline. Ginger curls boiled from under his skullcap; his earlocks were like scrolled ribbons, his eyes echoing the emerald of the mirror glass. All in all, Hershel thought he made quite an affecting bridegroom.

As Shloyme Aba completed the nuptial formula, Muni Misery, never so antic, placed a goblet near Hershel's foot for him to stomp. A stickler for protocol, however, Hershel came suddenly back to himself.

"How can I crush the glass," he wanted to know, "before I put the ring on the finger of my betrothed?"

The question was calculated to abort the ceremony, which to Hershel's mind had gone far enough; and since he was confident that the ring remained in the safekeeping of his future father-in-law until tomorrow, he assumed the horseplay was at an end. But Muni Misery again rose to the challenge. He presented Hershel with a loop he'd fashioned from a tuft of fur belonging to the perpetually molting study-house cat. (A brindled and querulous animal whom the rebbe suspected of being the reincarnation of Menachem Mendl of Kotzk.) Hershel, for whom the charade was effectively over, received the loop a little impatiently, but having committed himself thus far, he accepted his cue to proceed. He began to recite, albeit halfheartedly, the sacred *qiddushin: "Harai at mekudeshet lee, b'ta-ba-at-zu, k'dat Moshe v'Yisrael.* Be sanctified to me with this ring in accordance with the law of Moses and Israel." Then he placed the loop over the crooked brass finger of a coat hook.

The boldness of the gesture made him shudder, the shudder reverberating around the room—because no sooner had the ring encircled the coat hook than the surface of the mirror began to stir.

Hershel wondered if the vinous breaths of the other *bochers* had distorted his own perception, inducing a dizziness that blurred his image in the glass. He momentarily lost his balance, stepping on the goblet, which made a sound like a jaw munching bone; but more fascinated than frightened, he steadied himself, observing how the rippling glass resembled watered silk in a breeze. He watched his image begin to fragment and dissolve in the murky oval—as if a reflection on a pond were being replaced by a body floating to the surface. Then the body acquired dimensions that contradicted the flat face of the mirror, assuming the form of a young woman, tall and lean, with billowing midnight hair. She was wearing a loose cambric shift that clung to her sinewy limbs as she stepped from the mirror onto the swept clay floor.

With the exception of Menachem Mendl, screeching as he arched his back, screeching louder as he singed his fur on the stove, no one had the wit to utter a sound. Taking flight, they climbed over one another in their frantic efforts to escape through the solitary door. The slue-footed Yukie Etka Zeidl's stumbled at the threshold and was trodden upon by his cronies; Velvl Spfarb, already backed against the far wall, squeezed his girth through a narrow casement and tumbled out headfirst. Hershel himself would doubtless have been in their number, had not the woman—she seemed for all practical purposes a woman, of about eighteen in human years—had she not taken his hand in her own, which was brackish and cold.

"My pretty husband," she said, her voice as tart as prune compote, "*shalom.*"

Your garden-variety yeshiva scholar was never known for his discretion. So routine were his days that the least irregularity—one fainted from hunger, another suffered a nocturnal discharge—was likely to trigger a rash of *loshen horeh*, of gossip. Any deviation from the usual was subject to scrupulous inquiry; this was their habit. But what the boys had witnessed in the study house tonight so far surpassed their tolerance for abnormality that it confounded their ability to carry tales. Too prodigious and frightful a burden to pass on, this one was better left alone.

The few who boarded in town fled to their hosts; the rest sought sanctuary across the compound in the little stone shul. Despite the protests of Fishke the shammes, who reminded them that the small hours were reserved for the dead, they insisted on saying penitential prayers. Most remained in the synagogue—its haunted atmosphere notwithstanding—throughout the night, though some, more curious than chastened, girded themselves to return to the *besmedresh*. There they found Hershel Khevreman naked but for his ritual garment, huddled on the seat of the hall tree with unfocused eyes.

Nobody dared to interrogate him, nor did Hershel, absently accepting his trousers from one, his waistcoat from another, offer any enlightenment. He said nothing to counter their unspoken pact to forget this evening's incident altogether. Only Velvl Spfarb, who'd turned around after diving through the window and lost his smugness for all time—only he reported the story, first to the rebbe and again many years later, after Hershel himself had long since passed into legend. Then Velvl told how the paralyzed scholar had submitted to the woman's toying with his ritual fringes, her unfastening of his suspender buttons, the stroking of his chest; how she'd hunched her shoulders to let the shift slither down her tawny length, pooling like fog at her feet; after which they'd admired each other in the glass. And when, having touched the mirror to no purpose, Hershel turned to touch her umber flesh, she let loose a cry—like a sound that had traveled through three twists of a devil's shofar to rattle the study-house walls.

(The "three twists" were a bit of embroidery Velvl permitted himself despite the families who reproached him for recounting such an unsavory tale. Already sick with fear in a crowded box-car clattering toward *Gehinnom*, why should their children be further abused by the phantoms of a windy old man?)

When they'd expended enough guilty solicitude on him, the students nudged Hershel out the door, pointing him in the direction of the clockmaker's shop where he boarded. Tottering through the switchback streets of the Jewish quarter, the prodigy attempted to apply his talmudic logic to what had transpired, but found that once reliable faculty in sad disrepair.

With a borrowed key he entered the shuttered shop, its interior as alive with ticking as a field of locusts. Last week had been Kalman Tsensifer the blacksmith and his ringing anvil, the week before Falik the cobbler and his last; this week was Yosl Berg the clockmaker with his ticking, his wife with the swinging pendulum of her broom. Thus did the *shtetl* keep time with a pleasing monotony to the rhythm of Hershel's days. Parting a curtain, he slipped into the close compartment that served as parlor, kitchen, and bedroom for the Bergs. He crossed the floor, his footsteps muted by the clocks and the stormy snoring from behind a burlap screen, then climbed a short ladder to the loft above the ceramic tile stove. There, amid the risen odors of goose fat and human gas, he stripped to the flannel *gatkes* (it was cold for the month of Tishri) and crawled into the quilted cavern of his featherbed.

Raised on mealy potatoes by a lumpish mother, herself potato-shaped, and a father festooned in feathers like a flightless bird, Hershel had conceived, since coming to Stary Sacz, a fondness for creature comforts. He liked clean linen, warm rooms, and bakery goods. In fact, his affection for featherbeds might rival on occasion his passion for the conundrums of the Law. But such pleasures marked the limits of Hershel's indulgence. The wayward thoughts and temptations the rebbe described as the reverse side of the scholarly virtues seldom disturbed him. To resolve some thorny legal problem—the culpability, say, of a family into whose home a mouse brings unleavened crumbs on Passover, or how much farther to rend a garment upon the death of a near relation than of a friend—this was meat and drink to Hershel; of the commentaries of the oral torah, he could say along with the psalmist: "How sweet are Thy words unto my palate!" Nothing in the larders of the households on whose charity he depended had ever beckoned him more.

But all that was changed in an hour by a lady who stepped out of a mirror—which was of course impossible. It was a phenomenon that defied the rational categories, a thing that would never have been credited in the pandects of Maimonides or the Vilna Gaon. The Jews of Stary Sacz, *hasids* and *mitnagdim* alike, might be prone in their unworldly isolation to superstition. They might observe their watchnights, shooing demons from a baby's crib on the eve of his *bris*, incanting in the chamber of women in labor: "Womb, lie down!" But Hershel Khevreman, who had no patience with magic, discounted all irrational expressions of faith. He discounted them so fervently that he sometimes wondered if faith itself were not irrational. Wasn't God, when you thought of it, a somewhat absurd proposition? This was a line of reasoning Hershel rarely followed any further, always returning to a conscientious exegeses of texts. Study, that was his ruling impulse, overruled though it had been tonight.

So where had she fled to? For as soon as the boys began to creep back into the study house, she was gone, leaving him to crumple in a heap against the hall tree. To ask himself again if she were real was to belabor the question, for hadn't he already dismissed her as a figment, a dream—though it's said that "A dream is one-sixtieth of prophecy," and this one he recalled with uncommon lucidity. There were, for instance, all the things she had that, *l'havdil!* he did not: such as the hair in its abundant black whorls that could founder a frigate, the nipples that stood to attention with a look, the fluted ribs, the close-pored hollow where her navel should have been, her laughter like a glockenspiel . . .

According to the rebbe's precious Kabbalah, of which Hershel was deeply skeptical, one must yield to sin before attaining the higher status of penitent. But Hershel had argued from tractate Berakhot that "at the place reserved for penitents, no righteous man may stand," and surely he, by virtue of diligent study, was a righteous man. So what was he thinking? Only that, real or not, the lady from the mirror had awakened in him a desire that—God forbid!—he would trade Shifrah Puah and all the bounty that came with her to realize.

Then it occurred to Hershel the only logical explanation for what had taken place tonight was that he'd lost his mind. Coincidental with this conclusion the ladder creaked; it creaked once, twice, the planks giving gently, a body with a pungent odor (its flesh mingling fire and ice) sliding next to him in his goosedown cocoon.

"My man," her breath kindled his brain like an ember in a warming pan, "we got yet unfinished business . . ."

Around the same time the old bachelor rebbe, Asher ben Yedvab, was awakened by a knocking at the door of his cottage adjoining the *besmedresh*. Wearing only his nightshirt and *talis koton*, a shawl pulled over his scurfy head, he allowed himself to be tugged by an excited Velvl Spfarb into the study house. There he detached himself from the gibbering student and proceeded in his jerking progress—elbow, pelvis, and knee each attempting to go its own way—toward the hall tree. With the cat twined fretfully about his ankle, the Saczer struggled to maintain his balance as he inspected his trophy. He removed the loop of fur from the coat hook, held it a moment in his twitching palm, and smacked his bearded face, leaving the loop stuck in his eye like a monocle. Then he peered into the mirror whose surface had cleared of mist, which permitted him to see straight through to the other side.

"Come down, Hershel Khevreman!" Reb Yosl summoned from below. "The *kloger* rattled the shutter already. Would you be late for morning prayers on your wedding day?"

Torpid from too little sleep, Hershel opened a bleary eye, letting the phrase "wedding day" resonate sweetly in his head. He yawned luxuriously, stretched, extending his left arm from beneath the quilting, and endeavored to stretch his right—which was pinned beneath a breathing form. "Oy!" he cried, starting up from the pallet in consternation, as a hand gently squeezed him between the legs. He made a grab for the hand, and found there instead the warm head that had slid from his chest to burrow in his lap. Hershel wondered a panicked instant if he were giving birth.

"What's the matter?" called the clockmaker.

"Nothing!" Hershel chirped. "I banged my head on a rafter."

Rigid as the carved wooden figures that hourly emerged from the face of his clocks, Reb Yosl told him to hurry it up, he moved like a fart in brine.

"Go ahead," stalled Hershel, the hand having abandoned its hold to a pair of moist lips, "I'll catch up with you."

"Basha Reba," Yosl protested to his wife, who seldom spoke; although the fragrance of the tea she was brewing caused the prodigy's stomach to churn. Despite the circumstances, he still remembered that he was hungry; all his appetites, it seemed, were wide awake. "Basha Reba," complained the clockmaker, "it's a sluggard we got under our roof. Reb Sluggard, come down, you'll start your honeymoon tomorrow."

"Dawhahefing," said the voice from beneath the cover with her mouth full. ("That's what he thinks.") Her hair filled the scholar's lap like spilled lokshen noodles, her mumbling jaw made him whimper aloud.

"What's that?" asked Reb Yosl. "Basha Reba, what's he saying?"

"I'm coming!" cried Hershel with more emphasis than the situation called for, commanding all the heartsunk strength he had left to pry himself free.

He swarmed down the ladder still pulling his pants on, prompting the clockmaker's wife (who disapproved of young men on principle) to throw her apron over her vinegar face. Her husband squinted in puzzlement through cockeyed spectacles, suggesting "*Shpilkes?*" and pretending to chew his nails, as their boarder bolted past him for the door.

If he'd hoped to lose himself among the felt caps and gabardines crowded into the study house for the morning service, Hershel was soon disabused of the notion. Already distinguished for his status as *khasn*, bridegroom, he was made even more conspicuous by the presence of his prospective father-in-law. Chief elector of the merchants' synagogue—the ornate cedar pile behind the market platz—Reb Avrom had condescended, for the *khasn*'s sake, to pray this morning among Rabbi ben Yedvab's *hasidim.* For their part the *hasids*, devoted consumers of Reb Avrom's merchandise, fawningly acknowledged the honor. Throughout their semi-silent articles of faith, they winked at the bandy distiller, expressing their shared amusement at the bride-groom's nervousness.

They snickered at how Hershel had managed to entangle himself in his own phylacteries, as if—he feared—they could read his mind. Perhaps they perceived that, fatigued and famished from his unending fast, aching in every part, he was helplessly reliving the episode of the night before: when, after the first great wave of passion had subsided, he'd wished her gone. And when she refused to leave him, somewhat heartened by the un-broken snoring from the householders below, he'd summoned the courage to ask her, "Who are you?"

"I'm the black *neshomeh*, the soul below the belt," she whis-pered, a sulphur moon through the dormer aglint in her teasing eye, "I'm the naughty intention. Three groschen worth of asa-fetida I can eat on an empty stomach without losing my skin. Take a chalice from the smithy, fill it with pomegranate seeds, circle it with roses, and set it in the sun, and you got only an inkling of my beauty . . ."

Then she said she wasn't a woman at all but a succubus, a daughter of the demon Lilith named Salka, who'd been trapped in the mirror over half a century. This was owing to a spell in-voked by none other than the Saczer Rebbe himself, with whom she'd attempted to interfere during his own student days. But unlike Hershel he'd resisted her charms. He'd tricked her into ad-miring herself in the mirror of a hall tree in the home of the wealthy merchant where he took his meals. Then he'd uttered a swift incantation and *presto!* Salka found herself confined to the other side of the glass. But rather than abandon the hall tree, the young rabbi had purchased it, over his host's insistence that he accept it as a gift: let it be included as part of the dowry at-tached to the merchant's unwed daughter. But the youth, who'd developed a twitching that rendered him incompatible with do-mestic tranquility, took the hall tree instead of the girl; he lugged it over the mountains from Przemysl to Stary Sacz, where he installed it in a prominent place in his "court."

"And that's where I waited for you to release me, my fated one," said the succubus, nibbling the lobe of Hershel's ear.

He'd wanted to prove he was done with her, that his will was as strong as any apprentice tzaddik's; he wanted to disbelieve in her altogether—but he'd nevertheless responded to her touch with a blind urgency. And now, as Hershel watched the Saczer davening fitfully on the dais, his torso like a runaway metronome, he wondered why he should feel so jealous of such a comical old man.

After prayers the men dispersed, causing Hershel further annoyance with their conspiratorial pinches and backslaps. Reb Avrom, distributing noblesse oblige left and right as he departed, paused to chuck the prodigy's chin. "Torah is the best of wares," he announced, as if bestowing sound business advice. Then, while the room reverted back to a yeshiva, the boys, saying hasty blessings over milk-boiled groats before pairing off to pursue their studies, each stole private glances at the bridegroom. To avoid their scrutiny, Hershel took a seat at the end of a bench and buried his head in a volume of Talmud.

"If a fledgling bird is found within fifty cubits of a dovecote," he read, hoping to solace himself in the old familiar way, "it belongs to the owner of the dovecote. If it is found outside the limit of fifty cubits, it belongs to the person that finds it. But Rabbi Jeremiah asked: If one foot of the fledgling is within the limit of fifty cubits, and one foot is outside it, what is the law?"

Hershel thought the question unbelievably stupid. Clamorous dialogues were developing all around him; children ushered into the study house by the melammed had begun reciting their *alef-bais* to the beat of his leather knout. Again Hershel addressed the text, trying to decipher it with a speed that outran his critical judgment, let alone his gnawing anxieties. Had Basha

Reba discovered the creature in the loft and run shrieking into the street? Salka was nothing if not elusive, but she was also unpredictable, a quality he admired at the risk (he supposed) of his immortal soul. Unable to concentrate, Hershel asked himself when had he ever before been unable to concentrate.

Then a shadow fell across the page and Rabbi ben Yedvab, supported in his quivering by an abject Velvl Spfarb, stood before him. Hershel was aware of being the object of all eyes.

"I see your t-text is the B-b-bava Batra," said the tzaddik, his facial tics signaling the commencement of a standard catechism. "So tell me what three things ch-ch-ch-changed in the days of Enosh b-ben Seth?"

Hershel began his response with characteristic aplomb: "Corpses putrefied, men's faces turned apelike, and . . . ," he faltered. Was it possible that his memory had lost its steel-trap fidelity overnight?

"D-demons," reminded the rebbe, with alternately blinking eyes, "demons became free to work their will upon them. Hershel, it's your wed-d-ding-ding [Velvl dutifully swatted him on the back] your wedding day. You should visit the bathhouse."

Hershel straightened in his seat, wondering if his teacher, remarkable for his own rancid odor, could smell her salty essence on his person. Of course it was customary for a *khasn* to visit the bathhouse, not for purification—that was the bride's imperative—but to prepare himself through meditating on the estate he was about to enter. Still, he was distrustful, feeling almost belligerent toward the wintry old man, his shifting features as difficult to read as a map in a storm. Also, while tradition demanded that the groom not be left alone on the day of his marriage, was such a mob of attendants really necessary? Most of the key participants from last night's burlesque—Shloyme Aba, Salo Pinkas, Muni Misery—had zealously volunteered to accompany Hershel, and waited for him now with the air of hired strong-arms.

But having apparently no choice in the matter, Hershel rose and delivered himself up to his chaperons, resenting them nearly as much as he hoped they would stick by his side.

The bathhouse stood at the end of the butchers' shambles, its roof slates sprouting tussocks, its fissured brick walls breathing steam like a sleeping dragon. Serving on odd days as a *mikveh* for ritual immersion, the decrepit building was presided over by Moshe Cheesecloth—so-called for a skin condition resulting from his years of exposure to the sodden environment. It was to Moshe's good offices that the boys handed over the bridegroom, reluctant now to leave his protectors. Hershel also worried that the attendant might find, in checking his body for shmutz, marks left there by the talons of a lady demon. Never especially thorough, however, Moshe was too busy measuring the level of his rainwater cistern, fanning the copper furnace with a rawhide bellows, to make anything but a cursory inspection of Hershel's fingernails. Then he issued the scholar soap and towel, a birch broom to flog himself with, and sent him into the dressing cubicle off the entry.

Naked beneath the towel wrapped about his shoulders, Hershel padded into the humid tub room. He skirted a stack of smoldering rocks and, shedding the towel, lowered himself from the slippery platform into tepid, chest-deep water. He stirred the bilious green pool (in accordance with the precept against viewing one's own parts) and chased from his mind the water's resemblance to the surface of a certain looking glass. Then leaning against the moss-grown tiles, he allowed himself a sigh. Gone for the moment was his apprehension at being left alone, the events of the night before having again withdrawn to the distance of dream. This was weariness, of course, but with it came a resurgence of hope regarding his imminent marriage. He had the feeling he might be only a short nap away from the knowledge that his future was yet in place. Yawning, Hershel turned to climb out of the tub and collapse on one of the cots that lined the walls, when a hand took hold of his ankle and dragged him under.

He fought his way sputtering back to the surface, taking deep gulps of the muggy air, frantically rubbing open his stinging eyes: to find her also risen from the turbulent pool, lit by an amber shaft from the bull's-eye window overhead. Her damp hair was strewn like a cat-o'-nine-tails across her laughing face, her coral-tipped breasts jigglingly upheld by the water.

It was unconscionable that she should have appeared in broad daylight, however clouded in vapor. Clapping his hands over his face, Hershel recited the pertinent passage from the *Shulchan Arukh:* "Semen-is-the-vitality-of-a-man's-body-and-when-it-issues-in-abundance-the-body-ages-the-strength-ebbs-the-eyes-grow-dim-the-breath-foul-the-hair-of-the-head-lashes-and-brows-fall-out . . ."

When he peeked through his fingers, she submitted in a voice whose music thrummed his vitals, "Did I tell you that Salka is short for *rusalka*, a mermaid?"

"For God's sake," pleaded Hershel, "will you leave . . . ," forcing a whisper that was half a shriek, ". . . will you leave me alone!" Her presence in the mikveh was an affront to all things sacred, a violation of every law on the books.

Salka gave a careless shrug and began to pull herself out of the pool, the sleek, elongated S of her spine like a stem to the onion bulb of her glistening tush. Hershel wanted to tell her, "Demon, good riddance!" but a dreadful longing choked the words in his throat. Groaning, he threw his arms around her waist and squeezed mightily, hauling Salka back into the clammy water. He covered her with kisses so voracious that he felt they must constitute an untimely breaking of his fast, not that it mattered to a soul so already lost. A blessing came to his lips: "Praise God who permits the forbidden!" which was the phrase once invoked by the false prophet Sabbatai Zvi to excuse his sins. Afterwards Hershel couldn't remember whether they'd made love above or below the surface of the bath.

Outside, the bracing autumn breeze, laced with a bouquet from the slaughter yards, did nothing to lift the weight from his spirit. Weak-kneed and shamefaced, Hershel fell in among the ranks of his waiting comrades, but felt no safety in their numbers. Why, if sent by their teacher to guard the groom against his evil impulse—for how else explain their presence?—why had they even bothered to respect his privacy? Why hadn't they charged into the bathhouse, interrupting what he would never have forgiven them for? And to think that only yesterday Hershel Khevreman had been a master of logic. Yesterday all he'd needed to complete his contentment—the dowry of a rich man's daughter—was in easy reach; now the distance between himself and his wedding lay before him like a no-man's-land he feared to cross alone.

Huddled around by bodyguards, he nonetheless felt dangerously exposed. As they straggled across the open expanse of the market square, raucous with vendors hawking dried fish and caged foul, Hershel wanted to take shelter in some obscure commentary. A virtual orphan since leaving Zshldz, he reasserted under his breath his credo that the Book was his home, its many branches his family tree; Rashi, Nachmanides, the Rambam—these were his real *mishpocheh*, the only company in which he felt truly secure. Then a glance beyond the academy caps of his fellows, and Hershel was granted a sight that made him shrink even further, retracting his neck into his shoulders turtle-style.

For over the way, Reb Avrom's road-muddied Panhard touring car, complete with liveried chauffeur, had pulled up before the lime-washed façade of Berel Schnapser's inn. In the backseat were a pair of passengers: one a scarecrow in an undersized rug coat dusted in feathers, the other a stolid, potato-shaped woman holding a carpetbag. Hershel recalled how, at the contract-signing, Reb Avrom had offered to bring them to town for the wedding, but the groom had argued that his parents didn't travel well. "Nonsense!" replied the distiller, who couldn't do enough for the boy whose scholarship guaranteed his in-laws a share in Kingdom Come. And while he knew he couldn't postpone the meeting indefinitely, Hershel figured his afflicted conscience would scarcely register another offense: So for the present he gave Itche Chicken and wife a wide berth.

In the meantime, too depleted to do otherwise, he surrendered himself wholesale to the custody of his peers. They in turn saw to it that the scholar remained upright through afternoon prayers, then—though he reached for a scriptural codex like a drowning man—hustled him off to be outfitted for the ceremony. Practically asleep on his feet, Hershel was conducted by a growing convoy of students through streets thick with the aromas of baking kugel and potted meat. The entire quarter, it seemed, was busy making dishes for the nuptial feast, while the youth on whose behalf they labored swooned from hunger, begging his beleaguered senses to let him be.

His escorts, on the other hand, seemed to have recovered something of their mood of the night before. Putting aside their watchful solemnity, they grew livelier as the hour approached. They were jaunty as they marched the bridegroom through Reb Yosl's tiny shop, which (as Shloyme Aba observed) ticked like an anarchist's basement in Lodz. In the apartment behind the shop they twitted Basha Reba on the scythelike movement of her broom; a few made as if to steal the almond torte left cooling on an upended washtub, while the rest led Hershel behind the fabric screen. There they attired him—Salo Pinkas holding him erect while Shloyme Aba and Yukie Zeidl's manipulated his arms and legs—in the silk plus-fours and ankle-length black *kittl* that the distiller had provided. They crowned him with the beaver-trimmed turban and drew him around to face a tarnished pier glass to admire his finery, but having lately conceived a phobia of mirrors, the groom turned his head.

It was left for Muni Misery to describe what he was missing with a philosophical wistfulness: "All grooms are handsome, all the dead are holy," he said, prompting Hershel to steal a sidelong look. What he saw resembled a folded parasol, its tip through a wheel of cheese gone furry with mold. But so relieved was he to find himself alone in the mirror that his nerves relaxed their grip on his insides, and he had abruptly to excuse himself.

In the yard in back of the shop he pulled to the latchless door of the privy; he raised the stiff garment, dropped his breeches, and plunked his bare bottom on the splintered wooden seat. Given his empty stomach, Hershel wondered what was left to purge, unless—settling himself for a restful interlude—he might look forward to the emptying of his unquiet mind. Then the door swung open and the succubus swept in, lifting her shift to straddle Hershel's naked knees, entwining his tongue with her viperish own.

"Mmphlmph!" protested Hershel, fighting to retrieve his face. "Please, Salka, not here!" It was all so unspeakably degrading.

But the creature rocked her hips as if in a *shukeling* prayer— and despite his exhaustion and the fetid surroundings, despite everything he'd previously deemed to be decent, the scholar responded to her beckoning movements. For some moments he clung to her, sucking the pastille of a nipple through the thin cambric bodice, anticipating as best he could her fluid rhythm; until, with a cry that was equal parts rapture and shame, Hershel let go, experiencing a seismic release both fore and aft. Then slumped in humiliation against the still-heaving torso of the demoness, he wept guilty tears.

"Such an emotional boy," she breathlessly rebuked him, reaching for a cob from the pile on the floor: "Here, let me help you."

That's when Hershel heard the music, and once he'd determined that it originated on earth, that it came in fact from the street in front of the shop, he thought it might yet herald his salvation. Heedless of personal hygiene, he got to his feet, causing Salka to slide sprawling from his lap onto the spongy boards. "Impetuous!" she accused him even as he stumbled over her, snatched up his pants from around his ankles and staggered out to join the parade.

The groom's procession, led by one-half of Reb Dovidl Fiddle's klezmer ensemble, wound its way into the unpaved yard behind the hasids' listing stone shul. Although the date had been favorably fixed between the Days of Awe and Sukkot, it was late in the season for outdoor weddings. A brisk (if fair) afternoon, it would be nippy in the shaded court toward sunset. But bonfires would be lit to reduce the chill and—along with the garlands of garlic brandished by the guests—frighten the *sheydim*, the demons, away.

Ill-smelling and nearly insensible, jerked between the rebbe's dancing disciples (who'd hooked their arms through his), Hershel reminded himself he didn't believe in demons.

A path opened up for them through the crush of guests surrounding the canopy erected on four slender poles. In this way Hershel was made to run a gauntlet of shtetl society, from the crutched beggars on the periphery through the artisans, students, and hasidim, to the *machetonim*, the in-laws, seated just outside the *chupeh* in straight-backed chairs. Among the in-laws, (sitting together but for the aisle dividing men from women) were the bridegroom's own parents, whom Hershel hadn't seen face-to-face in almost three years. He acknowledged them now with what little filial deference he had left: a polite bow; and they returned his greeting with stony, befuddled nods, clearly uncertain of why they'd been asked to come. Hershel waited for the embarrassment to set in, and for the remorse that followed embarrassment, but the pair of rustics seated before him were strangers, people of the chicken and distaff, not the Book. They had no real connection to the prodigy about to make a brilliant match with a rich man's daughter; and for all his debilitation Hershel felt reassured.

He took in for the first time the magnitude of the gathering, indicative of the wedding's great significance; he remarked the string of lanterns, the trestle tables awaiting platters of stuffed goose necks, the cauldrons of golden soup and calves' brain puddings as large as drums. Neither ghosts from the past nor the nightmares of a treacherous present, he concluded, could lay claim to him here, safe in the bosom of his community.

Opposite Hershel, his erstwhile teacher, the Saczer Rebbe, had already begun his desultory benedictions, every feature of his face asserting its independence. Leaning on the humble arm of Velvl Spfarb, he nodded to the bridegroom, also bolstered by attendants, so that the two of them teetered like pugilists in a ring. Then came another flourish of fiddles and horns, as the other half of Reb Dovidl's orchestra ushered the bride's entourage into the compound. Flanked by her maids of honor, the *kallah*, the bride, came forward enshrouded in silk and brocade, her face mercifully concealed by a veil. Her venerable parents sashayed just behind.

When the bride had taken her place next to her intended, the music ceased and the rebbe curtailed his prayer. The guests shushed one another, as Rabbi ben Yedvab, his ceremonial sable as moth-eaten as his beard, was helped forward to perform the ritual lifting of the veil. Here was a moment Hershel had not looked forward to, when the *kallah*'s face would be revealed for his eyes only; for although entitled to call off the marriage if the face displeased him, he knew perfectly well what he must do: He must give his unqualified approval to the mousy, pinched *ponim* of Reb Avrom's daughter.

But the face beneath the mignonette veil, which the rebbe

raised like the lid of a covered dish, bore small resemblance (if memory served) to Shifrah Puah's. This one stunned Hershel with its narrowed onyx eyes and kittenish grin, the sooty ringlets spilling from under her pumpernickel loaf of a wig. Then the veil was lowered again, though not before the succubus had taken the opportunity to wink.

Involuntarily Hershel winked back, satisfied that he must be hallucinating. Fine, he thought, let it be *her:* Then last night's unholy wedding would be consecrated before Israel and all set right in the eyes of God. A shudder wracked Hershel's frame as he woke up to what he was thinking: He was contemplating his final disgrace, the mortal blow. The rebbe chanted the betrothal benedictions ("Who is m-m-mighty over all . . .?"), and Hershel told himself this was the authentic piety—the kind that scourged the devils that haunted the mikvehs and privies but would never, in any case, dare to venture in public. But despite his wishful silent endorsement, Hershel still thought the rebbe's performance less convincing than Shloyme Aba's spoof of the night before.

Then a commotion was heard from the courtyard, and all heads turned to see the distiller's daughter, a twig in a rumpled chemise, trailing rope from her ankles and wrists as she flailed through the crowd.

"Papa," bawled Shifrah Puah amid universal imprecations against the evil eye, "she tied me up!"

Madame Treklekh, clattering jewelry and flapping jowls, bustled headlong to her daughter's side, as her husband rose puffing from his chair. "Rabbi ben Yedvab!" he bellowed, his whiskers repeating the scimitar curve of his pointed finger, "What is this?" The rebbe looked ruefully from Shifra Puah to her usurper, and frowned; then with a swiftness that belied his frailty, he again removed the bridal veil, silencing the crowd with the savage beauty he exposed.

"S-s-s-s-s," stammered the Saczer, until Velvl respectfully

smote him between the shoulder blades. The old man caught his teeth in his hand, shoved them back into his mouth, and clicked them once to ascertain their working order. "Salka, sweetheart," he said tenderly, "you have to go back."

She'd assumed a defiant stance, arms folded over her breasts, shaking her head with a vehemence that dislodged the wig. Tresses tumbled from beneath it like unspooling yarn.

"*Hartseniu*," the rebbe was more sorrowful than threatening, a rare steadiness sustaining his speech, "don't make me have to lower the boom."

Visibly skittish, Salka sniffed and continued to stand her ground. Then liltingly for one so hoarse, the rebbe began to intone: "Return, return, O Shulammite, for love is strong as death, jealousy as cruel as the grave . . ."

Having expected some species of antidemonic humbug, Hershel was puzzled to hear the rebbe reciting snatches from the Song of Songs—and these in a throaty rendition that sounded less like a conjuration than a lullabye. It was evident, though, from the set of her damson lips, the exaggerated lift of her chin, that the words were making the demoness ill at ease. Had her brazen masquerade somehow proven a miscalculation? In none of their tumultuous encounters had Hershel detected in Salka the least hint of vulnerability; and seeing it now, as she stood there defenseless before the gawking multitude, he was filled with conflicting emotions. Desperately he tried to displace his feelings with sober concerns: How-does-one-determine-the-kosherness-of-apples-grown-on-a-tree-in-a-yard-where-a-pig-was-slaughtered? How-assess-the-property-value-of-a-tower-floating-in-air? But it was no use. Once again he was inflamed with desire, only this time the fire in his loins, try as he might to douse it with reason, reached his heart.

"Who is she that looketh forth as the dawn," warbled the rebbe, "fair as the moon, fierce as an army with banners . . .?"

Salka folded her arms more tightly, hugging herself.

Good, thought Hershel: Whatever their sentiments, the tzaddik's words were having the proper effect; soon the creature, assaulted by righteousness, would be banished forever from their midst. Then he thought what he dimly recognized as sheer madness: I can save her.

"Salkeleh," the rebbe was personal again, stationary and unstuttering, "the boy isn't for you. This one's destined for a teacher."

"Then," she countered, the tremor in her voice betraying her agitation, "let first the teacher learn to be a man."

"He's not your type. In the flesh he ain't interested."

Hershel coughed and Salka, for all her extremity, managed the shadow of a smile. "A man who's too good for this world is no good for his bride."

"This one belongs to the Book," the Saczer insisted—and Hershel's head, swiveling back and forth between the tzaddik and the daughter of Lilith, stopped at Rabbi ben Yedvab's ruined face. Never had it appeared so exalted, almost a young man's wearing the transparent mask of an old.

Then the creature spoke, so softly that she might have been inquiring of herself: "If he don't know from temptation, how will he know what to resist?"

His eyes having shifted back to her chastised radiance, Hershel could no longer contain himself. "I don't want to resist!" he cried, stretching his arms toward the object of his obsession. "Salka, I'm yours!" But instead of accepting his proffered embrace, she stiffened, confusion distorting her features, the last of her composure crumbling in the face of his need. It was as if, in disdaining the rebbe, Hershel had assumed his power over the creature, a daunting influence he had not sought. She shrank a step backward, her dark eyes aflicker with fear.

"Salka, don't worry, I'll save you!" declared Hershel, though he hadn't a clue as to what that might entail.

"Stay away from me!" she cautioned with outthrust hands.

". . . Behold thou art fair," the rebbe had revived his chant, "thy navel like a rounded goblet, thy thighs the links of a golden chain . . ."

"But Salka," said Hershel, bewildered, "what are you saying? Aren't you . . ." he had first to swallow ". . . my wife?"

". . . Thy teeth like a flock of ewes . . ."

"I'm nobody's wife, you *amhoretz*, you idiot! I'm a demon. All you did was break a spell, and that you didn't even do on purpose."

"But Salka, it's your Hershel! What are you afraid of?"

"It's you I'm afraid of."

"Salka, I love you!"

"Feh!" she spat, and was gone. She made a sudden reckless dash across the courtyard toward the tin-roofed study house, the guests parting before her like reeds.

Hershel turned back to the rebbe, who himself seemed abruptly deflated, requiring the aid of the faithful to raise his bony shoulders in a shrug. "It's love she c-c-c-can't stand," he said.

Suppressing an impulse to do the old man bodily harm, Hershel asked him, "How would you know?"

Again an assisted shrug. "Because I once loved her t-too." He explained that love had kept her trapped in the mirror, while desire brought her forth again. "But s-s-sometimes desire itself becomes sublime, and this the succubah-bahh [smack] the fiend cannot endure."

Aware of the intensity with which he was being regarded, Hershel stared back at the ogling assembly—at the row of would-be relations among whom the Treklekhs were trying to comfort their mortified daughter; at the poulterer and his wife who sat watching so complacently that they might have been enjoying a Purim shpiel. To them he felt oddly grateful: They were like some cozy couple who'd raised an imp the *sheydim* had substituted for their own lost child; and now the moment had come for the imp to return to his kind. Looking the rebbe full in his flinching face, Hershel reaffirmed the temptress's angry farewell: "Feh!" He shook off the groomsmen who tried to restrain him, picked up the skirts of his *kittl*, and flung himself after his bride.

Accompanied by students, disciples, and assorted wedding guests, Rabbi ben Yedvab entered the study house, finding it empty but for a petrified cat. He inspected the hall tree, then shakily (because he'd begun to twitch again), removed his *talis*, kissed it, and draped it over the mirror, as in a place where someone has died. No sooner had he done this, however, than the glass exploded in a hail of flying slivers and the prodigy crashed through the mirror from the other side. Tangled in the *talis*, Hershel plunged into the arms of the rebbe, who fell backward in turn into the open arms of his retinue.

Helped to his feet, the old tzaddik (muttering a blessing over broken glass) sought to help a disoriented Hershel, pulling the blood-flecked cloth from his head. His lacerated face, framed by lank silver hair, was utterly strange, an arcane text his one-time rival Velvl Spfarb endeavored the rest of his days to construe. What he gleaned from the scholar's expression was the story he repeated years later, though nobody listened, in the shadow of the chimneys belching yellow smoke: how the bridegroom had discovered that *yenne velt*, the other side, was identical to this one, except that the ghosts there had more substance than the living. The echoes there were louder than their original noises, and the ancient history of the souls you encountered was more vivid than their current incarnations. Beauty there had a density of meaning that no scholar could penetrate—a terrible beauty that had stopped Hershel Khevreman in his tracks; and frightened of his own ignorance, having lost the object of his pursuit in the dusky distance, he'd turned around and beat a path back to the world. Only to find that the house of study and the town on the Carpathian heights were too desolate now to accommodate his longing. There was nothing left but to continue the chase, charging out the open door and following to its logical conclusion the route already taken by his heart.

Sissman Loses His Way

The angel Sissman, despite a taste for tailored suits and his pair of magnificent alabaster wings, was in no way an illustrious angel. Neither was he dissatisfied with his position, but was content to remain the kind of functionary angel typically assigned to births of no special note. The current on his agenda was the birth of one Ira Bluestein, destined for a predictably drab and undistinguished life. In order to reach the site of Ira's nativity, Sissman had to follow the map of his life from its terminus in heaven, the angel's starting point, backwards through a prosaic history to the moment of his birth. Made of fine buff paper hand-milled from the pulp of glory trees by the celestial cartographers themselves, the map was soft as kid and somewhat elastic. It was indestructible in the timeless element of its manufacture, where it would endure in a heavenly archive for all eternity, but was subject to the usual ravages below.

Following the map was a perfectly straightforward operation, the route clearly delineated by an orderly procession of descending years. Its major crossroads were located at standard intervals, the rare points of interest graphically illustrated, labeled, and dated, highlighted in varying shades of gray and brown. The terrain was monotonously even, with no real obstacles to speak of and few unanticipated turns of events. Everything about this assignment was regular; Sissman had presided over a multitude of similar births in his time. His task was the usual one: to pinch the infant's nostrils, thereby depriving it of the wisdom it would otherwise have been born with. The wisdom in question was the ability to see without obstruction from the beginning of one's life to its end. It was a wisdom that also included the memory of paradise, a memory that would naturally make living on earth unbearable.

Having traced Ira Bluestein's chronology to its source, Sissman alit on the sill of a frost-etched window above Bluestein's General Merchandise. This was on North Main Street in the winter of 1927. He peered into a room where the coal-burning stove, the enamel washstand, the wardrobe, the tintypes, the busy pair about the iron bed, all glimmered from an intensity of hope and travail. Flouting physical law, a little luxury in which the angel liked to indulge, Sissman passed through the window and invisibly approached the bed. As always his timing was impeccable, a point on which he took particular pride. He'd arrived just as the doctor, puffing in his shirtsleeves and assisted by a hawk-nosed midwife (in this case the child's own grandmother Rebekah), was dragging Ira headfirst from his mother's belly.

Then it should have been simple enough to slip imperceptibly among them and tweak the infant's nostrils—this before the doctor, wielding scissors like a predatory beak, cut the cord connecting the baby to its mother. But when Sissman reached for the puckered blue and red bundle that was Ira, framed by the wings of his mama's splayed open legs, he encountered a problem. The *bubbeh* Rebekah had grabbed hold of the angel's arm.

Sissman had seen her type before: the raw cheekbones and steely eyes, rust-brown wig carelessly askew, her shirtwaist stained with blood. She was from the Old Country where it wasn't uncommon to find people with second sight, though few had retained it after coming to America. This one, it seemed, had kept intact her faculty for perceiving supernatural creatures. Sissman could have kicked himself for not taking proper precautions; a hasty prayer would have sufficed. Evidently the woman had mistaken him for Malech Hamovet, the angel of death, come to snatch the child before its time. It was a confusion that Sissman was not above being flattered by, since the angel of death was one of your more resplendent seraphim. But never ambitious himself, he merely wished the tiresome woman would let go her talon-like grasp of his arm.

Resourceful under pressure, however, the angel remembered his other hand, free but for the map which he dropped forthwith. Then, ambidextrous, he completed the pinching procedure, if not quite as effectively as he might have under normal circumstances: he left perhaps a vestigial grain of wisdom that could ripen over time, though Sissman seriously doubted it. Nevertheless, chagrined by the clumsiness of what should have been a routine affair, the angel yanked his sleeve out of the woman's grip. With as much dignity as he could muster in that swimming room (while the doctor *patsched* the squawling infant whom he held by the feet, saying, "*Mazel tov*, Mrs. Bluestein, you got here a fine baby boy."), Sissman spread his outsize wings. But answerable now to certain laws thanks to the error of his detection, he had to fold them up again to exit the window.

He'd flown some considerable distance from North Main Street, his silhouette briefly visible against a platinum moon, when he realized he'd left the map behind. Had Ira's been a more remarkable life, Sissman might have recalled enough of its details to follow them back to their destination (and his) in heaven. But without the map he hadn't a clue. Besides, it wouldn't do to leave celestial artifacts lying around on earth, where mortals might have proof of what they ought to take purely on faith. There was nothing for it but to turn around.

Almost immediately he was faced with another problem. In his haste to get away the angel had soared clear out of recorded history, into a spectral dimension where time is measured in eons instead of days. As a consequence, by the time he'd changed course and penetrated the thick yellow cloud cover over North Main Street, many years had passed. Bluestein's

General Merchandise was long gone, along with most other remnants of the original community: the kosher butchers and fishmongers, the cobblers and used clothiers, the movie house and the storefront synagogue, the trolley lines. Everything that wasn't boarded up was tumbled down into weed-choked vacant lots. God only knew where the map was, but Sissman could expect no advice from that quarter until he'd returned to Kingdom Come, the direction to which was anyone's guess from here.

Fortunately for Sissman he had the knack, as did the least of angels, of discerning the echoes of incidents and dreams. He could track down Ira Bluestein by the ghosts of events and fantasies he'd left behind him in growing up, and where he found Ira he was sure to find the map. Despite its urgency the enterprise didn't instantly appeal to the angel. It wasn't that Ira's experiences were so awfully disagreeable; on the contrary his youthful exploits—swimming the river, hide-and-seeking among racks of irregular pants, deceiving the rabbi, running errands for bootleggers, gambling with roustabouts, spying on the Widow Teitelbaum in her bath; the time he watched the burning Phoenix Athletic Club from the roof of his building and delivered papers by rowboat in the flood—were as sweet as any boy's. And his dreams—wherein he was often some bold composite of Natty Bumpo, Baron Munchausen, and the sorcerer Itzak Luria—made a colorful gloss on his adventures. It was just that the adventures hadn't lasted beyond his youth—they never did, a truth about humans which Sissman always found disturbing. They dead-ended on North Main Street, Ira's adventures, sometime during his thirteenth year, when a war was raging in Europe and his family had moved from the neighborhood. Neither did Ira's dreams survive the exodus.

Sissman dimly recollected having passed over the war years, which had appeared as an asterisk-studded trough on the map, on his way to the nativity. But now, moving forward in time as did the mortals, low to the ground without the benefit of navigational reference, he could feel how war had ruptured the very atmosphere. It had stunned the population, left them marooned from their pasts in a world unsafe for dreaming.

Mr. Bluestein had opened a hardware store in a shopping center near the treeless subdivision where the family lived. When he finished high school, Ira, who'd shown some promise at first then become an indifferent student, went into his father's business. (The war was over and it was said there were great possibilities in business, though Ira, never ambitious, had merely taken the path of least resistance.) Here the trail became more difficult to follow due to a tedious repetition of events which left only vague impressions in the air. Sissman couldn't help comparing them unfavorably to the indelible phantoms of Ira's boyhood, where even a walk to Catfish Bayou was a journey into uncharted fastnesses to battle rival magicians and so forth. Years that, on a map, should have required only brisk negotiation here slowed the angel down; they threatened to mire him in the wearisomeness that now seemed a betrayal of a once lively past. The angel's disappointment was so palpable it seemed to add weight to his wings, making the simple act of flight a hobbled chore.

Still, attuned as he'd become to the rhythm of human experience, Sissman relentlessly pursued the dull hum that was certain to lead him straight to his prey. He found Ira Bluestein—a frowning, multi-chinned man in an appalling plaid sport jacket, a pastel knit shirt, a few thin hairs combed over his freckled scalp—on a crisp Sunday afternoon in October of 1981.

He was seated at the bedside of his grandmother Rebekah, in a room redolent of disinfectant and stale gardenias at the Daughters of Zion Nursing Home. She'd outlived practically everyone, Rebekah, hanging on to her life with a tenacity that fascinated her grandson, who couldn't see why she bothered given the chronic pain she was in. He'd visited her dutifully over the years, every Sunday in fact since his last parent had died, attending her with the scrupulousness he demonstrated in all his affairs. But if pressed he might have conceded an unspoken bond between them, whose nature he'd never been able to define.

Now her health was rapidly failing, her sere flesh sprouting whiskers in inappropriate places as if she were already partly a tussock of earth. But even in sleep her wrinkled face assumed a certain ferocity, her fitful snoring half a snarl. Restless though not wanting to wake her, having exhausted his Sunday paper, Ira thought this might be as good a time as any to sort through her effects. Maybe there was something worth passing on, though he wondered to whom. He hesitated: this was possibly premature, then decided as well now as later, her end being only a matter of time. Besides, wasn't he at bottom a little curious? From the drawer of her metal nightstand he removed a ṣcuffed cigar box, donning bifocals to inspect the store of personal treasures inside.

What he discovered was an umber wedding portrait of herself and her long departed husband, of whom Ira remembered only a dry cough and unshaven jaw—the *zaydeh* Abe. There was also a scrolled marriage contract with Hebrew characters like black fire and a ticket stub for the steerage section of the Steamship Bratislava. There was an embroidered napkin containing almond cookies close to petrifaction, a silver amulet against the evil eye, a prayerbook out of whose pages fell indigo petals, and an atomizer with a bulb like a swollen thumb. There was a buff-colored parchment folded lengthwise like a map. Examining it, Ira noted its curious texture, brittle about the creases but otherwise soft as kid. He opened it to find that it was indeed a weathered map, though its loci were not so much places as incidents. The incidents were depicted in deep mahogany tones where they originated in the lower left-hand corner, fading to ashen grays in their diagonal advance across the years.

Following events in the order they seemed to insist on, Ira traced a boy's dream-appointed adventures to the place where

they dead-ended, the gulf—which was a war—separating North
Main Street from what the illustrations characterized as a desert
of subsequent years. A waste of time. Beyond the gulf the pic-
tures appeared more washed out, with less attention paid to detail, their dates more difficult to discern. You could just make
out the young man's ascendancy to manager of Bluestein &
Son's Hardware, allowing for his father's early retirement; his
marriage to Myra, a pliant but sickly high school sweetheart
with whom he'd been thrown together on account of the simi-
larity of their given names. There was a decade or two of mutual
recriminations, each accusing the other of responsibility for the
barren marriage, after which Myra passed quietly away. Meanwhile, through no particular fault of Ira's (who by this point in
his map-reading had no recourse but to acknowledge the life as
his own), the business had prospered, branches opening in several corners of the city. Well-to-do, he was on the board of di-
rectors of the new synagogue, a member of the Lion's Club,
active in the Temple Brotherhood and the B'nai B'rith bowling
league. He was often in attendance at weddings, bar mitzvahs,
and funerals, but persistently begged off attempts to "fix him
up" on the grounds that he was a confirmed widower.

He was lonely, according to the map, and frightened in his
bones of growing old, though he hadn't known it till now.
Watching at the open window, the angel Sissman knew it, which
was what had made it more than his job was worth to push on in
his search for Ira Bluestein. Having lost his own bearings in the
process, the angel understood what it meant that Ira had been
deprived of his at birth. And for this Sissman couldn't help but
feel sorry, unbecoming as it was in seraphim to sympathize with
the fates of mortals in their charge.

Retracing his steps via the same route that Sissman had traveled toward him, Ira also felt sorry for himself and his boring
life. But his sorrow changed swiftly to anger; the life was after
all only humdrum on the map, which had scarcely bothered

indicating instances that Ira clearly recalled as fraught with exquisite frustration and pain. Never mind occasional joy. Who
had drawn up this *farkokte* thing in the first place, that they
should represent his mature experience as a sleepwalking lock-
step toward death? All right, so he was only human, shivering in
his skivvies like everyone else, but for this was he entirely to
blame? No, Ira decided, the fault was not in himself but in his
mapmaker! At that moment Sissman, with his typical flair for
timing, threw up the sash and entered the room to snatch the
map away.

What happened next never should have. What should have
happened was that Ira, relieved of the map by an invisible force,
would also have been bereft of the memory of having seen it.
But that's not how things turned out. What happened was that
Ira saw the angel. This was maybe because Sissman's uncharacteristic intimacy with the earth had left him more dustily material. Or was it Ira's shock at perusing his own arid history that
had done it—jarred loose the long dormant grain of vestigial
wisdom that the angel had failed to expunge. The grain had
fallen into some fertile furrow of Ira's brain where it was
brought to instant fruition. In any case it suddenly seemed to Ira
that the promise at the beginning of one's life, rather than forgotten, ought to be realized later on. It seemed that the future
might yet hold some surprises. Of course there was always alarm
at seeing your life for what it was, but the fact remained that it
was your life, and no stuffed shirt of an angel in his tailored
worsted—now somewhat the worse for wear—had the right to
snatch it from you so rudely.

Launching himself from his chair, Ira made a desperate lunge
for the map, which prompted a tug-of-war.

"In the name of all that's holy-oly-ly," demanded Sissman,
employing his mightiest reverberation, "let go already!"

But Ira patently refused to do so, hanging on for dear life.
This was no easy exercise for a pudgy-fingered man in his mid-

dle years, who suffered from sciatica and shortness of breath. His bifocals slipped from his nose and he was certain he felt his hives coming on. Nevertheless he gripped the map as doggedly as his grandmother had clung to the angel's arm so many years before.

"I don't like to have to pull rank-ank-nk," barked Sissman, surprised to find that he meant it profoundly, "but you asked for it." Then he extended the awful width of his alabaster wings. Their shadow filled the narrow room in a manner that seemed ominous to the angel himself, as if an umbrella had been opened indoors.

Wondering that his heart hadn't stopped, Ira managed to hold firm. "You don't scare me," he blurted in unsteady defiance, giving the map a yank that pulled the angel momentarily off balance. Summoning outrage, Sissman retaliated by beating his wings. Their cool wind whipped the curtains, scattered molting feathers, caused a wheelchair to spin in circles, and lifted both the angel and his antagonist from the linoleum floor. Airborne, Ira still struggled to hang on.

"*Nishtikeit-tikeit-keit*," shouted the hovering Sissman, all patience spent, "you want I should carry you back before your time?"

Although they'd already ascended to the ceiling, Ira assured him through slipping dentures, "You're not taking me . . . *click* . . . anywhere!"

That's when the buff paper, aged considerably among Rebekah's keepsakes and moreover stretched to twice its ordinary length, tore apart. Ira fell to the floor with an earth-shaking thud and sat clutching his portion of the map to his heaving chest. Having retained the smaller portion—whose route led from the present moment (where a demarcation of recent vintage indicated a struggle) across the featureless expanse of Ira's last years—Sissman attempted to fly through the ceiling. But still corporeal, he bumped his silver head against the cork and was forced to fold his wings for a less exalted exit through the window.

No sooner had he set about following the map, however, than the angel became disoriented once more. What perplexed him was the way the lay of the land seemed to change before his eyes, the colors turning like a leaf aging backwards from gray and brown to a rich russet red. The previously flat thoroughfare of Ira Bluestein's hours, where they began the gentle grade toward their conclusion, was becoming as circuitous as a seam in a crazyquilt tossed by a gale. Incidents appeared where none had existed, bumps and declivities where before had been unbroken plain. There was mischief afoot, embarrassing behavior during business hours, liquidation sales, settled scores, withdrawn accounts, travel by night through a geography whose drama supplanted routine.

There was the bubbeh Rebekah who, having slept soundly through the commotion, sat up friskily in bed and called for her Jewish fish. Her grandson had kissed her parchment brow to bid her a tender so long, then returned the map for safekeeping to her treasure box before stepping off its ragged edge. He was headed who knows where, beyond the known world at any rate, into mysterious parts rumored to be the sites of lost neighborhoods, places dense with peril and romance. Here and there—as Sissman tried to make out his itinerary, the wilderness through which Ira journeyed was dotted with gardens, suggesting that the wayward shmo had recovered his memory of paradise. Nothing could be taken for granted anymore; thanks to the angel's bungling, a mediocrity was playing hell with the meticulous craft of the cartographers of Kingdom Come. A nobody was distorting his own destiny after a fashion that constituted an unauthorized miracle.

This wouldn't do. It was highly irregular and Sissman ought to put a stop to it at once, though he was currently at a loss as to how to proceed. All he knew was that he had to act quick. If he didn't turn around and stick close to Ira Bluestein for the wild remainder of the mortal's days—a proposition which promised to be, God forbid, interesting—he might never find his way back to heaven again.

The Wedding Jester

———

As for me, who called myself sorcerer or
angel, I have now returned to the earth,
with a duty to look for and a rough reality
to embrace. Peasant!

                      —Arthur Rimbaud

As he drove her toward the wedding in the Catskills, Saul
Bozoff's aged mother told him yet another of her stories.

"... so Lolly Segal wouldn't go with the girls to see *Chorus
Line* at the Orpheum last week ..."

While Saul, who wondered why he should care, withheld as
long as his conscience allowed a halfhearted, "Why not?"

"I don't know," Mrs. Bozoff expressed her own bafflement.
"She said her nipples ached."

Saul glanced at the crepe-hung little woman, her bosom like
a sat-upon ottoman, and tried to blame her for his life. Hadn't he
adopted his own rueful nature as a protest against her relentless
sanguinity?—which he knew to be only skin-deep.

Her he blamed for his feeling that, at fifty-three he was not
even successful at failure. An author, the books of his middle
years (there had been no books of his youth) had earned him a
small audience in what he considered "the ghetto." His fiction,
full of exotic Jewish legends translated to contemporary set-
tings, had been well-received among a generation that was already half legend itself, and a handful of a generation that was
tediously born again. Among his peers Saul Bozoff had no currency at all.

Of course, if he were honest, Saul would have to admit it served him right. Sometime in his early forties, after a protracted and largely fruitless literary apprenticeship, he'd been seduced by "heritage." But for a handful of short-lived absences (school, Wanderjahre, artists colony), he'd spent his life in an unlikely town in the Mississippi Delta, wishing he were somewhere else. He'd taken a job—one in an endless series of temporary positions—doing clerical work at a local folklore center, transcribing interviews with Baptist preachers who'd taught their hogs to pray, blind blues singers with half a dozen wives, a pawnbroker who'd sold the young Elvis Presley his first guitar. During this latter interview the retired usurer had alluded to a transplanted Old World community on North Main Street where he was reared; and Saul, recalling that he too was Jewish, made a pilgrimage to take a look.

What he found was a desolate street of crumbling buildings and weed-choked lots, a junkyard, a bridge ramp, an old synagogue converted into a discotheque of ill repute. But blink and there were ghosts—the immigrants crying hockfleish and irregular pants, pumping their sewing machines like swarming hornets in the tenement lofts, braiding Yiddish curses into their yellow challah bread. Not ordinarily given to ecstatic transports, Saul was as struck by the timelessness of his vision as was another Saul on the road to Damascus. Never much at home among the living (in whose company he'd managed only to botch a marriage and squander an education), he resolved to take up residence among the dead, whose adventures he was convinced made good copy.

Saul reported their picturesque antics in a book of stories that earned him a modest reputation, which he parlayed into a teaching job at a small New England college. (North Main Street being portable, Saul was hardly aware of the change of scene.) Noted for its Jewish studies program, the college was a place where Saul felt he could go native, immersing himself in a tradition he'd previously ignored. No longer confined to his Mississippi River outpost, or attached to any particular moment in time, he dwelled in the place where history and myth intersected; he was the contemporary of prophets, martyrs, and exiles, whom his spirit (he felt) had expanded to accommodate. From that vantage he sent back dispatches in the form of two subsequent books, each more saturated in Jewish arcana than the one before. Heedless of the tradition's rational ethos, he populated his tales with every species of its folklore, every manner of fanciful event—a labor that kept him occupied for about ten years. Then, just as abruptly as the spell had come over him, it lifted: Saul's vision of Yiddishkeit everlasting reverted back to rubble and unsalable real estate.

"What possessed me?" he wondered, astonished to find himself in his sixth decade the author of books catalogued as *Fiction/Judaica.*

Still, he mourned the loss of his *yenne velt*, his other world. It was cruel that spiritual afflatus should have abandoned him at an age when he had also to suffer so many other desertions: like muscle tone and a formerly thick head of wavy auburn hair. (Saul would have liked to draw a parallel with Samson, but such references now seemed distant echoes of a once joyful noise.) And things better abandoned, such as libido, had begun after a dormant period to reassert themselves. So, when his eighty-something-year-old mother asked him to accompany her to a wedding at a Catskills resort, Saul surprised himself by saying, "Why not?" Maybe a trip to the buckle of the Borscht Belt, the famed Concord Hotel itself, would be just the thing to revive his lost inspiration.

He'd forgotten, however, his mother's gift for reducing him to a childish petulance with her gossip, which Saul judged a poor substitute for an unlived life.

"So Wednesday night the women are playing canasta in Harriet Fleishman's apartment when Millie Blank can't get up from the table . . ."

His moody silence giving way to surrender, "Why not?"

"Oh, honey," replied his mother, "she was dead."

Mrs. Bozoff had flown into her hometown of Boston from Tennessee, where she'd remained despite the passing of her husband two decades before. Picking her up at Logan Airport, Saul had driven the Mass Turnpike into "the Mountains" of southern New York, wondering: What mountains? Because Sullivan County, heart of the Jewish Catskills, was nothing but gently rolling hills. The renowned autumn foliage had already flared and expired, leaving a scorched landscape of gray and tobacco brown. Then there were the towns, which in their heyday had supported conspicuous Jewish populations, boasting scores of kosher butchers and delicatessens; not to mention the hemlock-shaded boarding houses, bungalow colonies, cochelayns. Now their façades, where intact, were mostly boarded up, strangled in wisteria vines: providing backdrops for the local unemployed, who loitered in front of them as on blighted city streets.

Spotting a single hoary hasid beside an ashcan, Saul thought to himself, Reb ben Vinkl: He went to sleep in the golden age of the Mountains and woke up to this. "Looks like we're too late," he observed.

"What?" The battery of his mother's hearing aid was conveniently run-down.

"I said it looks like we're too late, all the Jews are gone."

Mrs. Bozoff smiled in serene denial.

The hotel was no less a disappointment. A good forty or fifty years out of fashion, the Concord was a cluster of boxy buildings, their rusting exteriors as forbidding as the Pentagon. Once inside, there was the sense of corridors measureless to man, though the acres of oriental sofas in flammable fabrics, the showy fixtures out of Belshazzar's salon, were faded, the enormous mirrors as shot through with cracks as with veins of gold. None of this was lost on Saul as he lugged their bags in a snail-like progress alongside his mother; while she, preceded by the clanking third leg of her metal cane, exclaimed, "It's like another world!"

Here and there you saw a woman with cat's-eye glasses and flashy jewelry, her husband in plaid pants, sporting the hairpiece that could double for a yarmelke; but these were far exceeded by the decidedly gentile presence of a regional convention of Emergency Medical Technicians. They were welcomed by a banner that spanned the lobby and eclipsed the bulletin board, which announced (among other weekend functions) the Supoznik-Shapiro wedding. Identifiable by their insignias, the paramedics also shared a generosity of girth—men and women alike wearing T-shirts bearing life-affirming logos stretched across medicine-ball midriffs. Parking his mother on a circular sofa surrounding a fountain, Saul resented her fixed smile, the rheumy eyes whose vision was as selective as her hearing. Had she even noticed the mixed clientele, which in this kosher-style establishment was the equivalent of mingling dairy with meat?

But he'd no sooner checked them in than Saul turned to find that his mother had become a rallying point. She was beset by what must have been *mishpocheh*—a host of relations she had perhaps not laid eyes on since migrating south with Saul's father over half a century before. Each was protesting that the others hadn't changed a bit.

Approaching them, Saul could hear Mrs. Bozoff unburdening herself: "You know I lost my husband," like the event had occurred only yesterday; and one or two of her listeners looked about as if Mr. Bozoff, a weary merchant who'd gone much too gently into his good night, might only have been misplaced.

Saul was introduced to a pint-sized character in bubble spectacles whom Mrs. B referred to as Uncle Julius, and his wife

Becky, a head taller though bowed by a sizable dowager's hump. There were a trio of thick-ankled maiden ladies with a neutered-looking fellow in tow, his trousers hoisted to the level of his pigeon breast. These were relations once, twice removed, hailing from places like Larchmont and New Rochelle, names that for Saul had a fabled resonance. And judging from the way they greeted him, making a perfunctory show of civility before dispersing wholesale, his name must have had some significance for them as well.

Back home, owing to his fecklessness, Saul had enjoyed the reputation of a confirmed (if harmless) black sheep. Writing books had only aggravated the perception, since most assumed without reading him that he'd merely graduated from private to public disgrace. That his notoriety should have preceded him to such far-flung parts, was in some way flattering, lending a slightly outlaw cast to an otherwise lackluster career.

"Help me up," his mother was entreating, sunk in the sofa's upholstery like a reclining Michelin man. Saul gripped her pudgy fingers and made a token effort to raise her, complaining that his back was sore from the drive. But even as he warned her she might have to sit there the entire weekend, a woman unsolicitedly grasped Mrs. Bozoff's other hand. Together she and Saul hauled his mother to her feet.

"Thanks," muttered Saul under his breath, "I thought I might need a forklift."

"Wise guy," replied the woman, whom Saul noted was nevertheless sizing him up with a heavily mascara'd eye.

"Thank you so much," panted Mrs. B with the excessive gratitude of a person pulled from the jaws of a beast. "I'm Belle Bozoff and this is my son Saul," who perhaps needed further explaining, "the author."

"Oh?" said the woman, circumflexing a plucked brow. The information seemed to have rung a bell. "Haven't I heard of you?"

"See," kvelled Mrs. Bozoff to her son, "everybody knows you," and to the woman: "He thinks he's a failure."

Clucking her tongue in sham sympathy, she introduced herself as Myrna Halevy and offered her hand.

Saul took it reluctantly, avoiding her eye. "Any kin to Judah?" he inquired in a pedantic reference to the Hebrew poet famous for declaring, "The air is full of souls!"

"Whodah?" asked Myrna. "Myself, I'm from the Great Neck Halevys. You maybe heard of Halevy's Fine Furs? That's my papa, the retired fur king, that dashing character over there—Isador, short for 'is adorable.'" She pointed to an ancient party in a sport coat the hue of a putting green, his ginger-gray hair back-combed over a freckled pate. Tall and ramrod-stiff, he was prominent among his cronies in their various stages of decrepitude.

As for his daughter, Saul thought he could read her history at a glance, though she was a type he'd seldom encountered outside of books and film. She was a "girl" in her forties trying hard to hide the fact, no doubt divorced and living on generous alimony. Her painted face was somewhat vulpine, her snuff brown hair (highlighted with henna) puffed high and as sticky with spray as candy floss. She was thin to the point of appearing malnourished, probably due to a diet of white wine and pills, though her breasts, which proffered themselves as on a platter, were disproportionately large. She wore an ocelot top and a tight leather skirt, below which—Saul had grudgingly to admit—her legs in their patterned stockings and heels were good.

She gave him a sidewise smile as if to ask if he were finished looking, and Saul flushed, adjusting his collar. A decade's hermetic devotion to dreams and outré texts had left him sensitive in the area of desire, and he resented that this aging princess, bracelets clattering like a Kristallnacht, should chafe him there.

"Is your mama with you?" Mrs. Bozoff was asking, to which Myrna replied that her mother had passed on some years ago;

and accepting Mrs. B's condolences with a dismissive wave, she assured her she'd always been Daddy's girl.

Saul's mother sighed. "You know my husband, Mister Bozoff..."

But Saul intervened, having realized that his mother, like the Ancient Mariner, might never stop buttonholing wedding guests to tell her tale. Clearing his throat, he piped, "I don't like to break up the party, but there's a tired old bellhop waiting to take up our bags."

Myrna Halevy gave him another appraising look, from which Saul recoiled. "Are you in the bride's party or the groom's?" queried Mrs. Bozoff, and when Myrna said the groom's, Mrs. B pooched her lip to signal an incorrect answer. "We're in the bride's," she stated with regret, "but it was nice to meet you anyway."

With his mother safely installed in her room for an afternoon nap, Saul was free to inspect the premises looking for ghosts. This was what he'd been anxiously waiting for. He strolled out under a leaden sky past a drained swimming pool the size of an inland sea, venturing onto a desert golf course called the Monster. Everything seemed to suggest that a race of giants had once walked these hills. But the visionary gift that had served him so well on North Main Street remained inactive on this brisk afternoon.

"Come back Eddie Cantor singing 'Cohen Owes Me Ninety-seven Dollars,'" Saul beckoned softly. "Come back Sophie Tucker, Sid Caesar, Fat Jackie Leonard, David Daniel Kaminsky né Danny Kaye; come back Mister Wonderful, Little Farfel, Eddie Fisher, Totie Fields..." Come back the mamboniks, the mothering waiters named Shayke ("Boychik, you want heartburn? go ahead and order chop meat"), the bungalow bunnies, the busboys from City College chasing the garment czar's daughter, the porch clowns doing Simon Sez. Saul could call the roll of all the talents that had their start in the Mountains, the gangsters and boxers and nabobs who'd watered there—he'd read the literature; he could trace the lineage of Yid personalities from the lion tamers, conjurers, and strong men of the Old Testament through the wedding jesters of the Diaspora, the shpielers and singing waiters of Second Avenue, right down to this late chapter in the long-running pageant, entitled "the Catskills."

What hadn't he missed growing up in the Delta? Poverty and diseases notwithstanding, he coveted the Lower East Side; Nazis, he'd missed, and Cossacks, Inquisitors, Crusaders, Amalekites. At least there would have been some compensation in summers spent hustling tips in the Mountains, oppressed by flighty hoteliers and drunken chefs. But no: Born at the wrong place and time, Saul Bozoff had been forced to abuse himself these fifty odd years.

Later on, trudging beside his mother (through a herd of paramedicals) toward the rehearsal dinner, Saul wondered why he'd agreed to come. What did this tacky terminus to the dream of a golden America, this Jewish wasteland, have to do with him—a lover of the "old knowledge"? Life prior to the discovery of North Main Street—the dead-end jobs, the brief dead-end marriage to a woman he scarcely remembered, who'd blamed him (as he blamed her) for its barrenness—had been a largely somnambulant affair. He'd had to wake up in order to dream. But now, bereft of the company of his wonder rabbis and hidden saints, Saul deplored his banishment to the ordinary world. What identity did he have beyond that of a dilettante, all passions spent? A bachelor professor of a certain age, squiring his mother to a faded resort half a century past its prime.

"So Kitty Dreyfus wouldn't go to her husband Moey's funeral...," Mrs. Bozoff informed him to the beat of her clanking cane. (All her gossip was homegrown within the walls of Ploughshares Towers, a geriatric high-rise wherein the Angel of Death—Saul surmised—kept his own efficiency.)

Said her son, reflexively: "Why not?"

"She said he wasn't her husband; sixty-five years they never, what you call it, consommé'd the marriage."

On their way past the neglected closet of a hotel chapel, mother and son were abruptly halted by the sight of a young woman leaving the Ladies Room in disarray. In completing her business inside, she had carelessly tucked the hem of an indigo cocktail dress into the waistband of her underpants. The panties, Saul could not help by notice, were a satiny eggshell white, scarcely visible (but for the ticktocking cleft at their center) against the cream of her perfect tush.

"Oo oo!" exclaimed Mrs. Bozoff, pointing. "Saul tell her before she makes an embarrassment."

"*I* can't tell her!" he objected. "It's not my place."

"Excuse me, dear!" his mother had begun to shout at the girl, when Saul clamped his palm over her mouth. At that moment the girl was met by several others, one of whom saw the problem and corrected it discreetly with a sweep of her hand. A crushed velvet curtain dropped over the girl's bottom, concealing the stockings that made her look as if she waded in blue water to the thighs.

Her friend whispered, giggling, to the girl, who turned to see who might have observed her: only a trundling old woman and her round-shouldered, middle-aged escort, neither of them apparently worth wasting a blush on. So why was it that Saul, removing his hand from his mother's sputtering mouth and assuring her he didn't know what had come over him—why did he feel as agitated as an elder who'd spied on Susanna? And why, even more than her fanny, should her face—distinctive for its cameo pallor among the artificial tans of her sisterhood—set his vitals vibrating like a tuning fork?

The cavernous Calypso Room, with its undulant walls and glittering terrazzo floors, reverberated with the noise of happy reunions. Everywhere families and friends reclaimed prodigal members and long-lost acquaintances to draw them into the larger fold. To insure his own exclusion from such scenes, Saul had contrived to leave his name tag in his room. At his mother's request that he go back for it, he complained to her much tested patience that such badges invoked for him bitter racial memories. It was in any case a relief to see how his mother, once again an object of warm regard, drew the attention away from him.

Seated next to her at their appointed table, Saul had assumed an expression so arch as to forbid anyone's attempting to engage him in conversation. The strategy was effective enough that he began in a while to feel sorry for himself; nor was he heartened by the notice of the Halevy woman, who fluttered her fingers at him from a nearby table. He nodded without altering the set of his jaw, and inwardly groaned. She was a cultural cliché, wasn't she?—the spoiled New World Jewess, her life organized around excursions to boutiques. The room was lousy with her tribe. Still, as a caricature, she seemed to Saul slightly larger than life—a condition in the face of which he was duly humbled.

Mrs. Bozoff was confiding to a lady with hair the blue of a pilot light (something about a nonagenarian neighbor no better than she should be), when a tinkling of silver on crystal was heard from the head table. A youthful rabbi with a neatly trimmed Vandyke was begging indulgence to perform, as it was Saturday evening, a brief havdalah service. Pushing back the cuffs of a sharkskin jacket as if to show he had nothing up his sleeves, he lit the candle, tasted the wine, and thanked the Lord for holding the line between the secular and the sacred. The guests amen'd, some with mouths full of chopped-liver salad, then pitched into the beef flanken à l'anglaise and the roast stuffed breast of veal with peach garni. They were gnashing asparagus spears, slathering baked potatoes in sour cream, when the crystal tinkled again.

This time a prosperous-looking gent, his spun-silk suit shooting asterisks of light, had risen to his feet. He introduced himself (unnecessarily for most) as Irving Supoznik, father of the bride. Deeply tanned, he was endowed with a regal nose and a two-tone head of hair—sandy on top and fluffy gray at the temples, like an inverted cotton boll. Observing him, Saul was troubled to note that, for one thing, he and the bride's father were approximately the same age, and that the daughter seated next to him was none other than the glimmering girl of the visible tush. Saul realized he'd been leering at her all along.

"You're probably wondering why I asked you all here," said Supoznik, waiting for the laugh. Someone called out, "A tummler you'll never make!" to which he replied, "Very cute. Who let Milton Graber in here? Will the ushers please escort that man from the hall?" Then confidentially, "Milt's still p.o.'d about last night's pinochle game. Anyway, I hope you're enjoying your nosh because I'm in hock to the eyeballs over this little soiree." Again polite laughter, while their benefactor assured them that, really, the house of Supoznik was in no immediate danger.

"Now if Nate Pinchas there can stop stuffing his face for a minute—I know the kishke is good, Nate, but this is my moment, okay? Gertrude, control your husband! But seriously, I'd like to thank you for traveling so far for this shindig. Everybody told me, who has weddings in the Catskills anymore? So call me sentimental, but when Ilka and I got married here thirty-two years ago, the place was lucky for us, and I'm betting some of that luck will rub off on these kids." With his pocket handkerchief he dabbed the corner of an eye.

Graber, the wag, shouted, "Shmaltz we had already from the herring!"

"You didn't blubber like a baby at your Tracy's wedding last spring?" challenged Supoznik, to which Graber: "That's because she married a bum," knuckling the burr-head of the lad beside him, who good-naturedly shook a fist.

"But all kidding aside," continued Supoznik, "I'd like you to join me in a toast to the happy couple." He lifted his glass. "Have I got *naches* or what? You young people maybe don't know *naches?*—that's when your daughter brings home a fine, clean boy like David Shapiro . . ." He bestowed a smile on the bridegroom at his left, a curly-haired, fresh-faced youth with a Clark Kent forelock, his blazer displaying a fraternity crest. ". . . who's about to graduate Yale Law School with a job waiting for him already at the firm of Klein, Klein, Klein . . ."

"Goes the trolley," sang Milton Graber.

". . . and Levine!" proclaimed Supoznik, ignoring his heckler. Young David, showing ivory teeth, clenched his hands in mock triumph over his head. Irving Supoznik then turned to his daughter, his tone becoming worshipful. "And now I give you our doll, our treasure, our Shelly—mwhaaa . . . !" He kissed his fingers, which inspired more needling from Graber. Saul asked himself if the literature of the day hadn't already *done* these people. Shouldn't they have been retired like old stage props? But for all that, he couldn't take his eyes off Irving Supoznik's languid daughter. Her fine-boned beauty seemed a bit out of place amongst the solid, aerobically contoured girls of her circle, her tranquil features opposing their constant animation. Her blue-black hair, whose lustrous profusion she'd tried to arrest with ribbons, tumbled over a milky brow. Occasionally she parted the tendrils to peer with dark eyes from behind them, but, the pert tilt of her head notwithstanding, she seemed drowsily unimpressed by what she saw. Here, thought Saul, was the meeting in one girl of Marjorie Morningstar and Trilby; for Shelly Supoznik appeared as if under an enchantment, her secret inaccessible even to one who'd spied the secret of her bottom drawer.

Having divested himself of platitudes ("Like they say, love is sweet but better with bread"), Irving Supoznik offered a health to the bride and groom. Saul sighed, trying to remember the last time he'd been intimate with a woman. During his driven years, abstinence was never an issue; so sated was his spirit that his physical self was a virtual irrelevancy. But now that his spirit had flagged, hadn't his flesh begun to go the same way? Although a restlessness in his pants argued to the contrary, he needed further assurance. What he needed was some fey creature like Shelly Supoznik to help him achieve, through the medium of his baggy body, the restoration of his soul.

"What am I thinking?" Saul asked himself, feeling that he ought to be ashamed. But while others fed on sponge cake, halvah, and petit fours, he nourished himself on fantasies of stealing the bride away.

Then Myrna Halevy, in a form-fitting, strapless tube dress that seemed to be made of mirrors, approached the table shadowed by her planklike father, whom she introduced to Mrs. Bozoff. Mrs. B, for her part, removed the napkin from under her chins and—a touch coquettishly if Saul weren't mistaken—invited Mr. Halevy to sit down. Myrna said they were on their way to the Imperial Room to see the bygone teen idol Frankie somebody, whom Saul had supposed long dead.

"Maybe you," she turned briefly from his mother to give Saul what he wanted to believe was an involuntary tic, but was clearly a wink, "maybe you and your son would care to join us?" He lowered his eyes, only to see himself dizzily multiplied in the scales of her gown.

"Oh, Saul," shrilled his mother, "let's go! It'll do you good."

Still preoccupied with thoughts of romance, Saul nonetheless wondered what she meant by "do him good." More curtly than he'd intended, he told her, "Go ahead, you'll have more fun without me," then conceding to universal objections, agreed to join them later on. First he needed a little air.

He made a wrong turn outside the Calypso Room and ended up in a dimly lit cul-de-sac. A dumpy couple plastered in paramedical emblems were in midtryst beside a faux-marble cherub, rubbing noses Eskimo fashion. As it was too late to back off un-

noticed, Saul asked them foolishly, "How do you get outside?"
The man scratched his muttonchops: "You mean this place has
an outside?" his moonfaced companion bursting into titters.

Eventually he found an exit that delivered him into an un-
comfortably chilly night whose fine mist was turning to drizzle;
though insulated by his visions of Shelly Supoznik, what did
Saul care? But out there in the elements it wasn't so easy to pick
up the thread of his imaginings. Still he tried: Reviewing prece-
dents from *Blood Wedding* to *The Graduate*, Saul endeavored to
picture himself snatching the girl from the altar; but who was he
kidding? What he felt had more in common with a pedophile
attraction than heroic passion. He turned up his coat collar
against the October wind, cursed the rain pelting his unpro-
tected head, and supposed he ought to be inside among the
guests. But inside he would doubtless want to be out. After all,
what did he have to say to the young go-getters and their fathers
who had already gone and gotten? From the worldly world Saul
had long since decamped for the society of his phantom Jews.
Now, excluded from their number, he was neither here nor there,
inside or out. Neither past nor present were hospitable, and his
people were not his people, and there was nowhere on earth that
Saul Bozoff belonged.

He decided it was time to go and check on his mother, since
what reason did he have for being here other than looking after
her? Suddenly Saul was resentful that others should have presumed to usurp his role. But as he was about to enter the lobby
under a massive porte cochere, who should he encounter but La
Myrna leaning against a stucco'd column. With a scarlet lamb-
skin jacket draped like an opera cape over her scintillating dress,
a cigarette wedged between talonlike nails, she was a thing of
smoke and mirrors. "The Dragon Lady," thought Saul, hoping to
get past her with some minimal courtesy, but the question she
posed brought him up short.

"So, are you getting good material or what?"

He uttered a querulous, "Come again?"

"Admit it, we're all just kitsch for your mill."

Saul thought he caught her implication: She was confusing him with writers of a more acerbic bent, the kind that made satirical hay out of affairs such as these. Not wishing to disabuse her, however, he replied mysteriously, "The mills of kitsch grind slow but exceedingly fine."

"What's that supposed to mean?" she asked.

Saul shrugged his shoulders. "You tell me. Look, I'll level with you, Miss . . . ?" He pretended to have forgotten her name but sensed she wasn't fooled. "I never draw from life."

"Then what do you draw from," Myrna exhaled a plume of smoke with all the éclat of the caterpillar in *Alice*, "death?"

Saul coughed. "You never heard from the imagination?" he said with undisguised condescension.

Myrna was thoughtful. "The what nation . . . ?"

"Now who's the wise guy?" asked Saul, irked with himself for having been lured into an exchange with this ridiculous person.

Then Myrna abruptly changed the subject. "Your mama's enjoying herself," she said, taking—as it seemed to Saul—credit for Mrs. Bozoff's good time.

"My mother always enjoys herself. She doesn't know any better," he apprised her, then attempting to beg off, "If you'll pardon me . . ."

"You got something against enjoying yourself?" asked Myrna.

Said Saul: "I have a very low fun threshold."

"I think you've seen too many Woody Allen movies," she submitted.

"Oh, very astute," replied Saul—was there no end to the woman's presumption? "Look, Miss . . . Halevy was it?" summoning patience. "You might think you know me, but you don't know me."

Then came what was probably supposed to pass for a sibylline remark: "Everybody's disappointed, sweetheart."

Sweetheart?

"You want disappointed, you should see the crowd in the Imperial Room," continued Myrna, upon which she threw down her cigarette and ground it with studied precision under a spiked heel. Suddenly frisky, she stepped forward to take Saul's arm. "C'mon, I'll show you."

"I'm not disappointed," Saul lied, reclaiming the arm. "I'm just damp from walking in the rain. I want to get out of these clothes and go to bed."

Myrna arched her brow, and Saul feared for a second she might offer to help him undress. "Naughty boy," she accused him, "you made a rendezvous with some college cutie, didn't you? Your type doesn't waste any time."

Would it were so, thought Saul, who allowed himself for the briefest instant to believe he was a lady's man. Of course, Myrna Halevy was only teasing him, wasn't she? She had about her, seasoning her character of the Long Island parvenu, a touch of the demoness. Shelly Supoznik, he knew, would never tease him; though Shelly Supoznik might not have the wit. In any case, rather than give the woman the pleasure of witnessing his chagrin, Saul adopted what he imagined was a roué's demeanor. He smiled enigmatically, made a careless little salute, and swept back into the hotel alone.

He woke the next morning wracked with guilt over his mother whom he'd neglected to see to her room the night before. To get even with her for having deserted him, never mind that the opposite was true, he'd gone straight to bed. There he tried again to conjure erotic scenarios featuring himself and the spectral Shelly, though images of Myrna Halevy kept intruding. Oddly, Saul had been nonetheless aroused. In vain he'd attempted to defuse his lust by recalling hasidic folktales, a proven remedy for insomnia in recent years. There was the one, for instance, about Rabbi Elimelech, whose seed, spilled in his effort to resist the temptations of the she-devil Lilith, turned to glowworms at his feet.

Dressing on the run, Saul hurried to his mother's room, separated from his own by two flights of stairs. (The hotel had been unable to provide adjoining rooms, for which Saul was much obliged.) He knocked at her door, called her name, and receiving no answer, began to pound. Had she died in her sleep or—unthinkable prospect—spent the night somewhere else? Aware that neither circumstance was likely, Saul still couldn't shake his unease, and as there remained no response from within, made a dash for the elevator. The lobby was full of medical conventioneers, to whom Saul in an irrational moment considered appealing, when he saw his mother shuffling toward the dining room. She was flanked by the Halevys, father and daughter, which gave him the impression she was being abducted.

Catching them up, Saul had it on the tip of his tongue to exclaim, "Thank God I found you!" but got hold of himself in time to utter a glib, "Remember me?" Myrna turned to greet him with a wry and knowing, "Hello, sleepyhead!"

Said Mrs. Bozoff, "We didn't want to wake you, tateleh," and Saul wondered who was this *we?* but vowed to keep his own counsel until he'd had his coffee.

At breakfast he was still wrought up. Why was he so wrought up? After all, his mother was well taken care of—she was regaling Mr. Halevy (who nodded either from compassion or palsy) about a friend's uterectomy and subsequent malpractice suit. They were in the common dining room where the wedding guests, though legion, were outnumbered by paramedics. Many of the latter said grace before eating, ending their devotions with "in Jesus' name, amen," but none of the Jews seemed aware of any menace. Instead, beyond an air of mutual tolerance, there was even a shared preference of attire among wedding guests and medical fellowship alike—namely, the nylon warm-up suits as brilliant as jockeys' silks. Dining, it appeared, was a friendly athletic competition.

Puerto Rican waiters brought groaning trays of food to the table, excess having remained a constant over the years. There were Danishes, jelly blintzes, bagels with lox, nova, and white-fish, baked herring, cream-cheese omelets. In light of such abundance Saul had ordered, perversely, a poached egg and toast. When it arrived, Myrna, wearing a shoulder-padded jumpsuit that looked like commando issue (but with spangles), leaned over to shovel some of her bounty onto his plate.

"*Essen un fressen*," she invited, taking the further liberty of unfolding a napkin and tucking it into his collar. Saul removed it, flinging it down like a gauntlet.

"That's it, isn't it?" he asked rhetorically. "That's all that's left, *essen un fressen?* The language of Mendele, Peretz, and Sholem Aleichem, Halpern and Leivick—poor consumptive Leivick, who came to the East Side via Siberia, and had to check his paperhanger's ladder at the box office before attending the debut of his play, *The Golem.* The language of Itzik Manger, Moishe Kulbak, and Israel Rabon, who crawled out of the corpse-strewn trenches at the Polish front to write *The Street,* then hung on long enough to be slaughtered by Nazis and tossed in a mass grave. The world's most resilient language, it survives every worst calamity of the past ten centuries only to dribble its last on the lips of a pampered Long Island minx at a Catskills hotel. O *essen un fressen,* yourself, and despair!"

Myrna batted her fake lashes the size of bats' wings. "I also know *gai kuckn in yam . . .*"

He stared at her with a sanctimony that crumbled in the face of her taunting admiration, then lowered his eyes. They lit on the lavender kerchief round her neck. Myrna followed his gaze, touched her throat, its tendons taut as bowstrings.

"You like the scarf?" she asked. "It's got sentimental value. I strangled my first husband with it."

Saul took a breath, odors of stewed prunes and cologne vying in his nostrils, taking him to the brink of a sneeze, which he suppressed. "Myrna," he said—it was the first time he'd used her given name, "can I ask you a question?"

"I'm all ears, kiddo," replied Myrna, bending an ear from which dangled a pendant like a loaded key ring.

"With all due respect, just what is it you think you're doing?"

She gave him a kittenish smile. "I'm throwing myself at you, can't you tell?"

Saul's mouth must have been hanging open, because Myrna took the occasion to stuff into it a thick piece of whitefish. He chewed tentatively, eyeing her like she might be Lucrezia Borgia, then succumbing to its savoriness, swallowed the fish, and took up his fork to skewer another piece from her plate.

Mrs. Bozoff was struggling to rise from her chair. "I'm gonna plotz," she jovially announced, and, suggestible, Saul had a brief panicked vision of his mother's exploding. "Let me help you," offered Myrna, getting up to take Mrs. B's free arm, and together they made their way toward the powder room.

Left alone at the table with Mr. Halevy, Saul felt obliged to break the heavy silence between them—while on the other hand, given the paces his daughter was putting him through, why should he pay court to her tight-lipped old man? If this was a standoff, Saul was damned if he'd be the first to fold.

Although you had to hand it to the geezer: He was certainly fastidious—his hair spread like tortoiseshell tines over a sun-speckled poll, his close-shaven cheeks (thanks to cracked capillaries) in perpetual blush. His safari jacket was complemented by a Hawaiian print shirt whose collar was tucked neatly outside the wide lapels. It was a nattiness, though, that didn't quite conform to Mr. Halevy's mummylike deportment; and it dawned on

Saul that the old guy's spruce aspect might be owing to the fact that his daughter dressed him.

Then Mr. Halevy's mouth had started working, distorting the stony dignity of his features—his fierce eyes asquint, face twisted from the effort, noises that scarcely resembled speech burbling up from his diaphragm.

"Your m-m-m-m, m-m-m-mah . . ."

"My ma?" guessed Saul. "My mother?"

The old man nodded. ". . . is whhh, a w-wha . . ."

Saul found himself mouthing the syllables by way of encouragement.

"W-whaaa . . ."

A Watusi? This was awful. "A woman?"

Again a nod; two out of two. "My mother is a woman . . . ," Saul restated what he'd gleaned thus far, but just as he felt he was getting the hang of it, the game was over: an ancient engine, Mr. Halevy's voice had apparently required a few false starts.

"Your mo-ther," he said, the words coherent if agonizingly deliberate, "is a whole lot of w-woman." And with what sounded slightly tinged with hoarse reproach, "K-character she got, and heart."

Then it was Saul's turn to nod, wondering was this an idiot or a madman? Or more sinister, were the alleged fur king and his daughter some kind of confidence team, gigolo and gigolette, who worked weddings and bar mitzvahs to fleece the unsuspecting? If so, it was clear that Mrs. Bozoff had fallen into their clutches past redemption. This was unfortunate, and while Saul wished he could help her, already lost, she would surely want him to save himself.

"Excuse me," he said, rising from the table and pointing to his slightly distended belly, "the fish isn't sitting too well." The phrase sounded inscrutable in his own ears.

The wedding was not until late afternoon, but according to the handouts there were meanwhile no end of activities to amuse and distract. There were organized water aerobics in an indoor pool with someone called Gilda, a cosmetic makeover workshop with Carol, a hair-replacement lecture, a lecture on "the sensuous spine," shuffleboard and horseshoe-pitching tourneys. There were gold clinics, investment clinics, bingo, duplicate bridge, instant art with Morris Katz, complimentary tango lessons with Mike Terrace on the promenade . . .

What, wondered Saul, no practical kabbalah with Rabbi Naftali? Still nursing the distress he'd brought away from the breakfast table, he felt disoriented to the point of nausea, whose antidote (he decided) lay in the pursuit of boredom.

He nosed about the shops, wandered past the solarium where off-season sunbathers lolled behind glass as in a human zoo. Leery of running into Myrna, he nevertheless tried to comprehend why the woman, any woman, should have set her coif for him: a mediocrity manqué. Though hadn't he once been a kind of poor man's Prospero? They were probably wondering where he was at that very moment, Myrna soothing his mother's worries by offering to go and look for him; and Saul supposed there were worse things than being found. But after a time it came to him that he wasn't so much eluding Myrna as seeking the sylph-like Shelly Supoznik.

She too might be wandering aimlessly, entertaining second thoughts. He would come upon her lingering before a wall of celebrity photos—Red Buttons, Jerry Lewis, Jan Peerce—and step up to recite their pedigrees: "Aaron Chwatt, Jerome Levitch, Pinky Perlmut . . ." They'd chat, establishing their distant cousinhood, and once he was technically no stranger, the girl would begin to confide in him. "The future seems so predictable," she'd admit, and Saul would delicately suggest it didn't have to be. She'd insist that she wanted the life her husband wanted, and Saul would ask who was she trying to convince, him or herself?

Then he'd tell her of the timeless world he'd discovered and lost, but might locate again with her help; and she would lift her Dresden face, open wide her sleepy eyes to behold a man . . .

When he came back to himself, Saul had strayed beyond the confines of the hotel proper; he was outside under a breezeway connecting the main building with the covered tennis courts. Entering on impulse, he was thrust into the big-top atmosphere of the Emergency Medical Technicians' showroom. Here was an even greater density of conventioneers than he'd seen at large in the hotel. Scores of them milled about the exhibits of helicopters and streamlined ambulances with computerized instruments for monitoring every vital sign. Sirens sounded, some in earsplitting squawks, some in arpeggios like Good Humormobiles. Broad-beamed men and women modeled the latest in emergency medical fashion, from insignia'd windbreakers to double-knit fatigues, their hips girded in utility belts worn with a military flair. Like stage magicians they demonstrated their ventricular fibrillators and blood/gas apparatus on live volunteers. A few diehards clung to hands-on procedures: artificial resuscitation and Heimlich maneuvers; but the majority seemed to glory in the use of their whirring and blinking machines. It was a technology, to judge from the reverence the paramedical community paid it, that put miracles in the shade; that rendered outmoded the devices of a Prophet Elijah or a Baal Shem Tov when it came to raising the dead.

Moving furtively among them, Saul felt like a trespasser who'd penetrated some forbidden holy of holies; he was thankful, once he was out of there, to have escaped (as he saw it) with his own wounds still unstanched. Making for his room, he dove between the covers of a recent translation of the mystical text *Palm Tree of Deborah*, but couldn't fathom it. For a couple of hours he alternated between dozing fitfully and longing for Shelly Supoznik, until it was almost time for the ceremony; though why he should bother to attend he didn't know. But knotting his tie—a task he hadn't performed since his own nearly forgotten wedding day—Saul experienced a vague twinge of anticipation, which he had actively to dispel. On the way he stopped by his mother's room, knocked fatalistically, and was surprised to find her in.

"Isador?" she called, a name Saul didn't answer to.

"Oh Saul!" Mrs. Bozoff greeted upon cracking the door, delighted to see him. She had a sense of time like a house pet, her zeal as fervent after an hour as a year. "I don't know why I thought you might be Mister Halevy—he said they would save us a seat at the wedding. Oh, we had a lovely day; we played bingo and I won seven dollars, and Mister Halevy . . ." She clucked her tongue, shook her head in fond sympathy. "The poor soul, you know in Great Neck they won't let him sit in a minyan."

Saul heaved a sigh, "Why not?"

"They say he had too many insides replaced with artificial— he's not a man anymore but a machine. So can you tell I'm wearing a girdle?"

Her dress, its material shimmering like an oil slick, was shapeless; it looked as though, to fill it, she'd been inflated to nearly life-size. Punch her and she might reel backward only to bob up again still smiling. Her rouged cheeks stood out like strawberry stains in oatmeal.

"You look fine," said Saul.

"So tell me, what did you do all morning? Myrna was worried you weren't enjoying yourself. I told her you never let yourself relax. You know she's crazy about you, don't you?"

Under his breath Saul muttered, "She's just plain crazy."

Mr. B tapped her hearing aid. "What's that?"

"I said Myrna Halevy has got a screw loose!"

"Oo oo," exclaimed Mrs. Bozoff, who could not abide unpleasantness.

Saul fairly shouted that he hadn't meant to shout, which elicited one of his mother's conciliatory non sequiturs.

"You know, Saul, we're more like good friends than mother and son."

Downstairs, as they inched along the corridor, Mrs. B, but for the clanking of her cane, was unusually quiet. She seemed to be pondering something, though since when did she ponder? When at last she spoke, it was to inquire experimentally of her son, "So how would you like a new papa?"

Saul ceased his forward progress. Incredulous, he would have liked to borrow her tactic of pretending she hadn't heard, but the question wouldn't go away. "You must be kidding!"

Mrs. Bozoff hunched her shoulders as if to say maybe she was and then again maybe she wasn't.

"But you only just met," gasped her son, thinking surely he could do better than this.

"Sometimes," replied his mother, reciting from what seemed the only available script, "these things happen." And on further consideration, "Maybe it's this place—don't you think it's sort of, I dunno, magical?"

"Magical?" The bite of his fingernails into his palms would leave fossil-like traces till doomsday. "This is the place where magic died!" Then making what he deemed a superhuman effort to control his emotions, Saul adopted a breezy tone: "Okay, fine, if you want to be the bride of Frankenstein, go ahead. So what if my father's not even cold . . ." His father was twenty years in the grave, but who was counting?

Then it pleased him to see how readily his mother acquiesced. "You're right," she said, her lower lip beginning to quiver, face clouding over, "I was just being selfish." Her eyes behind their fishbowl lenses were already aswim with tears, and pulling a tissue from her purse, she gave herself up to sobbing.

Having unmasked her for the forlorn thing she was, Saul tried to savor his triumph. The punishment, he told himself, fitted the crime. For, after all, hadn't she betrayed their unspoken contract, that they should each remain solitary and disconsolate throughout their days? But as he watched her brittle smile collapse before the deluge, Saul's victory began to turn hollow, and ashamed of himself, he wanted to take it all back.

"I didn't mean it," he declared. "It's just so . . ." discarding *ludicrous* and its fellows, ". . . sudden."

More to conceal their spectacle from the guests than to comfort his mother, Saul steered her between a potted rubber tree and the wall. There he enfolded her with arms whose circumference at first barely touched her. Then bracing himself, he put a hand in Mrs. Bozoff's crisp, silver hair and pressed her injured face to his chest.

The unsettling warmth of her tears seeped through his shirt. Patting her back, Saul asked himself why, after her years of carrying tales, shouldn't she be allowed to become an item of gossip herself? Just because he lived with ghosts didn't mean she had to as well. But the truth was, he didn't live with ghosts, and he couldn't live without them, and but for the fact that his narrative fund had dried up while hers remained bottomless, he was every inch his mother's son. Her misery having awakened his own, Saul too surrendered to a quiet blubbering.

At length he managed to swallow the lump in his throat (it sank into his heart, increasing its burden) and make an effort to humor his mother: "Mama, why don't you tell me a story."

Still snuffling, Mrs. B disengaged herself from her son's embrace, corrected her lopsided glasses, and blew her nose. Her pout dissolved the moment she began to talk. "Did I tell you Sally Blockman asked to be buried in her apple green nightie, but her husband Myron, the momzer, said not on your life . . ."

"Why not?" asked Saul, wiping an eye with his jacket sleeve.

But before the mystery of Sally's nightie could be disclosed, they were apprehended by Myrna Halevy, nudge extraordinaire. "Where have you two been?" she said, appearing as if out of the mushroom cloud of her own hair. "Do you want to miss the show?" She hooked her arms through those of Saul and his mother, coaxing them in the direction of the converted nightclub.

As they entered, Myrna quipped, "Look at us, we just met and already—" "—we're strolling down the aisle," Saul dryly coopted her remark; and to further cover his vulnerability, when Mrs. Bozoff exclaimed, "Oh, isn't it beautiful!" he responded,

"Sure, if you like beauty."

Transformed yet again, the Calypso Room was a bower, its capaciousness reduced to almost cozy by the long wine red curtain dividing it. Rafts of flowers in unnatural shades of yellow, pink, and blue decked the walls and trimmed the stage that doubled as an altar; flowers overwhelmed the wedding canopy like a garden gazebo, suffusing the air with their sickly perfume. It was a scent made audible by the cloying strains of a Broadway musical that Mrs. Bozoff identified as *Phantom of the Opera*. She allowed that she'd always loved the music of Andrew Lloyd Wright.

Ignoring the business of bride's side versus groom's, Myrna conducted the Bozoffs into an aisle where her father sat poker-stiff beside three empty chairs. Mrs. B was deposited next to Mr. Halevy, Saul plunking himself down beside her, while Myrna took the folding chair to his right. Thus hemmed in, Saul was interested to see how his mother took the furrier's hand in her own: how, laced together, their gnarled fingers looked as if they held between them a liver-spotted brain.

In his ear Myrna buzzed unrelentingly, "Don't they make a nice couple?"

"Yeah," said Saul, "like the Trylon and the Perisphere."

"I bet that's very witty," replied Myrna, and gave him a playful elbow in the ribs.

Saul made a face at the woman, her shoulders and glossy legs left exposed by her bustier'd jack-o'-lantern of a frock, and thought she didn't look half bad. Then he wondered was he losing his mind, or had the generations of love matches inaugurated at the Concord contaminated the atmosphere? How else account for the ease he'd begun to feel in his adversary relation to this impossible female?

"Myrna," he said, to try and sink their intimacy, "why me? This place is full of millionaires."

She narrowed her eyes in a burlesque of indignation. "So that's what you take me for, a gold digger? Well, I can assure you sweetie," lifting a hand to let the bracelets rattle down her forearm, "I don't have to dig."

Saul backpedaled, lowering his voice in the hope that Myrna would do the same, for heads had turned. "All I'm asking is, what the hell do you see in me?"

She looked at him as if amazed he didn't know. "You're the *author*," she informed him, giving the word the romantic dash of, say, *scourge of the Spanish Main.*

Saul struggled to keep from glimpsing himself through her eyes—God forbid she should lend him any unwonted self-esteem—and remembered that he knew her type: hadn't his wife been one of them? Women who believed the cure for what ailed him was to show him a good time. Well, he didn't want to have a good time.

He was about to give her reasons why the title of author no longer applied, but when he opened his mouth, she put a finger to his lips and said, "Shah!" The theme from *Exodus* had started up over the public address, which was apparently the cue for the wedding procession to begin.

First the groomsmen then the bridesmaids marched in in double file, their full-dress ensembles repeating the pastel floral scheme. A crinolined toddler strewing rose petals waddled behind them, herself followed by a boy in a Tom Thumb tuxedo bearing a ring on a cushion. In their wake came the bride, escorted by her father—and the sight of her gliding over scattered petals, her breasts nestled dovelike in the empire bodice of an alabaster gown, her face tantalizingly obscured by a chiffon veil, chased every other consideration out of Saul's mind.

Her intended waited on the altar, imperially handsome, his slender frame flattered by the white cutaway with its crimson boutonniere. Beside David stood his own flushed father, pot-belly corsetted in a silk cummerbund, looking either smug or pickled in his capacity as best man. Giving his daughter a melancholy kiss, Mr. Supoznik handed her up the steps to the altar before taking a seat next to his wife. There the girl was greeted with a wink by Rabbi Lapidus, rocking on his heels at the center of the chupeh. Smart in a madras dinner jacket, the rabbi clutched something Saul at first took for a staff of office, but turned out to be a handheld microphone; for once the participants were in place under the canopy, the wedding suite fanning out behind them like a choir, the rabbi brought the mike to his mouth with a practiced panache.

"*Barchu haba ha-shem adonai* . . . ," he crooned, while Saul wondered why such a showbiz production should even bother paying lip service to tradition. Of course, he didn't know Hebrew himself, nor had he set foot inside a synagogue since the confirmation of his sixteenth year—an ecumenical affair that in the reform movement replaced bar mitzvah. Saul had not been bar mitzvah'd: his Jewishness, like his connection to his mother's family, was several times removed. But for a brief bibliography of fables he felt increasingly had been written by someone else, Saul regarded himself an artificial Jew. So what made him think that his presence among this company should have anything to do with providence?

The first sign that something was wrong occurred after the second benediction, when the rabbi invited the couple to drink alternately from a goblet of wine. The Shapiro kid took a modest sip, but the bride, when her turn came, upended the cup and greedily slaked its contents to the dregs; then she emitted a most unladylike belch and wiped her mouth with the back of her hand. A shocked murmuring rose up among the guests, subsiding only after they'd assured one another (at least those in Saul's hearing) that Shelly was just a little high-strung.

The ceremony proceeded on a note of tension, which relaxed a bit as the groom began to recite, after the rabbi, the marriage formula: "Blessed art Thou, O Lord our God, Who hast made man in Thine image . . ." Vows were exchanged, the bride's with an especially breathy deliberation; then the groom, receiving the ring from his father (who, to the delight of the crowd, rifled his empty pockets before remembering the ring bearer), tried to place it on the tapered finger of his betrothed. But before he could succeed in this, the girl snatched the ring from his hand. She threw back her veil, disarranging a complicated black braid, and examined the stone through the loupe she made of her fingers; then wresting the mike from Rabbi Lapidus, she blurted in a Yiddish-inflected voice that bore no resemblance to her own,

"You say rock, I say shlock—let's call the whole thing off," nevertheless dropping the ring into her bodice.

The wedding guests collectively forgot how to breathe.

Turning toward them, Shelly Supoznik appeared for all the world like some callow ingenue with stage fright, though the words that came out of her conveyed no hint of trepidation.

"Maybe you heard about this fellow started a line of maternity wedding gowns?—*un iz geshvoln zayn gesheft!*" The room was deadly silent. "I said, you should see how his business is growing!" Not a sound, though the girl, or rather the voice that had borrowed her, remained undismayed. "It's not every line can bomb twice," it declared. "So Ethel and Abie are discussing Einstein's theory of relativity. Explains Abie to Ethel, 'All this means, everytink is relative. It's like this but it's also like that, it's different but it's the same, *farshteyst?*' 'Neyn,' says Ethel, 'give to me an example.' 'Okay, let's say I shtup you in the fanny. I got a prick up the fanny and you got a prick up the fanny. It's different but it's also the same. Now you understand?' 'Ah,' says Ethel, 'but I got only one question: from this Einstein makes a livink?'"

The party onstage, but for Mr. Shapiro who guffawed, remained frozen in place, while the only movement among the folding chairs was from seniors reaching for pills.

"The doorbell rings at a *nafkeh byiss*," continued the bride who was not herself: her body rigid, a helix of hair dangling over one eye. "You know *nafkeh byiss*, dear? A whoorhouse. So the madame answers and finds there a poor soul with no arms or legs. 'What do you think you can do here?' she asks him. The cripple says, 'I rang the doorbell, didn't I?'"

Standing on either side of her, the groom and the rabbi traded glances of stunned bewilderment, both of them afraid to touch the girl. A susurrus of murmurs was again heard throughout the cabaret.

"Don't laugh so loud, you'll start a *landsleit*, I mean startle the landslide, a *nechtiker tog* . . ." None of the mordancy escaping Shelly's lips was expressed in her face. The bridal veil trailed like vapor from her inky tresses which—though she'd yet to move a muscle—seemed to have grown even wilder; her gown had fallen off a pale shoulder. "*Gornisht helfn*," said the voice, "we got here tonight the undead. So what should I say to make friends? I want to sleep with each and every one of you, and I mean sleep! I ain't had a moment's rest since I croaked . . ."

The murmuring had swelled in volume to the hum of an aerodrome.

"But seriously," the voice went on, "it's great to be here in the bosom of Shelly Supoznik—and such a lovely bosom it is. Forty years I'm in the cold, I can't find shelter to save my soul, and believe me, I wasn't so young when I died. When I was a boy, the Dead Sea was only sick." The hand she lifted to quell the laughter that wasn't forthcoming looked as if raised by a puppeteer. "But this one, this *maidele*, so delicate, so graceful like a gazelle, so ... empty. I mean, hello?" The girl knocked mechanically at her temple as the voice echoed from within. "Is anybody home-mome-ome ... ? But don't you think I ain't grateful. Who else can accommodate a whole extra person without doing a time-share? Oy, Shelly Supoznik, such a princess! Ever see her eat a banana?"

Pretending the microphone was a banana, the bride made-believe she was peeling it, then placed a hand behind her head to force her open mouth toward the fruit.

Gasps of revulsion greeted the pantomime, the bridal party beginning to break ranks. Mr. Supoznik, having mounted the altar, appealed to the rabbi to for God's sake do something; while Rabbi Lapidus, checking his watch, replied that the episode was outside his jurisdiction, then screwed up his face as if to ask himself what he meant. Infuriated, Supoznik gave him a shove, which jarred the rabbi into asking if there were a doctor in the house.

A half dozen or more men and women got officiously to their feet and began to make their way toward the altar spouting conjectures: "Cataleptic dementia," "paraconvivialis," and "Trepuka's syndrome" among the infirmities heard bandied between them. Consequently, before they'd reached the foot of the stage, the neurologist, the psychoanalyst in her stretch-velour original, the hidebound osteopath dredging the bowl of a pipe—each identifiable by their respective theories—were at an impasse. Fixed on diagnoses peculiar to his or her own area of expertise, they were stalled by their differences, quarreling before any had bothered to examine the girl.

As other guests weighed in with their theories ("Her mouth you should wash it out with soap!"), Mrs. Bozoff turned to her son and said, "Nu?" Saul shifted in his seat and conceded that they were certainly witnessing a one-of-a-kind event. On his right hand Myrna Halevy leaned a spongy breast into his shoulder, the teasing tone as ever in her voice.

"This is up your alley, no?"

"No," Saul denied unequivocally, then sheepish: "What makes you think so?"

"Your mama gave me one of your books."

Saul didn't know which was more surprising, that his mother carried around his books or that Myrna could read. Moreover, he was aware that she was aware he was lying: for wasn't he familiar enough with the sources, both canonical and apocryphal?— S. Ansky's classic drama and Paddy Chayevsky's heretical spinoff; he'd read Scholem and Steinsaltz, *The Path of the Name*, *The Booth of the Skin of Leviathan*. He might be a dunce when it came to observance, but ask him about King Solomon's necromancy or the properties of an herb called *flight of the demons* from Josephus' *Antiquities*, and he'd give you an earful. He understood, for instance (though he was much too agitated to say so), that the girl was possessed of an alien essence, a *dybbuk*, and that this one was the restless spirit of a dead Borscht Belt comedian—whose name, as it introduced itself following the gangbusters opening, was Eddie Romaine.

"My parents changed their name to Rabinowitz when I went into show business." Eddie's voice waxed nostalgic. "Ach, I played them all, Kutscher's, the Nevele, the Concord, the Pines— this was back in the days when you came up from the City by the Derma Road. I started in the Mountains eighty years ago at a place called the Tamawack Lodge. This was a bungalow colony run by a Jewish farmer famous for mating a Guernsey cow with a Holstein to get a Goldstein—instead of moo it said, 'Nu?' The Tamawack was just thirty miles from here, and look how far I came in this business," nostalgia giving way to resentment, "thirty *farkokte* miles! This is the end of a career, ladies and gentlemen; on your way out leave a stone *afn meyn kop* . . ."

Under the canopy David Shapiro, his forelock dripping sweat, pleaded with his bride to admit she was having a joke— wasn't she? (Though not even her father, in his recital of her virtues at last night's banquet, had counted among them a sense of humor.) Chastised by Supoznik, David's dad had buried a rufous nose in the bib of his shirt, trying unsuccessfully to choke down his wheezing laughter–this while his counterpart Irving Supoznik tore the hairpiece from his own head and, inconsolable, stood wringing it in his hands as if strangling a rodent.

"Anybody helps her can have her!" he cried out in his desperation, which brought his wife in her yards of sequins and tulle to her feet.

"Irving, what are you saying?"

Again Myrna tickled Saul's ear with the feather of her breath. "Go ahead, Mister You-Don't-Know-Me, I dare you."

Saul turned to her in annoyance–she had a nerve! Though on the other hand, with all his yearning after the supernatural, wasn't he at least partially to blame for this visitation? Wasn't Eddie Romaine in a sense Saul's guest, and therefore, in a manner of speaking, his ghost to lay? Although he fought it, his vexation with Myrna fizzled into gratitude; he was beholden to her for calling his bluff.

Still he sat chewing his lip, emotions battling in his heart like cats in a bag. Who, after all, was Saul Bozoff, flash in a pan whose sheen had since rusted, to imagine himself the hero that saves the day?–to say nothing of a fundamental conflict of interests: because how could he not help feeling a certain sympathy for the dybbuk, who like himself was stuck between this world and another? Wavering, he asked himself where he got off even contemplating such a trespass, or for that matter even believing that this could happen. But somewhere between not wanting to seem a coward to Myrna and the growing conviction that he'd been elected, that no one else could release the girl from her spell, Saul stood up.

Instantly he felt it was too late to sit down. Exactly what he was going to do he didn't know, but excusing himself to his mother and Mr. Halevy ("Nature calls"), he slid past them, hearing nothing but the hammering of his heart in his ears. Between him and the girl the physicians debated, Mrs. Supoznik, breaking a heel, stumbled to all fours as she clambered onto the stage—all of which appeared as in a dumbshow to Saul. He was conscious of little else but the babbling bride and his stinging left buttock, where Myrna had pinched him to speed him on his way.

"The Concord, *gottenyu*," repined Eddy Romaine from his situation inside the girl. "Today I don't know, but forty years ago the Concord was swank, the barbershop so deluxe you had to shave before entering. I said, *you had to shave before entering*, badabum. You would eat like there's no tomorrow, check into the hotel as people and check out as freight. We had a waiter in those days, Shmuel—a *k'nacher*. 'Shmuel,' you'd say to him, 'what do you get with the brisket?' 'Severe vomiting and diarrhea,' he'd tell you. Ask him, 'Shmuel, you got matzoh balls?' he'd say, 'No, I walk like this from my arthritis.' Ask for Russian dressing, he'd bring you a picture of Stalin putting his pants on . . ."

Under cover of the general disorder, Saul passed virtually unnoticed up the aisle, taking the stairs to the altar at a couple of stealthy bounds. Mr. Supoznik was busy dragging his rumpled wife to her feet, David Shapiro handing over his father—whose hilarity was now indistinguishable from sobbing—to the long-suffering Mrs. Shapiro, who'd come up from the floor to lead her squiffy husband away. Solacing one another as at a graveside, some of the bridesmaids wept openly, as Saul warily approached the girl.

Possessed by another, she appeared to him more desirable than ever. Her ebony eye, the one not hidden behind her hair, remained moist but unblinking despite the fingers he waved in front of it. Her gown had slipped low enough on one side to reveal a breast, the aureole of a nipple just visible above the lace of her wonder bra. Attempting to cover her, Saul gingerly lifted the strap of the gown to her shoulder, though it instantly slipped down again. Sighing aloud, he made a mighty effort to subdue the tremor in his voice and address the dead comic inside her.

"Mister Romaine," Saul greeted respectfully, and was ignored.

"It was a regular sexpool in those days, the Concord. We had this house dick, you'll excuse the expression—Glickman; he was all the time kicking in doors. He hears shouts: 'Murder! Fire! Police!' so he kicks in the door. How's he to know it's only Sadie shouting, 'Furder, Meyer, p'lease!'"

Clearing his throat to summon what was meant to pass for forcefulness, Saul tried again, "Excuse me, Mr. Romaine."

"You got to love a wedding," declared Eddie, who began pensively recalling his own wedding night. "I'm strutting my stuff in the buff in front of my new wife: 'Look by me,' I say, 'one hundred fifty pounds pure dynamite!'"

"Mr. Romaine, you have to leave this girl."

"'That's right,' says the wife, 'and with a three-inch fuse . . .'" Then Shelly's head swiveled in Saul's direction, the movement drawing with it the attention of the entire room—upon which the commotion died down.

"What is this, audience participation?" The dybbuk's delivery was arch. "Did I ask for a volunteer? Do I look like Mezmar the Great? All right, you're in my power: Quack like a duck. No? Then quack like a chicken, I don't care." The voice becoming oily, "*Gib a keek* on this nice gentleman, so young, God bless him, he's just getting his hair. Nice gentleman, buttinsky, what's your name?"

Saul cautioned himself to stay on his guard, but for all his shuddering saw no reason why he shouldn't tell her, or him, or it, who he was.

"Okay, Mister Bozo, buzz off," said the dybbuk, "but first repeat after me: 'The sight of her behind . . .' What are you waiting? 'The sight of her behind . . .'"

"Pardon?"

"C'mon, be a sport. 'The sight of her behind . . .'"

Hesitating, Saul was nonetheless conscious that this was a beginning: He was involved in a dialogue with an un-disembodied spirit; it was a step. Gathering courage, he forced himself to look past the violated beauty of the bride to the job at hand. He even found the temerity to propose a condition. "If I repeat, will you leave the body of this girl?"

"Sure, sure," replied the dybbuk. "Now say it," holding the microphone up to Saul's jaw: "'The sight of her behind . . .'"

Uneasily, "The sight of her behind . . ."

"Forces Pushkin from your mind. Then you say: 'Forces Pushkin, Mister Romaine?'"

"Forces Pushkin, Mister Romaine?"

"Pushes foreskin, Mister B."

Shelly's expressionless head swiveled back toward the guests, some of whom chuckled only to be met by a barrage of angry "Shah's!"

"How do you like that?" said the voice. "We're a double act—Weber and Fields, Sacco and Vanzetti . . . Of course our people ain't had a *pipputz*, what you call a foreskin, for three thousand years, which reminds me of a story. A guy's watch has stopped so he goes into a shop with a giant watch hanging outside . . ."

Saul was squeamishly aware of his kibbitzers. The groom and the Supozniks, man and wife had edged close to him and the girl, themselves pressed from behind by members of the bridal suite on tiptoe. Wiping the incipient grin from his face (for God help him, he'd taken pleasure in the exchange), Saul made an attempt to dispel any hint of complicity, exhorting the dead jester, "Now will you leave this girl?"

"Was that the shortest partnership in history or what?" remarked Eddie Romaine. "Anyhoo, the guy asks the shopkeeper to fix his watch. Shopkeeper says, 'I don't fix watches.' Guy says, 'But you got a big watch hanging outside . . .'"

"Will you leave her?" Saul reiterated with warmth.

"Shopkeeper says, 'I know, but I don't fix watches—I'm a *mohel*, a circumcisor.' 'So why do you have a watch outside?' '*Tahkeh,*' says the *mohel*, 'what should I have?'"

Saul started again. "Will you . . . ?"

"No!" roared the dybbuk, its attention once more engaged, then sweetly, "but you can come in too if you like—there's plenty of room."

"What about our deal?" asked Saul, who knew better than to ask.

Said Eddie: "I lied."

No longer able to contain themselves, Mr. Supoznik and the bridegroom erupted simultaneously: "What do you think you're doing!" / "Shmuck, get away from her!"

Saul held up a placating hand and tried to explain that he was there to help.

"Help? You call this funny business helping?" said Supoznik, mopping his brow with the rug that he flung down in disgust. His wife begged him to remember his blood pressure.

"Listen to me," pleaded the intruder, "I'm Saul Bozoff," which made no impression whatever, and grasping at some straw of a credential, added, "the author." Then speaking hurriedly lest he be interrupted: "Your daughter Shelly has been occupied, that is possessed, by the spirit of a dead comedian. What she needs is . . ."

Inserted Eddie Romaine, ". . . an enema."

"What she needs," insisted Saul through gritted teeth, "is an exorcism."

Voices of outrage and disbelief were raised from all quarters, the shrillest emanating from the girl herself.

"*Nisht gedugedakh!*" shrieked the dybbuk, mimicking the shock of the assembly, "We shouldn't know from it!"

In the hush that followed Eddie's outburst, Saul tried to reassert himself. "With all due respect, I believe that with your help," steering a tricky course between humility and resolve, "I can expel the uninvited spirit from Shelly's body." Again a stirring in the room. "Rabbi," appealed Saul in an effort to curry favor, "you know better than I what's required."

Rabbi Lapidus, though he raised his anointed head, showed no signs of having a clue, nor did he seem especially disposed to indulge Saul on the subject.

"A rabbi?" asked the dybbuk, perhaps repeating Lapidus's own thoughts. "This is a job for a nice Jewish boy?"

"Of course," continued Saul with forced optimism, "we'll need a quorum."

"Nonsense!" barked Supoznik, and through Shelly's coral lips the dybbuk voiced its hearty accord.

"I know what I'm talking about," argued Saul, though he was frankly riddled with doubts; and had an unexpected party not come forward in his defense, he might have been persuaded there and then to give up the cause.

"Irving," submitted Mrs. Supoznik, tiara askew, "my mama from the Old Country and all of them, they believed in dybbuks and the evil eye. Who knows but this Bozoff is maybe right?"

Saul lifted his weak chin like a prow.

Others from among the gathering, all admittedly in their twilight years, began to mutter their solidarity with Mrs. Supoznik: Bozoff should be given a chance. Her husband rolled his eyes. "Ilka, you're playing dice with out daughter's welfare," he warned, but moved by the urgency of her plea and otherwise stymied, he asked the rabbi if it wasn't worth a try. Rabbi Lapidus remained sullenly unresponsive, but from the floor the stretch-velour psychoanalyst opined that, in some cases, ritual could have dramatic results; though she cautioned it should only be used in the last resort.

"If the Concord ain't the last resort," shouted the joker Milton Graber (without irony) from his third-row seat, "I don't know what is."

In the meantime a dwarfish old man with one blind and one basilisk eye, whom Irving Supoznik greeted as "Papa," had begun a slow ascent up the steps to the altar. He was aided by an equally aged peer, head bald and veined as a marble egg, the two of them followed in turn by an assortment of antiquated gentlemen. Among them, in defiance of the Great Neck interdict, was Mrs. Bozoff's suitor Isador Halevy. Why his presence should've mattered so much, Saul couldn't say, but at Mr. Halevy's arrival he felt a surge of confidence—the kind he suspected sorcerers must feel upon creating a golem.

Still it was daunting how these alter kuckers, constituting a quorum and then some, had so readily placed themselves at his disposal. What if he should disappoint them? But once he'd recovered his tongue, Saul impressed himself with the poise he now seemed to have at his command.

"We'll need the Torah scrolls and the ram's horn from the little chapel, the *shtibl*," he advised, "and also some black candles—I think I saw some in the gift shop . . ."

A couple of the old men relayed these requests to the floor—"Eric! Kevin! Kimberly!"—whereupon a gang of eager grandchildren bolted from the room in pursuit of the specified items. One of the doctors petitioned Rabbi Lapidus to put his foot down, but the rabbi was absorbed in the study of his oxblood shoes; and besides, the whole place now seemed galvanized by the sense that something was finally being done. Scarcely believing what he'd set in motion, Saul began to think he might actually be equal to the dreadful responsibility he'd shouldered.

Meanwhile the dybbuk kept up its tireless monologue: "Back in the thirties I'm dating this shikse—you know *shikse?* a girl who buys retail. So she calls me, says, 'Eddie?'" Shelly held an imaginary receiver to her ear. "'Who is this?'" Eddie waxed falsetto: "'This is Matilda.' 'Matilda?' I say, 'Which Matilda I'm having the pleasure?' 'This is the Matilda which you already had the pleasure.' 'Oh, that Matilda. I remember the wonderful weekend we spent together. Oy, what a weekend! And did I forget to tell you what a good sport you were?' 'That's why I'm calling, Eddie. I'm pregnant and I'm going to kill myself.' 'Say, you *are* a good sport.'" Shelly hung up the receiver. "But seriously . . ."

Shepherded by Milton Graber, the children's crusade returned bearing ritual objects. Further heartened at having been so quickly deferred to, Saul thought he should try and consolidate his authority.

"Irving, David . . . ," waiving the formalities since they were all united in a common cause, "why don't you light the candles and arrange them in a circle under the chupeh."

Clearly of two minds, the groom hung back with Rabbi Lapidus, but Supoznik, having placed his wife in the care of the maids of honor, began dispensing black candles. He kindled them one by one with his monogrammed Zippo, releasing their incense, as Saul called to the back of the house for someone to turn down the lights. The star-studded ceiling expired and the flames grew brighter, making goatish masks of the old men's faces. There was a crackling of joints as they bent to plant the candles in the puddles of dripping tallow until the bride and minyan were circumscribed and all others banished to the dark periphery.

Skullcaps and prayer shawls having also been issued, the men began putting them on, and Saul followed suit. He pulled a yarmelke over his bald spot, a tallis over his yarmelke like a cowl. Then, though he hadn't asked, Mr. Halevy presented Saul with the scrolls of the Law in their velvet mantle, the silver breastplate mirroring the old gold of the surrounding flames. Cradling the Torah, Saul imagined that in the darkness beyond the candles lay a courtyard instead of a nightclub; and in the courtyard the guests held cocks and hens and garlands of garlic, and were accompanied by the ghosts of ancestors on furlough from paradise.

Filling his lungs with all the righteousness conferred upon

him, Saul was more than himself; he was exalted as he hadn't been since his decade mirabilis, back when he was a fine-tuned instrument for the telling of tales. Intoxicated by an energy that cleared his head of any lingering reverence for the dead comedian, he set his sights exclusively on saving the girl. "Spirit," pronounced Saul, "in the name of all that's holy, leave this child!"

Replied the dybbuk: "So this Jewish lady's on the subway when a pervert opens his raincoat. 'Feh,' she says, 'you call that a lining?' Then there was the time I asked my wife, 'How come I never know when you're having an orgasm?'"

"With the power of the Almighty and with the authority of the sacred Torah . . . ," said Saul, taking his text from S. Ansky who'd taken it from the ancients.

"'Because you're never around,' she tells me," continued the dybbuk.

". . . I, Saul Bozoff son of Belle, do hereby sever the threads that bind you to the world of the living and to the body of the maiden Shelly, daughter of . . ." In a whispered aside to Supoznik, "Ilka?" Supoznik nodded.

". . . daughter of Ilka . . ."

"Not until I get a spot on the *Sullivan* show," interrupted the dybbuk, Shelly's head having rotated once again toward Saul.

He stopped in mid-invocation. "Come again?"

"You heard me, I don't leave the girl till I get a spot on the *Ed Sullivan Show*, which is my deepest regret that I never had in my life."

"Eddie," Saul was consolatory; he knew that unfinished business was a common reason for a spirit's inability to find eternal rest. "I hate to have to tell you but Ed Sullivan is dead."

"So give him an enema."

"He's dead over twenty years," said Saul, "it wouldn't help."

"Nu, so it wouldn't hurt."

Realizing he'd walked into that one, Saul attempted to regain

lost ground. "What's the matter, Eddie," he asked, "didn't anybody say kaddish for you when you passed away?" Because the
old wisdom had it that failure to say the prayer for the dead over
a corpse could result in an insomniac soul. To the circle Saul
proclaimed, "Let us recite the mourner's kaddish."

"*V'yish gadol v'yish kadosh sh'may rabo . . .*" the men chanted
inharmoniously along with Saul, loudly reciting one of the few
prayers he had by heart. "May His great name be magnified and
sanctified throughout the world . . ."

While Eddie proceeded: "It's Abie and Ethel's wedding night,
and Ethel—she's old-fashioned, you know; so the groom goes
down to the hotel bar while she gets ready . . ."

". . . *Yisborach v'yishtabach v'yispoar v'yisromam v'yis-
naseh* . . ."

". . . In the bar Abie has a couple of drinks then returns to the
room, where he finds his bride in bed with three bellhops . . ."

As the kaddish seemed to be having no effect, Saul called for
Psalm 91, known as the antidemonic psalm. "O thou dwellest in
the covert of the Most High and abideth in the shadow of the
Almighty . . . ," which was all he could remember, though he
mumbled along as others carried the tune.

". . . 'Ethel,' says Abie, 'how could you!' Ethel's got a little
something in every orifice, see, so she lets loose a bellhop from
her mouth mit a—" Shelly stuck her thumb in her mouth to make
a popping sound, then said via Eddie as Ethel, " 'Well, you know
I've always been a flirt.' But seriously . . ."

Rather than discouraged, Saul welcomed the opportunity to
employ yet another item from the repertoire. "All right," he bellowed, "let's take off the gloves. Blow the ram's horn!"

With the help of his son the elder Supoznik raised the spiral
horn (double-twisted and as long as he was tall) to his bearded
lips, but could make only the feeblest farting noise. He passed
the horn to one of his brethren, whose lungs proved no stronger
than his own. It was then that Rabbi Lapidus began to come

around. Apparently offended by the out-of-key bleating and
tired of his supernumerary role, he shook off his funk; he picked
up his trouser legs to step over the candles, borrowed a tallis to
cover his head, and prized the shofar from crooked fingers. Lifting the horn, he ballooned his cheeks and brought forth a long
unbroken note that ended abruptly. Then he sounded the note
again.

This was *tekiah*, whose echoes Saul could trace back to his
childhood: The first chilling blast of the shofar sounded during
the Days of Awe, it was guaranteed to chase demonic intruders
back to the other side.

"Which reminds me of the lady," said the dybbuk, "who during the Yom Kippur penance, the *al chet*, she beats herself below
the pipik instead of on the chest. 'Why do you beat yourself
there?' I ask her. '*Dezookst mir vi ich hob gezindikt*,' she tells me.
'That's where I sinned.'"

"Give it up already, Eddie," demanded Saul, doubly rein-
forced now that the rabbi had come onboard. "Don't you know
you're dead?"

"So it wouldn't be the first time—but give me a minute, I'll
warm this bunch up."

Again the ram's horn, and Eddie adopted a minstrel dialect:
"Dem Jewish folk got curious customs; on dey holidays de head
ob de household, he blow de chauffeur . . ."

"Rabbi," said Saul, still feeling his oats, "blow *shevarim*,"
and Rabbi Lapidus, wielding the horn like a virtuoso, trumpeted
a short series of three unbroken notes. Then Saul pressed the
dybbuk in a voice so withering he hardly recognized it as his
own: "Face it, Eddie, you're just not funny," notwithstanding
those maverick members of the audience in stitches; "Don't you
know when you're not wanted anymore?"

Once again the shofar, and Eddie: "Ach, didn't nobody ever
want me. I couldn't get booked for love or money, and then I

dropped dead. Sometimes I wish I was never born—but tell me, who should be so lucky? Not one in a hundred."

Saul wondered if it was his imagination or had the dybbuk's voice grown more subdued. Had the hectoring perhaps struck a nerve? Then girding himself against pity, he seized the advantage: "*Teruah!*" Saul clamored for the traditional climactic flourish, a succession of bloodcurdling staccato blasts alternating with eldritch trills.

A slightly winded quality was now detectable in the dybbuk's locution: "Guy goes to the doctor, tells him, 'Doc, I got five penises.' Doctor says, 'How do your pants fit?'"

"Like a glove," answered Saul, still the bully. "I heard it already, your material's stale."

"*Gay avek*, go away from me why don't you," said Eddie Romaine in exasperation. "I got my memoirs yet to write." And attempting to bargain, "You could be my whatsit, my ghostwriter; we'd split the royalties. I'd call it *The Catskills and Beyond*."

"Memoirs?" scoffed Saul, satisfied that of the two of them his own will was the stronger. "You've got no memories, Eddie, only stale jokes. You're a cheap, two-bit Borscht Belt tummler, which is what you are for all eternity, so die already and let live. Leave the girl!"

"What do you expect from what I got to work with?" complained the dybbuk, its anger mocked by a throaty delivery. "By which I don't mean the shtik but the shtiff. Look at me, or rather *her*—a *shaineh maidl?* This is a beautiful girl? Look at her eyes, like railroad tracks they cross." Shelly tossed her hair to reveal crossed eyes. "This is not Miss America but *Meis* America. Lips like petals? Like bicycle pedals, *gib a keek*."

Here, as if to defend the honor of his bride, David Shapiro stumbled into the circle, then in lieu of throttling his frail intended, lowered his fists and donned a yarmelke.

"Beautiful teeth? A *kolyerah*, such buck teeth she's got, she

could eat watermelon through a picket fence." The girl manufactured an overbite. "Body like a treasure?" Shelly slumped, allowing the gown to slip to her waist, exposing lace-cupped
breasts and the creamy hollow of her abdomen. "It should have
been buried already five hundred years. Let me be, *a nechtiker
tog*—this totsie's no great loss."

Such rancor toward the vessel it occupied was a fair enough
sign to Saul that the dybbuk was on the ropes. And oddly, the
more abuse Eddie heaped on the head of his host, the more
comely appeared the girl in Saul's eyes. All that was left was for
him to deliver a swift coup de grâce, and then to hell with Eddie
Romaine!

"Leave the body of the maiden Shelly," he commanded, the
borrowed lines become his own in the saying, "or be cut off forever from the community of Israel!"

Another, more violent reprise of the ram's horn.

Although reduced to mere curses, the dybbuk fought back:
"You should wear out an iron *shiva* stool, you should fall into an
outhouse just as a regiment of Cossacks finishes their prune
stew and twelve barrels of beer . . . ," its voice losing volume
with every syllable.

"In the name of the most holy, submit to the will of this con-
gregation!" cried Saul.

"May your son meet a nice Jewish doctor."

"Dybbuk, submit!"

"What do you call it," Eddie's utterance was profoundly
weary, "when a Jew has got only one arm?"

Student of exotic lore, Saul reckoned himself no stranger to
the popular. "A speech impediment!" he crowed, tearing the
mike from the girl's hand to speak into it himself: "Now do you
submit?" Electronic feedback rivaled the wail of the horn.

The dybbuk was barely audible: "Why do Jewish women do
it with their eyes closed?"

"Because God forbid they should see their husbands having a

good time," replied Saul, who—inspired—ordered his minyan to "Snuff out the candles!"

One by one the flames were extinguished, permitting the throng of gawking faces to become discernible once more in the dim cabaret.

So faintly was the dybbuk speaking that Saul muffled the mouth of the shofar with his hand; he leaned near enough for Shelly's lips to brush his ear. "What happens," peeped Eddie, his words souring the girl's ragged breath, "when a Jew walks into a wall . . . with a hard-on?"

"He breaks his nose!" Saul shouted triumphantly, as the last candle was put out.

"*In alle shwartz yor,*" moaned the dybbuk, "my time has come. *Ach un vey,* what a world, what a world!" Then the bride crumpled to her knees.

Her father and David, along with several old men, lurched forward to take hold of her arms. For a moment the girl sagged between them like washing on a line, her loose gown pooling at her feet. But as they started to lift her, her knees went rigid, her limp body snapped back to attention, and flapping her arms to rid herself of would-be samaritans, she spoke again through the medium of the deceased, "Had you going there, didn't I?" Eddie's voice was restored to its caustic vitality. "So where was I? Oh yeah, this swinger walks into a barroom . . ."

Saul trembled from a rage that made the room swim before him as in the eyes of a drowning man. He wanted to grab hold of something, as for instance the girl's swanlike throat; he wanted to strangle her for the sake of expelling the spirit. But with the candles out, he was once more aware of the size of the assembly onstage, never mind the mob of guests on the cabaret floor. Dumbstruck by the magnitude of the task he'd undertaken, amazed at his own presumption, Saul shrank accordingly.

And deflated, he was his old familiar self, ready to take up the theme of failure again—when he remembered a trump card he'd yet to play.

"... He's all *farputst*, the swinger, dressed to the nines," continued the irrepressible Eddie; "he's got the diamond stickpin, the Cuban cigar, the cathouse aftershave; when he sees this *kurveh*, this whoor sitting on a barstool, her legs crossed high, y'know, the garters showing ..."

Saul knew the risks involved in what he contemplated, that only perfect masters should attempt so advanced a technique; all others would be in peril of their lives—which, in his case, seemed little enough to lose. Returning the Torah scrolls to Mr. Halevy, the microphone to Rabbi Lapidus, he gazed on the drooping but still luminous Shelly Supoznik.

"So the swinger, call him Marvin—he saunters up to the whoor, asks her, 'What would you say to a little fuck?' Whoor gives him the once-over head to toe, from his single slick strand of hair to his Doctor Scholl's," at which point Saul took Shelly in his arms, "says mmphm ... ," and stifled the voice from inside her with a kiss.

He kissed her hard with what the kabbalists called *kavannah*, deep intent, and clung to her with the cleaving called *devekut*. Straightaway a force invaded his body; a black bird seemed to have entered his chest, searing its wings in the heat from his heart till they melted like wax. Hot liquid filled his lungs to overflowing and gathered in his loins, so that his spine became a wick dipped in oil. A spontaneous flame at the base of the wick shot up its length and flared like a Roman candle in his skull. Saul could have wished that the fever was mutual and would fuse them in their embrace; but instead the jolt to his brain pried his lips from the girl's, and with a cry of exquisite pathos— "Hello, little fuck!"—he plummeted into oblivion.

Then I'm hovering just under the wedding canopy. Below me is pandemonium: Irving Supoznik, steadied by his father (himself supported by others), is holding up his swooning daughter, while his wife Ilka fans the girl's cheek with the cast-off toupee. A tousled David Shapiro is trying on and rejecting a variety of solicitous expressions to greet his slowly reviving bride. Meanwhile Rabbi Lapidus entreats the still-debating specialists to help the fallen man—who is myself, evidently not breathing. A couple of doctors do finally break from their huddle and step onto the stage, where they lean over my horizontal body swapping opinions. Nobody seems to know basic CPR.

But somehow the paramedics have been alerted, because a team of them is lumbering down the aisle with apparatus in tow. Mounting the altar, they push past the indecisive physicians and set straight to work looking for vital signs. Having hoisted their machines onto the stage, they turn switches that start them whirring and blinking, attach wires to various parts of my lifeless form. Like pachyderms come to the aid of a fallen ape man, they hunker around me, their trousers dipping to show toches cleavage in back.

Fresh from the disbanded minyan, Mr. Halevy is stationed beside my mother, attempting to still her fidgeting with a withered hand. His daughter has left him to join those bending over me under the chupeh, where she practically rides the backs of the paramedicals. "Hooray!" she bawls once the fibrillations have restored a pulse to my body, which the monitors had shown to be technically kaput. A funny thing, though; for while I recognize this as the moment when I ought to be sucked back into my sad sack of bones, it doesn't happen, nor do I feel the least pang of regret. In fact, I don't know when I've been so relieved.

The one I'll hereafter refer to as Saul Bozoff, breathing but still unconscious, is lowered from the stage onto a gurney, which the EMTs, under Myrna's gratuitous direction, begin to wheel up the aisle. Then in another interesting development (though I confess my level of interest is beginning to wane) the suspended marriage ceremony resumes. This is doubtless due to

a collective amnesia: Since the preceding events have not figured in any rational categories of understanding, they've conveniently dropped from everyone's mind. The rabbi, picking up
where he left off, pronounces the final benediction; the groom
stomps the goblet and, to salvos of flashbulbs and resounding
"Mazel tovs!" kisses the bride. Vacantly she receives the kiss,
which does little to rekindle in her cheek the bloom that was
never there.

When the stretcher has been rolled as far as the hallway—
whose high windows are ablaze with a burnt orange dusk—Saul
opens a furtive eye, then closes it. He snakes an arm about the
waist of Myrna's rustling pumpkin gown, and abruptly pulls her
down on top of him. She screams in a fright that dissolves into
giddy laughter, which Saul chokes off with a kiss. This is not the
beatific Kiss of Moses, which only I could've inspired him to
perform, but judging from Myrna's ardent response it will do.
The paramedics, though impressed, remind Saul he's suffered a
trauma and should lie back down; he's too weak for such
shenanigans. But against their advice, only halfheartedly seconded by Myrna, he rises from the gurney. He agrees that, pend-
ing the results of a battery of tests, his discharge will remain
unofficial; he promises them in addition a testimonial and a
photograph.

By the time Saul and Myrna reenter the Calypso Room, it's
been converted yet again. A brigade of waiters have struck the
canopy, removed and stacked the folding chairs; they've parted
the curtain bisecting the erstwhile altar to reveal a space as large
as the original on the other side. In it, laden with steam trays and
the centerpiece of a seven-tiered wedding cake, the smorgas-
bord trestle meanders along a wall. Dining tables surround the
parqueted dance floor, and a paunchy, middle-aged orchestra in
mambo shirts with ruffled sleeves, dragging fiddles, concerti-
nas, and music stands, have taken over the stage. They are
launched into the overture from *Hello Dolly*.

Posed beside her husband for the ritual cutting of the cake, the new Mrs. David Shapiro, herself a wilted lily, flings her bridal bouquet. It falls short of the assembled maids of honor, who dive for it like scavengers. In the ensuing scuffle the blossoms are so mangled that no single girl emerges with enough to comprise a bouquet. When they sulkily disperse, Mr. Halevy abandons his sentinel post to creep forward; and in an act of unexampled agility, he approximates a deep knee bend to retrieve a sprig of baby's breath from the floor. He returns to Mrs. Bozoff and, bowing from the waist, deposits the stray sprig in her lap; but before he can straighten, she's stuck it in his buttonhole.

Then the band breaks into an obligatory "Hava nagilah," and in a nod to (or parody of?) tradition the bride and groom are lifted in their chairs by spirited youths. Carried in a wild ride around the dance floor, the couple hang on apprehensively to either end of a lace paper napkin.

Following Myrna's lead, Saul loads a platter with potted meat in mango sauce, gefilte fish in honeydew, noodle pudding with smetana, poppyseed strudel; then he and Myrna approach the table where their parents are seated. Mrs. Bozoff smiles absently at her son to acknowledge the food, then picks up the thread of her discourse. She's relating to Isador the predicament of one Minnie Horowitz—who, during a fit at a Hadassah meeting, began to speak in the voice of a girl kidnapped from a Russian shtetl three centuries ago.

"We were gonna try and give her a whaddayacallit?" says Mrs. B.

Suggests Saul: "An enema?"

"No," replies his mother, who wasn't supposed to have heard, "one of those things like what you did with the Supoznik girl—only the dybbuk was better company than Minnie."

Saul knits his brow, rummaging his brain for a memory that won't come. (Because it's *my* memory, though I hereby relinquish it forever.) Giving up the search with a shrug, he inquires

of his mother, "Would that be Minnie Ha-Ha-Horowitz, the In-
dian maidele, to whom you refer?" Then he tenderly assures her,
"Mama, you're a stitch, I'm gonna put you in a book one of these
days." He stoops to kiss her forehead—he's a regular kissing fool
tonight—and Mrs. Bozoff, absorbed again in her story, touches
the spot as if to dab a drop of rain.

The orchestra has begun playing a bubbly version of "Never
My Love," to which the bride and her father are waltzing, somewhat shakily, alone in the limelight. Having stepped to the edge
of the dance floor, Saul watches the ethereal Shelly Supoznik
Shapiro with a philosophical appreciation, as if he rather than
her father had given the bride away. Then a hand tugs at his
sleeve and he turns to face a barrel-shaped matron wearing
what looks like a vintage prom gown, who introduces herself as
his aunt, or cousin, Rosalie.

"I was just talking with your mama, she's such a love," she
informs him, "and I wanted to meet her son, the author."

"Ah, my mama, God bless her," sighs Saul. "Y'know, we may
be here next year for *her* nuptials. Can you believe this is the
same woman who last week went to the doctor? Doc says, 'How
do you feel, Mrs. B, sort of sluggish?' 'If I felt that good,' says
Mama, 'I wouldn't be here.'"

There's a moment when the woman's broad face seems perplexed, her eyes closed as if in pain, just before she gives way to
a loud, braying laughter. Some of her intimates bustle over to
see what's so funny.

"She's got three sets of dentures, my mama," Saul persists,
"one for milchik, one for fleishik, and one for Chinese."

His little circle of admirers cackle like a henhouse, attracting
a larger audience.

"She's a card all right—what am I saying, she's the whole
fershlogener pack. She gives me a pair of neckties, and when I
wear one she asks me, 'What's a matter, you don't like the
other?' A shnorrer comes up and complains to her he hasn't

eaten for days. 'You should try and force yourself,' she tells him. I ask her how's the champagne and caviar; 'The ginger ale was fine,' she says, 'but the huckleberries tasted from herring.' She says she feels chilly, so I tell her, 'Close the window, it's cold outside,' 'Nu,' she replies, 'if I close the window, will it be warm outside?'"

He's surrounded now by a knot of hee-hawing wedding guests, including Myrna Halevy who's sidled up next to him. In a motion that appears to be second nature, Saul hooks an arm about her shoulders and pulls her close; he leans toward her to accept her nibbling at his earlobe, and continues talking.

"When my father was dying, I asked him if he had any last wishes. 'All I want is you should fetch me a nice piece of your mother's coffee cake from the sideboard downstairs.' Then I have to tell him what my mama tells me, that it's for after . . ."

As you see, he was never a serious person, Saul Bozoff; I was the only thing that kept him in line. I tried my best to restrain his high spirits lest he squander them in the pursuit of happiness, and for a while it worked: the lost cause of his sorry self was found. But it didn't last; it wasn't enough he had me and the run of a Yid Neverland. He got lonely just the same.

Well, no hard feelings: May he be as at home in his shambling body as I am to be out of it. Anyway, I've stuck around long enough. A vagabond now, I'm content to let the winds of fancy blow me north or south, forward or backward in time. It's all the same to me. And if I sound a little wistful, I can assure you it'll pass; I've already as good as forgotten the container I came in. Still I suppose I ought to look for another—a worthier that can manage, with grace, to live in two worlds at once; though I'm in no hurry, savoring as I do the life (so to speak) of a solitary wanderer. Of course, you couldn't exactly call this flying solo; I'm not really in any immediate need of companions, since the air is as full of souls as falling leaves.

A String around the Moon:
A Children's Story

Old Mr. Aharon Notowitz was a complete failure as a sorcerer. He'd been at it longer than he could remember and had yet to produce a single miracle. Still, he stayed alive in case something might some day come of his experiments, though he doubted that anything ever would. Besides, he was very tired. He'd been tired for several generations, and lately he was given to nodding off at his work.

He lived alone in a room at the top of an otherwise deserted building on North Main Street in a rundown neighborhood called the Pinch. He'd lived there more years than he could recall. He couldn't remember the last time he'd left his cluttered room, which he liked to think of as his laboratory, or even lifted the window shade. (He believed the window overlooked rooftops, a broad river, and the fields beyond, but who could say?) For that matter, no one remembered the last time they'd seen Mr. Notowitz, since there was hardly anyone left to remember. There were only the poor Abrahams who ran the failing delicatessen on the corner, which had been in their family for many generations. The last remaining business on North Main Street, it seldom had any customers.

Every morning the Abrahams' teenage son Kippy left the stuffed cabbage and beet soup on the landing outside Mr. Notowitz's door, and every evening he took away the empty plate.

In the mornings, as was his habit, he called out, "Good morning, Mr. Notowitz," and in the evenings, "Good evening," then pulled off his transistor headphones to listen. But nobody ever answered. And were it not for the evidence of the empty plates— and the pale yellow light behind the window shade, which was the only light in the Pinch after dark beside the moon—Kippy wouldn't have believed that anyone was there. Then there were even times when he doubted the evidence.

Of course he might have simply tried opening the door, but he'd long since stopped being curious. Anyway, he'd been cautioned by his father, who'd been cautioned by his own father and so on back through the generations, never to disturb the sorcerer at work. "It's a tradition and you have to have faith in tradition," said Mr. Abraham, a gaunt man with a dignified mustache. So Kippy faithfully delivered the meals each day, though he failed to see the point. Nor did he understand why no one ever asked the old man, whom he wasn't convinced was there, to pay his rent or settle his bill. He figured the bill must be in the millions by now. But they were that sure, Kippy's parents, that Mr. Notowitz would one day present them with a miracle that would more than pay back for having fed him all these years.

Sometimes, when he thought about his long solitude, Mr. Notowitz was inclined to feel lonely. He might feel sorry for himself and think that, while the door wasn't locked and no one prevented his leaving, he was a prisoner of his own fruitless labors. Then he would try his best to shake off such feelings.

Brushing crumbs from the seedy bathrobe he never removed, having only holey underwear beneath, rubbing the film from his bloodshot eyes, he would turn his attention to his books on practical magic—ancient books with moldy pages written in languages that Mr. Notowitz had mostly forgotten. Seated at his worktable, he dusted off the smoky glass beakers and the crucibles shaped like stomachs, lit flames under green and blue elixirs that quickly boiled away. He recited what little he could recall of the sacred incantations that were supposed to turn beetles and june bugs into jewels. Moth-eaten suits were supposed to turn to spun gold, fish scales to doubloons, dead river rats to monsters and fabulous beasts, even angels. But nothing ever changed into anything other than what it was, and Mr. Notowitz was tired of everything always staying the same. The fact was, the old sorcerer was just tired.

Tonight, as he gazed at the books, beakers, and dead animals on his table, he felt finally defeated. "All right, okay," he muttered, hanging his head, drying an eye with the edge of his scraggly beard, "I give up." It was a warm spring night and the window was open, but the rustling shade was still drawn, keeping out the breeze. The stuffiness of the old man's room made him drowsy, and folding his arms cradle-wise on the table, Mr. Notowitz lay down his head. In seconds he was fast asleep.

He was awakened by a radiant light, which he saw in his mind before he'd even opened his eyes. Opening them, he was momentarily blinded. He scrambled from his stool as fast as his creaking bones would allow and stumbled backwards across the room, shading his eyes until it came into focus, the source of the light. It was a thing Mr. Notowitz hadn't bothered to look at for many years, though he nevertheless recognized it now. It was the full April moon, which must have somehow drifted off course, floating through his window to plunk itself down on top of his worktable.

This wasn't right. The moon was supposed to set out of sight in some faraway place beyond the horizon, wasn't it? But here it was, round and still and oozing buttery light, practically eclipsing the four walls of his room, taking up precious space a sorcerer needed for his experiments. It had upset his distillery, crushed his dead animals, and displaced his books, which had fallen on the floor.

"Such a nuisance!" exclaimed Mr. Notowitz, wringing tears from his whiskers with his bony hands.

Naturally it wasn't lost on him that this was indeed a strange turn of events: The pale yellow moon didn't plop down on your table every day. But shouldn't the moon be big enough to contain a room this size several times over, rather than vice versa? Scratching his scalp beneath a crumpled skull cap, Mr. Notowitz seemed to recall from his distant store of sorcerer's wisdom that the moon could change shape at will. It could sometimes even become something other than the moon. In any case, he had the distinct impression that, instead of the moon having shrunk to fit in his room his room had grown large enough to accommodate a glowing heavenly body.

What's more, Mr. Notowitz felt that he had grown as well. All of a sudden he wasn't a weary, disappointed old man in an itchy bathrobe anymore. He was Aharon Notowitz, a larger-than-life wizard, a legend in his own time, who accidentally or not—it was immaterial—had conjured a visit from this bright celestial orb. It was enough to restore your faith and make you feel young again. It made you feel as if your antiquated arteries were flowing with swift and beautiful moonlight instead of tired blood.

It made you want to dance, which Mr. Notowitz directly proceeded to do. For a man so many decades out of practice, his joints badly in need of oil, he got the hang of it pretty quick. He kicked off his slippers and lifted his sticklike legs, flapping his bathrobe, spinning in his laboratory like the moon's own satellite. Then he was struck with a mad idea: He'd had enough of dancing solo and thought he might invite the moon to join him. Bashfully he sidled toward the table, remembering a night long ago in his student days, back before sorcery was everything. It was a time when he was living in the great wide world instead of in just one room, and having attended a wedding banquet under the stars, he'd asked the blushing Miss Bialy for a waltz. He believed he could still hear the lilting strains of violins.

But when he touched the moon, pressing his cheek against its surface, which was cool and spongy but tender as velvet flesh, Mr. Notowitz was lonely all over again. Only now it wasn't Miss Bialy he missed; it wasn't his student days when he strolled by the river leisurely collecting rats and scorpions, gathering roots and herbs in the fields. What Mr. Notowitz missed were his frustrated labors. His work was his destiny—how could he have forgotten for even an instant? His studies and experiments were what he was about, and he longed to get back to them with a passion he hadn't known for generations. Suddenly it was clear what he had to do: He had to remove the moon from his table so he could busy himself with his sorcery once more.

The problem was that Mr. Notowitz wasn't keen on having to give up one thing for another. He wasn't ready to sacrifice the sweet companionship of the moon even for the sake of his labors. But ticklish as he'd become with lunar energy, bursting with ideas, the old sorcerer thought he saw a solution. From a shelf that bowed from additional books and odd skeletons, he took down a fat ball of twine. He began to march in a circle, un-raveling the twine until he'd wound it around the entire circum-ference of the moon. Then he tied a knot, gave a yank, and watched the heavenly body roll lightly off his work table, bob-bling balloon-wise across the laboratory floor. At the window Mr. Notowitz hugged the moon. He squeezed it small enough to fit between the sill and the sash and shoved it past the rustling shade, leaving it to float like a kite in the early morning sky.

Breaking the twine with one of his few remaining teeth, he tied it to his pinkie finger, then set about restoring order to his room. He piled his fallen books on the table, opening them to admire words that would have looked to us like crows in flight—though their long-lost languages had begun to speak to the sor-cerer again. Sitting down to apply what he'd learned, he righted his upset beakers and lit flames beneath them; he recited sacred incantations that caused the flames to dance and the green and blue elixirs to froth without boiling over. Then into the elixirs Mr. Notowitz sprinkled zombie dandruff, perspiration from the

Patriarchs of Israel, and other ingredients that must not be revealed even here.

Later the same morning young Kipper Abraham, a skateboard tucked under his arm, came up the stairs as usual with a plate of stuffed cabbage and a thermos of beet soup. No longer troubling to take off his headphones, he opened his mouth to say, "Good morning," when the word, "Awesome!" came out instead. For there on the landing outside of Mr. Notowitz's door was a golden crown set with bug-shaped precious stones. Snatching it up in exchange for the food, Kippy bolted down the stairs and coasted back to the delicatessen in record time.

Mr. Abraham propped his glasses over his forehead and wiped his hands in his apron before hefting the crown. With a conoisseur's appreciation he declared it authentic. "This ought to do it," he said, and gave his wife a wink.

"Do what?" wondered Kippy, still breathless.

"It ought to take care of Old Man Notowitz's bill." Then he gently placed the crown over his haggard wife's thinning gray hair and called her, "Queen Natalie."

"Oh Myron!" squealed Mrs. Abraham, coloring like a girl, after which she and her husband went on about their business. Having expected a miracle daily for the whole of their lives, they weren't particularly surprised now that one had come.

Kippy, who on the other hand had never expected anything, was beside himself with glee. He was elated when he returned that evening for the old man's empty plate, and found a giant river rat with the tail of a scorpion (which despite its fierce demeanor was perfectly friendly) outside the sorcerer's door. And in the morning he found a curly-headed infant holding a bow and arrow and flapping its snow white wings.

"So, Kippy," said the infant angel familiarly, "you are maybe in the market for a pretty bride?"

That's how it went: Every day another couple of miracles appeared on the landing outside Mr. Notowitz's door. There were magical wishbones encrusted with cockroach- and spider-shaped jewels, suits and gowns of spun gold, fabulous beasts unseen since the time of Noah's Ark. There were angels and other assorted creatures with wings. Soon the word was out that the tumbledown neighborhood by the river had become the site of an epidemic of wonders, and the curious came from all parts.

Some stayed, so charmed were they by the idea of living in a place where anything seemed possible. They fixed up the dilapidated buildings, opened shops and groceries until the Pinch began to thrive as it had in bygone days. In fact, the name of North Main Street came to be known the world over as a street of miracles—the street above which the moon hung in the sky both night and day. Even those unable to visit were said to be a little happier at the knowledge that such a place existed on earth.

But ask as they might, no one could discover exactly where all the marvels came from. This was because the Abrahams were careful not to let on for fear that someone might interrupt the sorcerer at work. The secret of Mr. Notowitz should be kept in the family, handed down from mother and father to daughter and son. Time passed and Mr. and Mrs. Abraham grew fat and wealthy in their golden years, famous as proprietors of the world's most popular delicatessen. There was even an *Abraham's Deli Cookbook*, including recipes for Mrs. Abraham's Enchanted Noodle Pudding, Minced Mystery Fish, Borsht Magic, Stuffed Cabbage à la Fantasy, and angel food cake—to be prepared with only super-natural ingredients.

When they retired, his parents handed over the business to Kippy. By then he'd gotten on in years himself; he'd put away his skateboard and transistor radio, grown a dignified mustache, and taken a pretty bride. He and his wife had an enterprising young son of their own named Herbert. When Herbert came of age, he inherited his father's skateboard and transistor (to which he seldom listened because the clamor of North Main Street was music to his ears); and he took over the job of delivering meals to Mr. Notowitz and collecting the daily miracles. Sometimes, being a normally curious boy, Herbert was tempted to steal a peek at the creator of such marvelous prodigies, but he'd been cautioned never to disturb the sorcerer at his labors. Besides, he had it on his father's authority, who had it on his own father's and so on back through the generations, that the sorcerer was a giant of a man. He was strikingly handsome, with a silky white beard, robes of many colors, and a satin skull cap embroidered with crescents and stars. And that was good enough for Herbert.

Meanwhile Mr. Notowitz had been making miracles longer than he could remember. He'd been at it so long that the manufacturing had become second nature to him, and the miracles didn't seem all that miraculous anymore. They were merely the products of an endless, grinding routine that had left him feeling empty and in need of a break. Slumped at his table, the old man shoved aside the books and bubbling beakers to make room to rest his weary head. He yawned like a rusty hinge, patted his mouth with his hand and noticed through his flickering eyes a piece of string tied to his pinkie finger. What in the world, he wondered, was this supposed to remind him of?

Stiffly he slid from his stool and followed the trail of string across his dusty laboratory to the window, where he lifted the shade. It was night out but North Main Street was still lively, as bustling with activity as in the days of Mr. Notowitz's youth. Neighbors in suits and gowns of spun gold, their pockets spilling doubloons strolled from shop to shop under ruby and emerald streetlamps, past diamond windowpanes. Fabulous beasts mingled peacefully among them—dragons and abominable snowmen, walking catfish and unicorns. Over the rooftops he could see the broad river shimmering from the reflection of a full April moon, across whose face soared angels and phoenixes with wings of flame.

Mr. Notowitz also saw how the string on his finger sagged across the dizzy darkness, stretching like an immeasurable clothesline toward the moon. On impulse he gave the string a little tug, and likewise felt a tug at his heart. While this caused him to tremble, at the same time it filled him with a warm rush of ticklish energy. Suddenly he felt refreshed, ready to do ... you name it! He might wrestle with the angels of his own invention if he wanted, or reel in the moon.

Then he thought: "I must be crazy! Aharon Notowitz, where's your humility? Just who do you think you are?" But he knew perfectly well who he was, and the knowledge made him giddy, scarcely able to contain his pride. Brimming with ideas, he rolled up the sleeves of his tattered bathrobe. He returned to his table without even bothering to take the string from his finger, and went straight to work. There was so much left to do.

STEVE STERN is the author of two novels, *The Moon & Ruben Shein* and *Harry Kaplan's Adventures Underground*; two collections of stories, *Isaac and the Undertaker's Daughter* and *Lazar Malkin Enters Heaven*; and a book of novellas, *A Plague of Dreamers*. He has also published two children's books, *Mickey and the Golem* and *Hershel and the Beast*. His stories have received the O. Henry Prize and the Pushcart Prize, and Stern was awarded a Pushcart Writer's Choice Award for *Isaac and the Undertaker's Daughter*. *Lazar Malkin Enters Heaven* won the Edward Lewis Wallant Award for Jewish American Fiction in 1987. Steve Stern was born in Memphis, Tennessee and lives in Saratoga Springs, New York, where he is a writer-in-residence at Skidmore College.

The text of this book has been set in Rotis, a typeface created by Otl Aicher in 1988. This book was designed by Wendy Holdman, set by Stanton Publication Services, Inc., and manufactured by Bang Printing on acid-free paper.